With and Without you

EMILY WIBBERLEY
AUSTIN SIEGEMUND-BROKA

VIKING

VIKING
An imprint of Penguin Random House LLC, New York

First published in the United States of America by Viking,
an imprint of Penguin Random House LLC, 2022

Visit us online at penguinrandomhouse.com.

Library of Congress Cataloging-in-Publication Data is available.

Printed in the United States of America

ISBN 9780593326879

10 9 8 7 6 5 4 3 2 1

CJKV

Design by Kate Renner
Text set in Elysium Std

To everyone who's ever had to say
"I miss you" over phone or text

End of Summer

One

"I WANT TO BREAK UP."

The words feel weird passing my lips. I can't quite believe them even though I'm the one saying them. Maybe there's just no way to prepare for the end of stories like ours.

The whole thing is made weirder by the fact I'm floating in a swimming pool, sheltering from the hundred-degree Phoenix sun. On days like this, I never know where the droplets of chlorinated water on my shoulders end and where my sweat starts. Right now, though, I'm pretty sure I'm mostly sweat. Not just from the heat, either.

"Patrick," I continue before I lose my courage. I have a whole speech planned out, and I'm determined to give it. "You know how much you mean to me," I go on, working hard to keep my expression contrite yet respectful. "You've honestly been the best boyfriend—"

From across the pool, he interrupts me. "And you've been the best girlfriend." He's treading water in the deep end, sweat beading on the brown skin of his brow.

I grimace. "Thanks," I say through my teeth. It's the worst kind of *thank you*. Not grateful, just necessary. "But what I'm trying to say is that we've been together for nearly three years. I'm just wondering if . . . maybe we're too young for this kind of commitment." I hear my voice grow stronger by the end of the sentence, which is good. It's the only thing making this bearable, really. I believe what I'm saying.

"Siena, you're my world," he protests. "You're my everything. You have been since we were fifteen."

My mouth flattens. Some stinging combination of sunscreen and water has slipped into my eye, and I rub it, grateful for the moment to regroup. "That's my point, though. It's been almost three years." There's more I don't say. We haven't even said *I love you*. We haven't had sex. We discussed early in our relationship wanting to wait for the "right time." Which . . . somewhere in these three years, shouldn't I have felt like it was the right time? "Do you want to graduate high school having only dated me?" I ask.

His reply is immediate. "Yes! I literally only want to date you!" He looks genuinely confused by my question. Then his expression clouds over. "Wait, who else do you want to date?"

I've been bobbing lightly on my toes in the pool, but when I sink down, I realize I've drifted into the five-foot section. I'm only five foot six, and I find the water rising past my mouth. I've lost my footing, conversationally and literally.

Paddling into shallower water, I force myself to remain clear and calm. "Nobody in particular," I say. "I just feel like I need freedom. Not to date exactly, but to explore who I am."

I breathe out. That's it. That's what I've been feeling this summer, in the months leading up to Patrick's and my senior year. The truth is, if I examine who I am right now, I'm not very interested in what I find. I'm incredibly, painfully *normal*. I just exist, filling days with the routines of life. I go to school. I do Model UN. I'm not very good—I never gavel. Besides, I joined the extracurricular for Patrick. On Saturday nights, I go to the movies or McDonald's with the same group of friends I've had since elementary school.

Honestly, my most defining feature is my boyfriend. Patrick and I are The Couple. The couple our circle of classmates can only imagine as a unit. No one even says our names separately. It's only *SienaandPatrick. PatrickandSiena. SienaandPatrick are in our prom limo. PatrickandSiena were the only people not drinking.* Which isn't Patrick's fault, not in the least. But it *is* our relationship's fault. When everything I do involves or centers on him, it's hard to figure out how to be my own person. I just know I can't stand it much longer—I'm desperate for something to change.

His voice cuts harshly into my thoughts, louder now. "So, what? We're over? Three years, and you're throwing me away?"

I'm caught off guard. I flatten my feet on the rough concrete of the pool for some sense of stability. "It's really more like two and a half years," I point out, then wince.

"Like I'm *garbage*?" he goes on emphatically.

"Patrick, you're—you're not garbage." I kick under the water to move closer, reaching out for him.

He pushes away from me, splashing dramatically. "You were everything to me," he says. "I guess I was nothing to you. I don't even know who you are anymore. The Siena I knew would never do this to me," he wails.

I open my mouth to reply, then—

Instead, I sigh. Dropping the contrition from my expression, I frown. "Okay, this isn't helpful," I inform him.

He stops flailing immediately, mirroring the change in me. "Too much?" he asks apologetically, his expression completely changed.

"Way too much," I confirm. "You have to be realistic, Joe. Patrick won't make a scene."

My best friend nods, considering my feedback like an actor hoping this performance wins him his Emmy. "He will be heartbroken, though," Joe says matter-of-factly.

Ruefully, I realize he's not wrong. While Joe obviously doesn't know Patrick quite as well as I do, he's received more secondhand knowledge of Patrick Reynolds than anyone on the planet. I made a point of having the three of us hang out often so that Patrick never got jealous of Joe and Joe didn't feel like I ditched him when I got a boyfriend.

Joe's my closest friend and has been since we were five years old. We met in kindergarten, our friendship founded on having the same Wonder Woman lunch box. These days, Joe is much cooler than me. I can't explain why we're friends except to say we just get along. On paper, we don't have much in common—Joe is Black and wealthy, plays drums in the jazz band, and hangs out with athletes and drama kids instead of my friends in Model UN—or MUN for short, as in, rhymes with fun. But it doesn't matter.

It's why I'm here. When I decided today was finally the day I would break up with Patrick, I texted Joe, who promptly invited me over.

I didn't hesitate. First, Joe's house has a sweet pool, and it's ridiculously hot out. Second, I needed to get out of my apartment before my brother, Robbie, started making out with his new girlfriend on the couch. Most importantly, however, I wanted to rehearse my speech.

Joe agreed, probably out of boredom, when I explained I needed him to play the role of Patrick. We've spent the past final weeks of summer supposedly enjoying the homework-less emptiness of each day, but really doing nothing. I know Joe has more parties, more obligations, more unread group chats on his phone than Patrick and I do. Even for him, though, I think summer has started to feel a little listless.

Hence him getting carried away with the role of Patrick, my soon-to-be ex-boyfriend.

"Patrick's too nice to get argumentative," I point out. "Honestly, he'll probably end up consoling *me* after I dump him." The thought douses me in guilt. Despite the heat, the water feels cold and clammy on my submerged skin. I don't *want* to hurt Patrick, partly because he really is that nice.

Joe ducks his head under. Coming quickly back up, he blinks water out of his eyes. "Well, you know he's going to be crushed, even if he doesn't show it."

"Are you trying to make me feel worse?" I'm going for joking and end up sounding miserable.

"No," he replies gently. "Just—are you sure about this?"

I weigh the question seriously as if I haven't asked myself the same thing every night for weeks, staring at the small photo of Patrick and me from a Model UN conference in the craft-store frame next to my pillow. It's not that I don't love Patrick. I'm just not *in* love with him.

Deep down, I know it's not just lack of passion driving my decision, either. I'm scared of staying the same girl I was when I was fifteen, when I started dating Patrick. I feel stilted, confining myself to fit my relationship, to stay the person who fell for Patrick three years ago.

The thing is, I know it doesn't *have* to be this way. I've been friends with Joe longer than I've been dating Patrick. But my friendship with Joe hasn't kept either of us from changing over the past eleven years. Joe, with his enormous video game collection, his skateboarding scabs. I never felt trapped into being that kindergartener with her Wonder Woman lunch box in order to stay friends with him.

Yet with Patrick, I'm stuck. Our relationship is routinized. We have every excuse to do the same things, have the same conversations, see the same people. It's why I really haven't changed since we started dating. I'm afraid if I stay with him, comfortable in our complacency, I'll be forever the fifteen-year-old who watches YouTube home renovations late into the night, does puzzles for fun, goes to the same café every Saturday afternoon. The girl Patrick loves.

Everyone else gets to change. I look at my friends, look at Joe's older sister, Hailey, who's home from her freshman year at Rice. She's vegan now. She listens to music she calls chill-wave and deep house. She's training to run a marathon. It's like she discovered this whole other person within herself.

I don't want to run a marathon. I did not enjoy the chill-wave she played for me. But I do want to discover new sides of myself.

"Yes," I say honestly to Joe. "I'm sure. Breaking up won't be easy, but it's the right thing to do."

"Then you don't need to practice," Joe replies. "Just be honest with him."

I smile weakly. I hate this, even though I know it's right. Patrick is the kindest boy I've ever met. He's probably the kindest *person* I've ever met. Breaking up will hurt us both. But that's no reason to put it off.

I hoist myself out of the pool, immediately feeling the oven-like heat. The pavement sears my feet, and I spring lightly for my sandals. Wrapping my towel around my shoulders, I turn back to the pool.

"By the way," I call to Joe, *"you're my world?"*

Hearing his words repeated, Joe waves a hand carelessly. "I don't know what Patrick says to you in your intimate moments."

I laugh despite myself. "Well, it's not *you're my world.*" I pull on my dress over my wet bathing suit, knowing the fabric will dry in minutes. Glimpsing my reflection in Joe's glass sliding doors, I notice the damp boob stains outlined on my dress, my hair—dark brown, usually straight—hanging tangled and stringy down my back. "Should I shower and change before I meet up with him?" I ask Joe.

Joe climbs up onto one of the rafts floating in the crystal water. "You're about to dump the man and you're worried about how you look?"

I wind my hair into a bun using the hairband I keep on my wrist. It looks a little better. "I just want him to know I respect him," I say.

Joe closes his eyes, stretching out on the raft. "Siena, don't procrastinate," he says. "Go put him out of his misery."

I cross the hot concrete to the glass doors. "Okay, I'm going," I grumble. "The next time you see me, I'll be single."

It's unexpectedly reassuring to say. I'll be single. Once I get through this conversation, I won't be Patrick Reynolds's girlfriend. I'll be someone else—me, or the beginning of who I might become.

Two

I WALK INTO REX'S just like I have every Saturday afternoon for years. The café felt sort of grown-up when we started coming here—a coffee shop, where we hung out on our own, with caffeinated drinks and no parental supervision.

Now, it just feels like Rex's. It is exactly the model of an independent coffee shop, no different from the kind where characters meet in old TV shows. Wooden booths along one wall, old couches in the center of the room, dusty bookshelves of unread books, local artists' paintings near the windows. I could sketch every detail of this place from memory if I could draw. Which I can't.

I know Patrick will have ordered a single cappuccino and an almond croissant. If they don't have almond croissants today, he'll have gotten a blueberry scone. It's his routine, every week. From the door, I see him sitting at our regular table, the one in the corner with the cushioned booth, which he always leaves open for me. He knows I prefer it.

When I get closer, I find—sure enough, his single

cappuccino and almond croissant. I recognize the book on environmental activism he's reading, which he got when we went to the bookstore last weekend.

Under different circumstances, I know how the rest of the day would go. I'd finish his croissant, because he always saves me the final bites. We'd spend the next hour reading, then he'd walk me home, ten minutes through streets of nondescript houses with cacti and gravel in the yards, and talk about Robbie's newest girlfriend or the funny thing Patrick's cat did that day. Then he'd either come up to my room and we'd make out for twenty minutes or he'd head home, regretting not having the time to come up to my room and make out for twenty minutes.

Except today, none of that will happen. Because today, I'm breaking up with him.

I nearly lose my nerve when he glances up, noticing me. His grin fills his face, his eyes lit with enthusiasm.

Patrick. Patrick Reynolds. He's objectively cute. I know every feature of his face, which doesn't change how handsome I find him every time I see him. The light summer tan of his skin, pale in the school year. His wavy brown hair, the dusting of freckles over his cheeks, his solid chin, lips I'm honestly envious of. In ways, he's the best of a bunch of worlds. He's got a jock's looks, gentlemanly charm, impressive intelligence, and a goofy sense of humor. The problem isn't with him.

It's with *us.* With *SienaandPatrick.*

We're chronically coupled. First, I enjoyed it, the glow of

having a boyfriend, not needing to find a date for home-coming or Valentine's Day. Then I got used to it, used to knowing exactly what every Saturday would look like.

Now, I'm seventeen and I'm scared real romance is behind me.

I feel like I've been married for twenty years. When people ask how we met—mostly my mom's friends—it's like I'm dusting off some old fairy tale instead of describing myself. No one wants the details of our love story now. Frankly, they're boring. Which leaves me, Patrick, and our routines.

It's not like I want to date someone else, or like I'm passing up prospects left and right—while Patrick compliments me often, I don't have eye-catching curves or long legs. I'm not popular. I don't have indie-girl charm or some intriguing hidden side. I like Netflix and pumpkin-flavored coffee. I'm just me, and I don't feel like settling down in high school.

While Rex's cappuccino machine hisses, Patrick rises and gives me his customary quick kiss, the way he has hundreds of times. I can't help comparing it to how Robbie clumsily but passionately makes out with his girlfriend—can't help noticing the listlessness between Patrick and me.

"Hi," he says. "How are you? You look nice."

I sit, already uncomfortable. My hair is probably frizzy, my forehead sweaty. If Patrick notices, he doesn't mind. "Oh, thanks," I say. "Um, actually, I have something I wanted to talk about."

Patrick's expression changes. "Me too," he says heavily, looking forlorn.

I frown. "You do?" *Is he about to dump* me? The idea hits me suddenly, which makes me feel vain and naive. It's an awesomely impressive oversight, never wondering whether the boyfriend I was planning on breaking up with was planning on breaking up with me. Shouldn't I feel relieved if he is? It would save me having to hurt him.

Still, it stings. I have no right to be hurt, obviously. Just, on every late night I've spent wondering how I would do this or how Patrick would react, I never imagined realizing he no longer saw in me what he once did.

"I'm moving," he says.

I don't really have a reaction to this. I'm sort of surprised, sort of confused. "You're moving," I repeat. "Like, your parents bought a new house?"

"They did," he replies. "In Austin."

For some reason, I suddenly start to notice details I hadn't when I got here. Details I wasn't looking for, because that's what familiarity does. The tension in Patrick's shoulders, the fidgetiness of his fingers on the tabletop. What he's saying hits me with a fuzzy, dizzy feeling, uncertain and unsettling. "Wait, what?" I start to understand. "Austin? As in Texas?"

Patrick's mouth tightens, like he might be holding back tears. The weird feeling knocks me over, leveling me. My plans disappear under shock, incomprehension, and . . . sympathy?

He nods. "My mom got a position at the hospital there," he says. "We're moving in two weeks."

"You're—you're moving to Texas in two weeks."

Patrick doesn't point out I've done nothing except unhelpfully repeat everything he's said. I would think he's just being courteous, except his eyes have gone distant and moved to the café's windows. He's preoccupied, understandably wrapped up in everything he's feeling.

"But the school year starts in two weeks," I point out softly.

Patrick's eyes glisten. He wipes his cheek, then looks back at me. "I'm transferring. My parents told me yesterday. I—I'm so sorry we won't be together for our senior year. I hate that I won't be in Model UN with you, and our friends . . . I feel horrible that I'm leaving them."

He swallows hard. I study him, realizing he's phrasing everything as apologies despite the fact he's the one hurt by it all. This is *his* life he's leaving behind, his senior year. He was going to be president of MUN. It makes me do something I really hadn't planned on.

I reach over, taking his hand.

He forces a feeble smile. "It'll be okay," he says reassuringly, comforting me as much as himself. "It's my mom's dream job, and my dad's excited to move. You know how he hates Phoenix. It'll be good," he finishes, his voice upbeat like he's convinced.

My heart cracks a little. The thing is, he probably will be okay. Everyone will love him in his new city. Patrick wins over every room he walks into. His new Model UN team will learn how eloquent and hardworking he is. He'll be fine without me.

He squeezes my hand. "Siena, I know this affects our relationship," he says like he's reading my mind, if not catching everything. I bite my lip.

"Yeah," I say. "About that . . ."

I can't meet his eyes. This is my window.

Yet, I'm guiltily relieved when he goes on. "I know a long distance relationship wasn't your plan for senior year," he says gently. "I'd understand if, you know . . . you want to break up."

I sort of can't believe our conversation's unexpected, circuitous route has led us here so perfectly. He's opened the window wide. It wouldn't even hurt him the way I was prepared for because I could pass it off as about the distance, not about him.

I say nothing, working out exactly what's holding me back.

Slowly, I figure it out. If I break up with him now, it's the end of Patrick in my life. While I'd been counting on ending our romantic relationship, freeing myself to try new things, I'd figured I would *see* Patrick. We'd stay friends. In this new future, he'll be nothing to me. Old photos on my phone, signatures in dusty yearbooks, texts fallen to the bottom of my messages app. The idea is unexpectedly painful, and the pain threads doubt through my conviction. I'm not in love with him. But I don't know if I want to completely lose him, either.

I need more time to know for sure.

Time and . . . possibly distance.

I put my other hand on top of where ours are clasped on

the table. "Do *you* want to break up?" I ask. It occurs to me that Patrick's suggestion might be exactly the kind of courtesy I've learned to expect of him. Maybe he hid his own preference within a guess about mine.

His eyes widen. "God, no. I want to be with you, no matter what. I just want you to have the best possible senior year."

When I smile, it's genuine this time. "We could try long distance. It might not work, but I think . . ."

With Patrick watching me, his eyes sincere, I pause. Ending our three-year relationship is not to be done lightly. Maybe I was being impulsive, hasty, careless. Maybe I would regret dumping Patrick. Maybe—just maybe—I'm being given the chance to spare us from needless heartbreak.

"I think I want to try," I finish, uncertain but certain enough. I don't want to close this door and have him lock it behind me.

Patrick's entire expression transforms. He beams at me, sitting up straighter, looking renewed. Only then do I understand how much he wanted this, how he was only giving me the option to be kind. "Okay, great," he says energetically. "Resolved. We're staying together. Seriously, Siena, I'm so glad. I could stomach the idea of leaving Phoenix, but losing you, too . . ." The gleam in his eyes fades.

I swallow. "I'm—I'm glad, too." In fact, I'm more like *not miserable*, which is different. But the idea of dampening Patrick's enthusiasm is not one I enjoy. Instead, I continue cautiously. "What . . . do you think long distance will look like?"

Patrick's focus is immediate, his brown eyes turning intent. "Well," he starts, like he's brainstorming policy resolutions. "We'll text. We'll video chat. You know, FaceTime and stuff. We'll"—now his voice takes on bright vigor—"we'll visit. Visits will be great. Thanksgiving, winter break. We'll see each other."

I've sometimes found Patrick's enthusiasm infectious. Right now, I'm trying to follow his positive outlook, but it's not easy. I'm weighed down by questions. Do I like the sound of the relationship he's describing? Will it give me the room I need to discover myself—the reason I wanted to break up in the first place? Is it even fair to subject Patrick to long distance for *his* last year of high school?

I settle for the smallest form of those questions. "Will . . . those things be enough for you?"

This, I instantly see, does dampen Patrick's spirits. I feel guilty, though not unjustified. When *I* imagine long distance, I have the dull feeling our relationship will only get colder with intermittent texting, separate lives, and no twenty-minute make-outs in my room.

Patrick pauses, and in the stretching silence, I know he's really evaluating the question like I did. He must be entertaining a similar outcome. And that's before we even factor in that there's no real end point here. Next year, we'll be going to college, and in all likelihood it won't be in the same place. Is this really what either of us wants for the foreseeable future?

When he speaks, his voice is heavier. Not with defeat.

Just realism. "It can be a trial," he concedes. "If at any point we decide it's not what we want, we'll just say the word."

I shift in my seat. I . . . really might say the word. This could very well be over by Thanksgiving.

But by then, I will have had time to adjust to Patrick out of my life. He'll have had time to adjust to me out of his, too, I console myself. This is better for us both. We can slowly submerge into the cold water instead of dunking our heads and shocking our systems.

"Sounds great," I say, reaching for the confidence I felt seconds ago. I give his hand a final squeeze before pulling mine free.

Patrick takes a bite of his almond croissant, then passes the final piece to me to finish. I stare at the flaky crust, fighting doubt. I walked in here ready to end us. I'm glad I didn't. Still, with the complicated conversation over, I realize I'm left with . . . more of the same. We're just stretching every unworkable *same* over hundreds of miles. Same Patrick, same me. Same problems.

I finish the croissant, knowing exactly how the rest of the day will go.

Three

THE NEXT TWO WEEKS have the feeling of life on pause. We don't finish summer the way we normally would—the rotation of lazy days, Saturday dates, and family dinners I'm used to. But the new shape of this year hasn't started yet, either. We're in the between.

We fill it with packing, fitting the contents of Patrick's entire bedroom into cardboard boxes marked with Sharpie. It's surreal how swiftly years of memories and signs of life can be removed, leaving bare walls and empty shelves. I accompany Patrick as he says heartfelt goodbyes to our friends, watch him promise to come visit. I wonder what he's feeling. I wonder, if I were in his position, whether I would be glad to leave.

On his last night in Phoenix, we sit out in his backyard. While Patrick doesn't shed a tear, I can feel how hard this is for him. We talk, our conversation made sparse by the circumstances. Patrick focuses on the future.

"We'll be together again before we know it," he says. "The time will fly by."

I nod, saying nothing. Whether the time flies or drags isn't the question on my mind. It's what it'll carry with it. The next time we're together, will it be for the last time? Or in these months apart, will I miss him enough to not want to let him go?

It's not an answer I can possibly know right now. Instead, I just let Patrick hold me while we stare up into the wide, dark sky.

Hey, call you in 10?

Can we do in 15?

Sure thing!

September 5, 7:14 a.m.

Hope you have a good first day!

Miss you.

September 5, 1:30 p.m.

Day went well. They don't have MUN,
so I have to figure out what I'm going to
replace it with. But the people seem nice.

September 20, 3:16 p.m.

How's everyone doing? Tell me everything
that's happened at school so far.

Nothing to tell really!

I find that hard to believe.

They moved mac and cheese day to Thursday. Oh, and Marcus and Jenny broke up.

Siena! Those are two MOMENTOUS changes!

Okay, shifting mac and cheese from Friday to Thursday maybe has rippling effects that might alter the very core of our school.

And Marcus and Jenny! What happened?

They got in a huge fight about how Jenny didn't like Marcus's favorite movie or something.

Wow. They broke up because of a movie?

I know.

That's very depressing to me.

October 9, 12:57 p.m.

Hey, just got your text and tried to call

you, but you must be out. Hope you're
doing something incredibly exciting.

Sorry, I missed you! I was not doing
something incredibly exciting, unless
you consider finding a new optometrist
thrilling.

Everything is relative, I suppose.
New contacts?

Glasses. I'll send you a pic. Hold on.

Hey, can we talk at 8 your time instead
of 9? I need to get more sleep this week.
First midterm coming up.

Sure!

Marcus and Jenny got back together.

Oh thank god.

Happy Birthday! What's the birthday plan for the day?

Thanks. Wish you could be here to celebrate. I miss you.

Miss you too.

As for what I'm doing today, I'm registering to vote!!

Oh my god. Did you know about this? My mom called your mom and I'm coming out to have Thanksgiving with your family! The flights are my parents' gift to me. I am so excited!!!

Thanksgiving

Four

FOR NEARLY EVERYBODY, THE Wednesday before Thanks-giving is one of the most checked-out times of the year. Plenty of my classmates don't even come to school, already on planes to visit grandma and grandpa wherever. Those who do show up spend every hour watching the clock.

Not Model UN. I'm in the government room after school, where MUN has meetings. Alicia, the new president replac-ing Patrick, is discussing our upcoming conference in January and who will be on Security Council. Everyone is riveted, hoping for a good assignment.

Except me. While the meeting stretches on, I realize I just . . . don't care. Not like everyone else here does. Not like Patrick would.

Searching myself for the reasons why I'm sitting here, I can't find them. I chose Model UN freshman year because it fit my schedule. I wanted four years of my extracurricu-lar on my résumé, the way everyone told me I should. Then, when I started dating Patrick, my center of gravity shifted to

Model UN friends, my Model UN responsibilities, my sense of myself here.

The more I reflect, though, the less enthusiastic I become. I don't like the competition in Model UN, and I'm not particularly passionate about the subject matter. *This* is what I've felt for months, this persistent vague discomfort—like I'm out of place in my own life. The pieces I put together three years ago no longer fit.

Nevertheless, I try to force them. Effortfully, I tune in to what Alicia's saying. When she mentions the Non-Proliferation Treaty, I Google the term on my phone under my desk.

It doesn't work. The words warp and scatter in front of my eyes. I sigh quietly in frustration.

I thought without Patrick here, I could come into my own in this club, be more than the president's girlfriend. Now I'm wondering if Patrick was the *only* reason I was here. It's not something I'm proud to admit. I want to do things for myself, not because my boyfriend does them.

Hastily, I delete my previous Google search. Instead, I type in *quarter-life crisis*.

I scroll unproductively for the next twenty minutes. When Alicia finally ends the meeting, I shoot out of my seat immediately.

Next to me, Garret, one of Patrick's and my closest friends, catches my eye. "Hey, is Patrick getting in tonight?" he asks.

I plaster on a smile, hiding the nerves Patrick's visit twists in my stomach. "Tomorrow."

"You have to say hi for us," Alicia says, coming over to collect her bag. "Tell him we miss him!"

"Yeah," I say. "I will."

I duck out of the room, frustrated that even with Patrick in Texas, he's the focus of every conversation people want to have with me. In the empty outdoor hallway, I find I'm speeding my steps, rushing for no reason except the pressure mounting in my chest. I have the oddest sensation, like I need to run or scream or both.

I do neither, wrestling the feeling down. Reaching the library, I take a deep breath and walk in. Past the checkout desk, someone is working on one of the computers, typing furiously. I don't recognize the program, but I do know what long, tight tiers of web- or app-design code look like.

Since the summer, I've noticed myself doing something sort of embarrassing. When I see someone interesting or passionate or skillful, I'll . . . imagine I'm them. Like, not them literally. But the them version of me. Like now, my mind flashes to *For Dummies* books piled on my desk for programming languages—Java? C++?—and whiteboards in my room filled with hand-drawn interface designs. Me, hoodie-clad, powered by espresso, working late into the night on my next ingenious idea. *Coder Siena.*

One day, maybe, one such image will excite me enough to stick in my head, instead of vanishing the next second the way this one does. Still, the momentary diversion is enough to calm the pressure in my chest.

I continue toward the back of the library, where I know I'll find Joe. His mom is a guidance counselor, and Joe and I usually work here until she's ready to leave for the day. I drop my bag on the floor, then collapse into the seat across from him. But when I open my math book, Joe flips it closed again.

"I need a milkshake," he says.

I slouch forward, pretending to pout. "I just got here," I say. "I have so much homework to do before Patrick gets in." While it is the long weekend, I doubt I'll have time during Patrick's stay for the lengthy calculus assignment Ms. Jones dropped on us.

"We can drink it on the walk back," Joe points out with the ease of someone who expected this objection. "It'll only take fifteen minutes."

I sigh. I know his timing estimate is dead-on, what with how often we've made this very walk to Bentley's Burgers. Besides, I'm too restless to deal with differential equations anyway. "Fine," I concede. "But we're getting strawberry today." The size of Bentley's milkshakes renders them decidedly a collaborative experience. Even splitting, Joe and I sometimes don't finish.

"It's the worst flavor, but okay," he replies with a hint of judgment.

We leave our bags in the library. Walking out, I have to quicken my pace to keep up with Joe, who's clearly eager even for strawberry. Reaching the large street running next to our school, we start our familiar route to Bentley's.

"When is Patrick getting in, anyway?" Joe asks. "What do you guys have planned?"

I groan. "Can't I have one conversation that isn't about Patrick?" My voice comes out a little shrill.

Joe eyes me. "You're touchy."

I exhale, calming myself again. Joe's not wrong—today does have me touchy. "I know," I say. "Sorry. I just thought Patrick moving away would mean I'd be seen less as Patrick's girlfriend and more as . . . Siena."

Right then, my phone vibrates in my pocket. I check the screen, finding it's Patrick wondering how Model UN went. I ignore the message for now.

"What does it mean to see you more as Siena?" Joe asks, sounding like he's giving the question real consideration.

I say nothing for a moment. In the harsh daylight, I suddenly feel just like I did in the hallway. Joe's put forward exactly the question I find so stressful. "That's the problem," I say softly. "I don't know."

Joe nods, either contemplative or, possibly, not riveted by my existential dilemma.

Needing to get these thoughts off my chest, I stubbornly press on. "I guess I don't know what I want the real me to look like. Like—have you ever been starving but didn't know what you wanted to have for dinner?"

"Honestly, no," Joe replies. "My dad's cooking goes hard."

I laugh. *"Metaphorically."*

"Well, *metaphorically*"—he matches my intonation—"I think if you're hungry, you should just look into your cupboard and make something."

The suggestion softens me. It's genuine and well put. But it's not easy. "Maybe," I say quietly.

While we walk, I work the question over. If Joe's right, I should just pick something—just decide. Coming down the street opposite us, a woman jogs in color-coordinated athleisure wear. I picture myself in her shoes—sleek Nikes. I could be *Runner Siena*, scheduling out my marathon practices and pounding pavement every morning.

Well, actually, that sounds terrible. So, not *Runner Siena*. But something. I should pick *something* and just . . . make dinner.

The weekend of my boyfriend's visit, though, does not feel like the ideal time to decide what. First I'll focus on my relationship, *then* I'll focus on me. It needs to be this way, I realize—I can't be *Fill-in-the-Blank Siena* while I'm still figuring out *PatrickandSiena*.

For the rest of our trip to Bentley's, our conversation moves to other subjects, and I hold on to this personal schedule. I *will* decide who I want to be, but this weekend is for the questions Patrick poses. And right now is for strawberry milkshakes.

Five

I'VE ONLY BEEN TO the airport three times. Once for the Model UN conference we went to in Washington, DC, the farthest I've ever been from Phoenix. Then once coming home from the same Model UN conference in Washington, DC. The third time was picking my dad up from a business trip.

Which means I only vaguely remember the emptily modern details of the Phoenix Sky Harbor International Airport. The cream-colored carpet, the long ceiling tiles, the rows of gray chairs. For somewhere evidently meant to be manageable and streamlined, it's doing nothing for my stress.

I pace in front of the baggage claim carousel. The place is packed with people flying in last minute for Thanksgiving. Over the stainless-steel conveyor belt, the screen reads Patrick's flight number. Next to it: ARRIVED.

Any minute now, Patrick will walk through the doors across the room. He'll be here, in person, for the first time in months. The thought has me jumpy. It's taken over from the personal identity crisis I was having yesterday.

"Siena, would you sit? You're blocking the exit," Mom says from the chairs.

It's not the least bit true. I know not to say this out loud, though—my mom will notice I'm on edge, and we'll have a passive-aggressive fight. I settle for rolling my eyes so she can't see. Joining her on the gray chairs, I fold my hands in my lap, hopefully showing no signs of what I'm feeling.

I don't know if I *want* to see Patrick again, and my uncertainty is wreaking havoc on my emotions. Our texting and phone calls over the past few months have been pleasant, like the neutral cheer of the airport decor. I enjoy texting Patrick, I do—just, in the way I enjoy texting friends.

Other friends. Who I haven't been dating for three years.

Patrick *is* my close friend, obviously, and conversation comes naturally with him, if sometimes predictably. I just don't think it's how texting my boyfriend should feel. Like we're . . . just pals. *My pal Patrick.*

When my mom told me that Patrick's mom, Mel, wanted to buy Patrick plane tickets for his birthday, I agreed to the plan mostly because I knew if I was going to break up with Patrick, I owed it to him to do it in person. Two and three-quarters years together shouldn't end in a text message beneath a conversation about homework or what we had for dinner.

My doubts about our relationship haven't faded since he left for Austin. In fact, they've gotten worse. Not just because of the strains of separation, either, the conversion of walks home and unconscious handholding to laboriously organized FaceTimes and time-zone forgetfulness.

The problem is, even *with* the distance, I haven't managed to start rediscovering myself. It's not Patrick's fault, but it's just . . . not working. I've started to wonder if maybe holding on to this relationship is making me hold on to pieces of myself that no longer fit.

It's like somehow, even from half of the United States' distance, our relationship is squeezing out room in my life I need for myself.

So I'm forcing myself to give us one final chance. This visit, I'll decide whether there's enough holding us together to *keep* us together—enough friendship, enough spark I couldn't feel over long distance—or whether I'm now ready to say goodbye to him. When the end of this weekend comes, I'll make a decision on whether we're breaking up.

Obviously, I'm not looking forward to it.

I bounce my leg in my seat, which leads my mom to look up from the historical romance she's reading on her phone. "You excited?" she asks gently, if not without genuine curiosity.

I look over, not sure how to respond. *No, Mom, I'm not* would prompt questions I don't want to voice out loud, questions I've wrestled with plenty on my own. I'm not even sure what I'm going to do with Patrick for the next few days. It's near-impossible to reconcile the fundamental pressure I'm placing on this visit with figuring out the mundane logistics of how we'll spend each unstructured hour.

My mom watches me with hazel eyes like my own. Some

people don't look like their parents, or they look half like one parent, half like the other. I'm not one of those people. I'm a weird carbon copy of what my mom looked like when she was my age. Even now, we're unusually similar, down to our perfect golden tans and our small noses. Besides our ages, the only difference between us is our haircuts, hers shoulder-length while mine spills lower. In moments like this, it's like I'm being interrogated by myself.

She continues without waiting for my reply. "Of course you are," she concludes. "I remember when your father and I did long distance for a few months."

"You and Dad? When? Why?" I welcome the distraction of the questions. My dad's worked in insurance here in Phoenix my whole life. Until now, I've never had much curiosity for my parents' dating life pre-me. I don't know why she's only mentioning this months into my own long distance relationship. I guess the airport is stirring up memories.

"It was when we'd just met," she says. "We didn't realize we lived in different states. He had been in Phoenix, visiting Uncle Al when we . . . Well, I'll tell you that story when you're older."

I grimace. Okay, now I would prefer my nerves.

"We really hit it off," Mom goes on. "For a while we saw each other every couple weeks while he lived in Los Angeles. It wasn't easy. I hardly knew your father and I already hated the distance. I can't imagine what it's like for you and Patrick."

I shift my eyes from hers. "Yeah, it's . . ." I cast around

for words. "Not great," I finish. While I know the *not great* my mom's envisioning is me heart-stricken and hugging Patrick's photo to my chest instead of serious existential soul-searching, I choose not to clarify. "But if a relationship is meant to be, the distance doesn't matter, right?" It's a more revealing question than I intended. Nevertheless, I'm hungry for the answer—for someone to just tell me whether I should break up with him or not. What if long distance is like the natural selection of relationships? If it only kills the weak ones? Does the fact that it's hurting Patrick's and mine mean we're not right for each other?

"Oh, I'd like to believe that," Mom replies. "But I think it requires maturity. Dad and I were thirty when we met, and we really wanted this to work. So we made it work. You and Patrick are young, but you have an incredibly mature relationship for your age. Most young people wouldn't even consider long distance. I know I wouldn't have when I was seventeen. I really admire that."

While it's a compliment, her words don't warm me. In fact, they only increase my doubt. I shouldn't be in this relationship because I'm *capable* of doing long distance. I'm *not* thirty. I'm *not* married. I shouldn't have to act like I am.

Just then, my concentration is shattered by an ear-splitting shriek.

My head spins in its direction. My mom's does the same. I find a girl in a Harvard sweatshirt rolling her suitcase with her. Her pace picks up, until she runs into the arms of a well-dressed young man waiting near the carousels. He catches her, sweeping her off her feet while her suitcase clatters to the floor. They kiss like they haven't seen each other in months. Her hands rise to his face while his encircle her waist. It's like something from a movie, like few kisses I've ever seen. None I've felt in a very long while. My face heats.

My mom clears her throat, then returns to her phone.

It's several whole minutes before the guy pulls back, grinning widely, the kind of goofy grin I wouldn't have imagined on his sleekly handsome features. I'm in earshot of their conversation. "Wow," he says, lightly goading. "You really missed me, Sanger."

The girl looks indignant. She's pretty, with perfect, understated makeup. A collared shirt peeks out from under her sweatshirt, and her high-waisted black pants are somehow unwrinkled despite her having just gotten off a flight.

"I did not," she protests. "I've been way too busy. No time to waste on missing you."

I watch them, entertained. Despite the obvious insult, the boy smiles wider. Neither of them releases each other. "I've been busier," he scoffs. I hear something practiced in his playful haughtiness, like it's not the first time they've had this sort of conversation. "While you've been in *class*"—he tugs gently on the hem of her Harvard sweatshirt—"I've been chasing leads and writing an incredibly important piece of investigative reporting."

"Can I read it?" the girl—Sanger—asks. She quickly hides

her obvious eagerness. "You really should let me edit what you have so far. Knowing you, you've stuffed your lede into the sixth paragraph."

I don't understand what's funny. Nevertheless, the guy laughs. Finally, he grabs her luggage, and they walk hand in hand toward the sliding doors. "I know it's hard for you to accept," he says with mock seriousness, "but you're not my editor anymore."

Sanger waves a hand, her nails painted pale pink. "Only for this year. Next year, you'll be a lowly freshman on the *Crimson*."

Watching, I fidget. I can't put my finger on why. It's probably just nerves.

"Oh, and you'll be my superior?" The boy raises an eyebrow, watching the girl out of the corner of his eye.

"Obviously, Ethan," she replies.

He stops instantly, then pulls the girl in for a kiss, no less passionate than the first. "I missed you," he says, his voice filling those three simple words with emotion. I don't know how I know they're words he's wanted to say for weeks, maybe months. Ones he's said into his computer's camera, or whispered to the text messages on his phone screen for no one but himself to hear.

The girl softens. "Fine. I really missed you, too."

They stare at each other, their squabbling faded under affection so apparent I can hardly stand to look at them. It makes me intensely jealous. Somehow, this realization stops my fidgeting. I clasp my hands in my lap while I sit, not wanting to examine what exactly I'm jealous about.

"Siena?"

It's Patrick's voice. I turn, finding . . . him. The real him. Not the version on my FaceTime or in my fading memories of summer. I freeze, my mind short-circuiting. I'd gotten so used to not seeing him that *seeing* him is something I can't react to immediately. Then, clumsily, my body unlocks. I stand, dropping my hands to my sides.

"Hey. Hi," I say. "You're here."

Patrick is grinning widely. His hair is shorter, the way I've seen on our past few video calls. Still, seeing it in person is somehow entirely different. He shifts on his feet in shoes I don't recognize. The contrast is jarring. It hits me suddenly, the only visual I've had of him for the past three months has been on my thirteen-inch MacBook screen. I haven't seen his feet or his knees or his legs in months.

He lifts a hand hesitantly. In view of my mom, we lean forward for a hasty brush of lips. Our arm placements and face-tilting are uncoordinated. We're out of practice.

"I'm here," he replies.

We stand still, not knowing what else to say, until my mom's voice cuts in. "Do you have luggage, Patrick?"

"Nope." Patrick holds up his duffel bag. "Only this."

Mom deposits her phone in her purse. "Perfect. Then let's get back to the house. I'm sure you two have so much to catch up on, and I have to check on the turkey. How was your flight?"

I follow them out, noticing how my mom is having an

easier time making conversation with my boyfriend than I am. I can't help comparing us to the couple whose reunion I very not-creepily just watched. Ethan and Sanger. Their fire. Their kiss. Their obvious happiness.

Nothing like us.

Six

WHEN WE REACH MY apartment, I lead Patrick down the hall and into Robbie's room. It's not like he needs leading, obviously. Patrick knows my place like he knows his own house. Or—his old house in Phoenix, I guess. He probably knows my place *better* than his new one in Texas.

The parents were very clear on the sleeping arrangements when they hammered out this plan. *Separate bedrooms.* Our apartment doesn't have a guest bedroom, and my mom wouldn't hear of sticking Patrick on the couch. Which means we're kicking Robbie out of his own room. I doubt Robbie minds. He falls asleep on the couch plenty, exhausted from practice for whichever of his sports is in season, and he certainly acts like the sofa is his bed for purposes of making out with various girls.

I push open the door, finding Robbie inside, grabbing clothes from his dresser. Objectively, I understand how Robbie draws his revolving door of girlfriends. At fifteen, he's knobby-kneed and round-faced, and it's obvious he's going to grow into a guy who's athletic and cheekily charming. His room, unsurprisingly, is calamitous. It smells like sweat, his Phoenix Suns posters hang crooked, and every day he leaves his finished cup of protein shake crusty next to his computer.

"Hey, Robbie," Patrick says. "Sorry for stealing your room."

Robbie grins when he glances up. It's sort of adorable how glad he is to see Patrick. Robbie's always liked him—it's one of the few things my brother and I have in common. It's not just inclusiveness from Robbie, either. When Patrick and I first started dating, Patrick worked hard to win him over. He'd even plan guys' nights where they would go to movies or basketball games without me. While Robbie would never say it, I know he's missed Patrick.

Lapsing back into sophomore-boy chill, Robbie shrugs. "It's cool," he says. "I wasn't, like, looking forward to sharing a wall with my sister while her boyfriend's here."

"How do you think I feel when you and Chloe treat the living room couch like it's the back row of a movie theater?" I fire back.

Once more, Robbie shrugs. "Mom won't let me have a girl in my room with the door closed. Feel free to get her to change her mind." He does one of those upward nods to Patrick. "Hey, we're going to watch the new Bond movie while you're here, right?"

"You bet," Patrick replies readily. "I refused to see it in Austin without you."

"Cool. I'll rent it." He flashes Patrick a grin, then leaves the room, boxers and basketball shorts bunched in one hand.

And for the first time in months, I'm alone with Patrick.

I'm hyperaware of the privacy. Patrick, obviously also aware, reaches out gently for my hand. I don't move, knowing my smile must look pasted-on and weird.

I love kissing Patrick. I do. It's just, with the memory of the airport couple in my mind, I'm caught up comparing what Patrick and I have to them, wondering if we'll measure up. Wondering if we've ever had real passion. Then there's the problem of how I'm 90 percent sure I'm going to break up with Patrick in a couple days. I don't want to give him mixed messages in the meantime. If we're making out or doing other things—because we have done *some* things, if not sex—in hindsight, won't Patrick feel like I was using him while planning on dumping him?

Which is why, with Patrick's face closing in on mine, I panic.

"We have to go to Joe's house!" I blurt out.

If my withdrawal hurts Patrick, he doesn't show it. He blinks, no doubt trying to follow my train of thought, which, he's right, has gone off the rails. This is one of Patrick's kind, good qualities. He loves debate—like Model UN—yet with me, he starts every conversation by trying to understand and find the sense in what I'm saying.

Right now, it is a noticeable strain. "We . . . do?" he finally asks.

I think fast. "Yeah. He . . . missed you. So much. He—made me promise to bring you over. Right away."

Patrick steps back. Watching how thoughtfully he takes this in, I feel my insides twist. "I didn't know Joe cared that much," he says. "We're friendly, but—"

I cut him off. "Oh, he cares. He just doesn't show it because, you know. Toxic masculinity."

"Wow." Patrick rubs his chin. His eyes refocus on me. "Okay, yeah, we should go see him."

Heart pounding, I'm guiltily glad my ruse worked, until I realize what this means. It might've worked *now*, but I'm going to have to keep Patrick distracted this way for the next two days.

I lead him back out the front door, covertly pulling out my phone to text Joe, telling him we're coming over and I'll explain later.

On the front steps of my complex, Patrick pauses.

I worry momentarily he's going to balk, to beg me to postpone with Joe for ten or twenty minutes. Instead, Patrick looks peaceful. He breathes in deeply. "It smells like I remember," he says.

I'm not sure how to reply. Phoenix doesn't smell like anything, except maybe dust.

Patrick doesn't expect me to, I'm relieved to find. He flashes me a smile. "It's just good to be home," he says.

While I wonder how he considers this place home even now, we head off down my nondescript street. It's temperate out, probably sixty degrees in the dry daylight, perfect for the ten-minute walk to Joe's through tract-home suburbia. Every building is a slight variation on every other, the neighborhood a combination of houses like Joe's and complexes like mine. Each front yard is gravel and cactus. Nothing else grows here.

"I missed how open everything is," he goes on. "How quiet it is."

I don't really hear the words he says. My brain translates them into something else. When he says *open* and *quiet*, I hear *empty*. "But there's so much more to do in Austin," I say. I'm not just trying to cheer him up. I'm genuinely confused.

"Yeah, but I still miss this," he says. "Like, look how wide this road is!" He wanders off the sidewalk into the middle of the smooth pavement. There's no traffic in sight, and if there were, we'd see it with plenty of warning. "It's great," he enthuses.

I can't help laughing. Not like I'm making fun—I'm charmed by how excited he is. "The wide roads? Really?" I tease. "That's what you missed?"

"Yes!" He returns to the sidewalk, entwining his fingers with mine. This time, I let him. "It makes me feel like I could go wherever I want," he says.

I smile a little. While we walk the rest of the way, Patrick occasionally pauses to fawn over boulders or street signs. By the time we reach Joe's house I've half forgotten why we're here. It's been a pleasant walk. When Joe opens the door, Patrick immediately pulls him in for a firm hug.

"I missed you, too, buddy," Patrick says.

Over his shoulder, Joe mouths, *What?*, looking understandably bewildered.

I can only muster an apologetic smile in reply.

Seven

JOE'S MOM PUTS US to work immediately. We're placed in charge of carrying folding chairs and tables into the backyard with Joe and Hailey, who's home for the holiday. The Crawfords have a huge Thanksgiving, with all of Joe's aunts and uncles coming later with prepared dishes. Joe's mom didn't even allow us inside the kitchen, wanting us nowhere near the sweet potato pies she's making.

Heavenly smells waft outside through the screen door onto the patio where we're working. It's unexpectedly easy how everyone falls into conversation, with Hailey explaining she's gotten into civil engineering, which she's interested in pairing with a minor in energy and water sustainability. I remember when she was leaving for Rice, she didn't know what kind of engineer she wanted to be. Hearing her now, it's not just interesting, it's exciting—what life looks like when you have the freedom to figure it out.

I'm grateful for the distraction, too. Hanging out with her and Joe gives me a much-needed break from my self-imposed ultimatum of figuring out whether to break up with Patrick, or figuring out how *not* to. Not worrying about how I'm acting around him, I can relax and just listen to him and Hailey exchange experiences of living in Texas. It makes me enjoy his presence more, even if that presence is more friendly than romantic.

The conversation changes to Patrick asking Joe and me how everyone's doing at our school. Caught up in my thoughts, I stay silent, half listening while Joe starts to run out of West Vista High School gossip.

I'm about to chime in when I have an amazing idea. The answer to one of the problems I'm facing for the rest of Patrick's visit. "We should have a welcome-home party for you while you're here," I say.

I set down the chair I'm holding, swept up in the ideas forming in my head. Patrick faces me, his expression once more written with the effort of figuring out where my thoughts are coming from. "A party?" he asks. "That's really not necessary."

Oh, it's necessary, I think to myself, *just not in the way you mean.* Party preparation will keep us occupied all day tomorrow, then at the party, we'll be around other people, without the expectations of what we might do if we were alone. Patrick leaves Saturday afternoon. I can break up with him Saturday morning without him feeling used or led on.

"Of course it's necessary," I say with excitement I know he thinks is at the idea of getting our friends together. "I should've planned it weeks ago. You're only here for two and a half days. Don't you want to see as many people as possible? We'll do it tomorrow night, and everyone can bring their Thanksgiving leftovers. It's perfect."

The more I explain the idea, the more I like it. It's not just evasiveness, either. I *do* want Patrick to enjoy his visit. Especially if he's about to get dumped. He deserves to spend time with the friends he'll actually want to keep in touch with instead of the soon-to-be ex-girlfriend he definitely won't.

"Joe," I say, seized with enthusiasm, "can you host it?"

My friend looks up from where he's placing chairs around the table. "Why don't you host it?" he replies, obviously not amused.

I frown. "We have to invite all of MUN, Joe, and my place would practically fit in your garage."

Glancing from Joe to me, Patrick works to catch my eye. "Siena, you really don't have to do this. I'd be happy to just spend the day with you."

I resist his efforts, focusing on Joe. *"Please?"* I repeat.

Joe closes his eyes for a moment, setting the chair down a little too forcefully. "Help me carry in the next table first," he tells me.

Hopeful, I follow him into the detached garage. Even with the Crawfords' Buick in the front, there's plenty of space for storage. I walk past Joe's old skateboards and the plastic ramp I've dutifully filmed him doing jumps off of in the driveway, but while I'm starting to pull out the table, Joe stops me.

"What are you doing?" he asks.

"I'm . . . getting the table." I pause.

Joe rolls his eyes. "No, with Patrick. You can't just avoid your boyfriend."

"I'm not . . . avoiding him," I say, hoping I don't sound as forced as a freshman delegate on Security Council. "I'm with him right now. Or I would be if you hadn't brought me in here."

Joe eyes me, clearly not convinced.

I sigh. It's frustrating how good his intuition is. "Okay. Fine. I'm avoiding him," I say. "If we're alone together, he's going to want to hook up."

Joe says nothing for a second, looking like he doesn't understand. Which is fair. I know my predicament is somewhat unusual. "If you don't want to hook up with him, don't hook up with him," he says slowly.

"No, I know," I reply immediately, feeling nerves in my chest like I'm walking into an exam. Not history or government, either. *Calculus.* "Honestly, I *would* hook up with him, but I'm pretty sure I'm going to break up with him on Saturday. I don't feel right using him."

Joe looks past me, thinking. Then he rubs his face, pained. "Okay, I understand that logic. Can't you just break up with him now?"

I gawk. "Joe, he's staying at my house!" I imagine the next couple days. Hearing him cry himself to sleep in my brother's room. Or if he's not upset at my ending our three-year relationship, the awkwardness of the rest of this visit would be unbearable. Waiting in the hall for him to finish brushing his teeth. Exchanging no words except *pass the syrup* over break-fast with my entire family. It would be comedically bad.

"Fine. Why do I have to be dragged into this, though?"

"Because you're my best friend, and you'd do anything for me?" I ask hopefully.

Joe crosses his arms. For the first time, something besides reluctance enters his expression. "Do better," he instructs me.

I imitate his gesture, sensing I'm halfway there. "Remember in seventh grade when you wanted to break up with Emma Goldberg? You had me hand her a note telling her you didn't like her anymore, and then I had to watch her cry for all of recess," I say. It was one of my worst memories of middle school. I liked Emma. We did a softball summer camp together one year.

Joe is starting to smile. "Fair point," he says grudgingly.

I eye him, expectant.

"I'll host your party," he goes on, and I beam. "*But,*" he says before I can revel in my victory, "you and Patrick have to leave, like, now. I cannot look at the dude knowing you're about to wreck him."

"Deal," I reply eagerly. I force out of my head the question of how I'll occupy Patrick for the next few hours. "You're the best," I tell Joe, meaning it. Then I hold up the heavy table with one hand. "Do you still need help with this, or—"

He laughs. "Just go, Siena."

Smiling, I hold up my hands in surrender. "I'm going!" I leave the garage.

Under the awning covering the patio, Patrick is eyeing

the chairs intently, studying them for perfect spacing. I know Patrick's mom has precise preferences on how she wants each piece of silverware placed, and while Patrick finds it sort of silly, in situations like this he can't fight his eye for table preparation.

"My mom called," I say when I walk up. "We have to go."

Patrick pulls his eyes from the chairs, then smiles. "Sure, sounds good."

We're heading down the driveway leading to the sidewalk when Joe comes out of the garage. Patrick walks right up to him and wraps Joe in another noticeably long hug. "See you tomorrow, man," he says, clapping Joe on the back.

I mouth *sorry* to Joe while trying not to laugh.

Eight

THANKSGIVING PREP IS IN full swing back in my apartment. The kitchen smells like spices and baking bread. Patrick and I are enlisted in peeling potatoes next to Robbie, who's cutting green beans and who I'm glad to have as our new buffer. What's more, we have the entertainment of hearing Robbie attempt to convince our mom to let Chloe come to dinner.

"I'm sure Chloe has plans with her own family," Mom says decisively.

Or *I* consider her reply decisive. Robbie does not. "Her parents are super chill," he insists. "They won't mind."

Mom turns up the heat on the stove. The blue flame grows under the pot of cranberry sauce. "Do you even know her parents? You two started dating like last week."

Dad, who's kneading bread at the counter, nods in silent agreement.

I hide my grin behind a potato I'm peeling when Robbie frowns, realizing he doesn't have a good defense. "What if she asks them and they agree?" he poses to Mom with renewed energy. *"Then* can she come?"

Mom opens the oven to check on the turkey, pouring the smell into the room. I know she's only half paying attention to this debate. "It's just not appropriate," she says. "We'll have her over for dinner another night."

"How is it not appropriate?" Robbie protests, sounding indignant. "Siena has *her* boyfriend here. Why can't I have my girlfriend?"

I exchange a look of amusement with Patrick. We know what's coming. It's not the first time Robbie has tried to include various girlfriends in holidays, family road trips, birthday plans. It never works. Invariably, the girlfriends do end up coming over for dinner "another night." I've made enough conversation with Katies and Sarahs over Macaroni Grill sides for a lifetime.

"Patrick is different," Mom pronounces. "He's family."

I cringe inside, guilty and stressed.

Robbie opens his mouth, but I'll never know what poorly planned point he was going to make because Dad chooses now to interject. "Your grandparents don't need to see you and Chloe making out before they eat, Robert. They'll lose their appetite."

Robbie cuts the edges off his green beans with vigor. "You can't compare me to Siena and Patrick," he complains. "They're . . . old."

I put down my potato. "Hey!"

He ignores me. "So you're saying I can't have my girlfriend

over until we've been together long enough to be *boring*? No offense," he adds to Patrick, and very deliberately not to me.

Patrick doesn't get the chance to respond because Mom fixes Robbie with a withering glare. "If you could demonstrate the maturity needed to stay with one girl for more than three months, then we could *maybe* invite her to Thanksgiving *next year*," Mom says with finality.

Under ordinary circumstances, I would love watching my mom dunk on Robbie like this. Even with three years of Model UN on my résumé, I don't have half of my mom's debating skill. Right now, however, I'm unable to enjoy the demonstration. Robbie's words have gotten under my skin like salt in a hangnail. Not because they were mean, but because he wasn't wrong. We *are* boring. I used to hide the word behind *stable, comfortable, drama-free*. The fact that my self-involved fifteen-year-old brother sees it proves how undeniable it is.

Robbie pouts into his green beans. Even he's smart enough to know not to press Mom further.

"You know, just because we've been together for three years," Patrick says to Robbie, "doesn't mean we're boring. It means we're special." I can't quite read his tone. Patrick is never ever less than graceful and enthusiastic with Robbie. Right now, though, there's something other than innocent observation in his voice.

Robbie glances at him. "Sure. Yeah," he says. They're even and flavorless syllables. Without elaborating, Robbie stands, pulling out his phone. I know he's heading outside for privacy to FaceTime Chloe.

While my parents start up a detailed discussion about the oven schedule, I'm left with just Patrick. I guess it was inevitable, which suddenly feels obvious. *Yes, Siena, you will end up spending time alone with your own boyfriend.*

Patrick slides his chair closer to me. I can only muster a weak smile, still hating how hard my brother's words were to deny.

"Hey," Patrick says, his voice soft. "I know what you're thinking."

I search his expression. Once, Patrick really did know everything I was thinking. Where I wanted to go for dinner, what conversation I was worrying over, what tests had me stressed. Does he feel this, too? How boring we've become?

"You're wrong, though," he goes on. "I'd be happy to make out with you in front of your grandparents to prove it."

A laugh escapes me, catching me by surprise. His face splits into a delighted grin. Despite the heat of the kitchen, his reaction warms me in a different way, even while it makes me a little sad.

He must notice, because sympathy shades over his expression. He leans closer to me, elbows on the table, hands clasped in front of him. "Whatever it is, you can tell me," he says, quieter.

He's only inches from me, smelling the way he does. While Patrick's kindness is genuine, I'm caught off guard. I'm certain he's got *no idea* what a huge answer I could give him. I chew my lip, working over what to say. With hours until *Thanksgiving dinner* with my entire family, I'm pretty sure it's not the time to unravel my every messy misgiving and uncertainty about our relationship.

Spontaneously, I reach for my reply—and grasp on to some smaller, more manageable truth. "I just wonder if we've been together so long we've forgotten how to flirt," I say.

I notice it's strangely relieving to confess. It's only one of my fears, but it's a real one. While I'm not ready to get into every problem with our relationship, I feel okay with maybe opening up this one. It makes me suddenly grateful for our privacy.

I watch Patrick closely for his reaction, which surprises me. He looks . . . amused. There's even relief in his familiar features.

"Me?" he says. "Forget how to flirt? No way."

Once more, I laugh. His amusement is contagious, even if it's the last thing I expected. Still, it's welcome, especially when privately, I sometimes wonder whether I'm not the only one whose passion has faded. For both of our sakes, I wouldn't want him to stay with me if he's not feeling a spark.

Looking pleased, Patrick leans just a little closer. "Need I remind you how I put the moves on you in sophomore year? You think those skills were a fluke?"

I don't need reminding. In AP European history, we had to do a "French Enlightenment Salon" presentation, each of us playing philosophers or social critics exchanging ideas in one unstructured conversation. He played Voltaire, while I was Descartes. He flirted with me so much our teacher wrote in his feedback that to his knowledge, Voltaire and Descartes never had a "romantic liaison" on account of them not even being contemporaries.

The memory is like melted ice cream. Sweet, but spoiled. It aches in a place I thought empty. "I don't think you've ever been so proud of a B minus," I say softly, holding on to the sweetness.

Patrick doesn't hesitate. "Absolutely worth the five hours of extra credit I did to rescue my GPA."

We share a smile. I don't know if it's at all sad for Patrick. It is for me. I have so many happy memories of him, of the Patrick I fell for. But memories aren't enough to hold two people together, I remind myself. What we had feels like history, no different from Descartes and Voltaire. Things I know happened instead of things I feel.

Like he's reading my mind, Patrick's expression shifts. I hardly recognize the way his eyes dance. "I have *not* forgotten how to flirt," he assures me. "I'll prove it to you."

Automatically, I scoff. Then I catch myself. I look over, studying him, not sure what I'm hearing. "How?" I ask.

Patrick doesn't move, his shoulders relaxed, his hands still folded. He looks perfectly comfortable. "Just prepare yourself to be flirted with," he says. "And while I'm at it, I'm going to challenge you to dust off *your* skills as well."

My stomach flutters a little, my smile loosening into something more like a smirk. I'm surprised and not surprised at the same time. On the one hand, my boyfriend wants to flirt with me. Super normal. On the other, *my* boyfriend wants to flirt with *me*, which hasn't happened in months, for sure. It's like how in a dream, stuff makes a weird sort of sense even when it's wildly different from real life.

What he's proposing would definitely count as giving him mixed signals. I want to do it anyway. And maybe, I realize, it's something I *have* to do to know for sure if we still have anything.

Patrick raises his eyebrows, waiting for my reply.

"Come on, Griffin," he says. "Show me what you've got."

The look he's sending me is one I'm distantly familiar with. I can't quite place it, like I'm squinting over an unfocused photograph. Until it hits me, and suddenly I'm fifteen, in the front of the class with Victor Hugo and the Marquis de Lafayette. The sparkle in Patrick's eyes, the smug curve of his lips. It's exactly the look Patrick-Voltaire gave me years ago.

I can't help it. "Game on," I say.

Nine

IN MY ROOM, I'M putting on earrings. I don't do earrings very often. When I'm just going to school or Joe's, they're not worth the hassle. The pair I've picked out now has small gems dangling from the ends, and I would have worn them even if Patrick and I hadn't had our conversation in the kitchen. Thanksgiving is occasion enough. Nevertheless, Patrick's promise to flirt with me rings in my ears, and I'm not unconscious of how I look.

With dinner starting soon, he and I went to our rooms to change. I put on a flowy yellow dress, one I bought early in the school year. It's long-sleeved, loose in the skirt, and fitted in the torso. I bought it even though it's like nothing I've ever owned—or because it's like nothing I've ever owned. I'm more of T-shirt dress and Vans kind of person, but this dress was too unique to ignore. I had to know what I'd look like in it. Like I was trying on a new version of myself. Which felt silly when I first thought it—it's a dress, not a personality. But on the other hand, I'm searching for who I want to be somewhere, and this striking dress seemed like not the worst place to start.

I only have one earring in when I hear a knock on the door.

Opening it, I find Patrick in the hall. He's wearing the black button-down I know his mom got him for MUN last year. He looks good. It shakes my focus for a second, the jumbled feelings of not being fully used to having him in front of me, of his smirk in the kitchen, of how I remember looking forward to seeing him dress up for MUN conferences. "I'm almost ready," I say, recovering. "Give me a minute."

Returning to my dresser to put in the other earring, I leave the door open.

Patrick pauses a moment. Then he walks in, closing the door gently behind him.

"You look beautiful," he says. "I've never seen that dress before. Is it new?"

"Um," I start, finishing with my earring. "Not really. I got it not long after you left."

New to you, I could've said. The months we've spent in different cities, the differences in our lives, sit behind my words.

With Patrick reflected in my dresser mirror, I watch those differences settle onto him. He looks sad, and it makes me wonder how he must feel, returning home and finding so much unfamiliar. The fact it's happened slowly doesn't mean it hasn't happened, like how clouds don't look like they're moving when you watch them—until you glance down, then look up minutes later and find the whole sky changed.

I wonder what other things he finds unfamiliar. I wonder if I'm one of them.

Of course I'm not, though. I'm exactly who I was when Patrick left, despite my flailing efforts to figure out who else I might want to be. It's uniquely disappointing, but undeniable. Patrick's hometown might look different to him, but me? The distinctions end with this dress. I try to ignore how itchy the sleeves suddenly feel.

"Well, you look amazing," he says, his voice revealing nothing.

Facing him, I find his expression expectant. Which confuses me. I don't know what he wants me to say. Patrick's not vain—he doesn't give compliments in hopes of receiving them in return—but there's definitely something he's waiting for.

"Wait," I say when I realize. "Don't tell me this is you flirting."

Patrick doesn't even look wounded. "Obviously this is me flirting!" he says. I can't help it. I laugh. "Don't laugh," Patrick responds despairingly. "Siena, I live in a major metropolitan area. I didn't need to leave Austin, get on a plane, and come to your house to get *murdered.*"

I laugh harder. "Sorry," I say, grinning with my hand over my mouth. "It's just, you always tell me I look nice."

He gives me a flat look.

"Yeah," he says. "Almost like I've been flirting with you for years and you never noticed."

Even though we're still joking, there's a hint of bitterness in Patrick's voice. I notice it not because I hear it often, but because I don't. Patrick is never resentful, not when he did everything on a debate group project in AP US without help from his partner, not when I had a period crisis and was late to homecoming last year. He's nice literally whenever he can be, which means my not noticing has genuinely gotten to him. It makes me feel a little guilty.

I speak gentler. "I just think flirting and compliments aren't the same. Flirting should be . . . fun."

"Actually," he starts, and while the sting isn't gone from his voice, neither is the humor, "the definition of flirting is to communicate—whether through spoken, written, or physical means—romantic interest or attraction."

My eyes widen. "Did you *Google* flirting before you came in here?"

"I wanted to get it right." His cheeks flame.

I feel myself soften. "That's sort of—" I falter. I know what I want to say, the word sitting on the edge of my lips. I know why I'm not saying it. In a split second, I decide to ignore my reasons. "Adorable," I finish.

Patrick overlooks the compliment. "Well, apparently I missed something in my online research," he says so seriously I almost laugh again, until he sits down heavily on my duvet. Looking dejected, he doesn't meet my eyes. "The difficulty is you already know I'm attracted to you," he goes on, like he's explaining a complicated international relations issue. "It's why I'm dating you."

"It's just nice to be reminded of it sometimes," I reply. "Nice to feel like you enjoy showing me." *Nice to feel like you even want to,* I don't say.

He looks up. His expression flickers with something else I hardly recognize. Something sly.

"I think I need a demonstration," he says. "Since you're the expert."

The little laugh I give now is different. I'm kind of embarrassed, kind of charmed. I have to hand it to him, it was a good line. It's put me on the spot—and fairly so. I'm only sheepish because I'm not exactly a black belt in flirting myself.

I stop overthinking it. *What the hell? Why shouldn't I flirt with my own boyfriend?*

I walk over to the bed. Sitting down next to him, I give him a long look, one I hope is smoldering, instead of an unlit burner clicking on the stove.

Patrick faces me, lightly questioning. "Yes?"

"*Shh.* I'm flirting with you."

He grins wide, and *god, okay,* it's possible I'm not doing this for purely demonstrative purposes. Patrick's smile was one of the first things I fell for. It's Hershey's-bar-melting-in-your-mouth warm. I slide closer to him and cross my legs, letting my knees graze his thigh.

Now he's silent. His eyes drift to our legs.

I'm close enough to smell his familiar scent. Memories steal over me of making out with him for the first time in his room, in the house where he no longer lives, on the plaid comforter I think every teenage boy has some version of.

Everything was new, exciting, uncharted. Just the scent of him now is enough to bring back some of those feelings. I put my hand lightly on his thigh.

"Wait, *this* is flirting?" he asks. I hear the excitement hiding under his incredulity. It's enough to bring back feelings, too. "I'm not sure it counts—"

I cut him off. "Are you saying you don't like it?"

"No!" he replies hastily. "Please, um. Carry on."

I laugh. Then I chew my lip, letting my eyes trail down his body while he watches. I stop forcing myself not to *over-think* and just let myself *think*. I realize I'm not just doing this for the hell of it. I'm enjoying myself. When my eyes return to Patrick's, his gaze is heated.

"Patrick . . ." I say, while he leans closer, his hand playing with the hem of my dress. I drop my voice lower, soft and sultry. "I think I'm ready . . ."

His face closes in. His eyes dip to my chest, which sends a pleased shiver down me, even though there's no reason for it to. Patrick has seen me shirtless plenty of times. Though maybe that's what thrills me. He's seen me with much less on, and still, here he is, looking.

Which makes me just a little sorry for what I say next.

"Ready for some turkey!" I finish my sentence with no hint of smolder. I spring up, holding my hand out for him. Patrick stares for a second. Then a laugh bursts out of him.

"You're extremely cruel, you know," he says.

I shrug. "You're having fun, though, aren't you?"

"Fun is one of a few things I'm having."

I flush a little, which I don't care if he notices. His mind is probably elsewhere. He takes my hand, and we walk into the hallway in time to hear the front door opening. My dad greets my grandparents warmly with hugs and smiles. He's great with his in-laws, and my mom says he has been since he first met her parents.

I feel Patrick's hand move to my back. Inconspicuously, it slides a little lower. He looks at my grandparents, then leans in, his lips a whisper from the shell of my ear. "Just say the word, Siena," he says softly.

Grinning, I elbow him lightly, remembering his earlier make-out offer. We walk into the dining room, flushed and holding in laughter.

I realize I haven't felt this spark with Patrick in months. It's like exercising old muscles, like waking up as a past version of myself. I'm happy—and I'm not relieved. I'm even more confused. A couple hours ago I was 90 percent sure I'd be breaking up with him. Now, I'm down to . . . probably 50. It's not comforting. In fact, it's left me in the furthest place from either decision. The middle.

With only two days to decide.

Ten

PICKING AT MY MASHED potatoes, I'm wedged in between Patrick and my grandma, who's leaning over me to describe to my boyfriend the plot of the novel she's reading. She's gotten really into the cozy mysteries where animals help solve crimes, featuring titles with pet puns and cute pictures on their paperback covers. She just finished *Ruff Justice*, and while she elaborates on how Lieutenant Spot and his wounded, wisecracking handler save the city, Patrick nods diligently, listening with real interest, even asking questions. His concentration doesn't falter even when he passes my dad the gravy.

My family's Thanksgiving is small. It's only me, my parents, Robbie, my grandparents on my mom's side, and Patrick. Of course, it's not like our apartment could hold crowds. The dining room is part of the kitchen, and the wooden table my parents have had forever, painted a dusty red, is wedged under their wedding photos on the wall. With seven of us seated at once, you can hardly move from one end to the other.

The intimacy of our celebration only emphasizes just how woven into the fabric of my family Patrick is. He knows my grandparents well even though they live in Flagstaff and only visit for special occasions. He's hiked with me in the woods near their cabin, listening while my grandpa identified birds from the guide he reads like it's the newspaper. He celebrated Grandma's seventieth in February. I couldn't imagine bringing anyone else home who would so patiently listen as Grandma completely spoils how Lieutenant Spot apprehends Mr. Abernathy, the mayor's killer. By the end of dinner, I know she'll hand him her copy of *Ruff Justice*— dog-eared—which he'll dutifully read. He might even write her a long email of his thoughts. It'll make her day.

Everyone in my family loves Patrick. My mom said it herself—he's family.

Except he *isn't*. The thought prods into me like a thorn. Everyone is eager to surround us with white picket fences, but I'm seventeen. He's my high-school boyfriend. Shouldn't we have some boundaries? Some sense that now doesn't necessarily mean forever? It's an unfair position they've put me in. If I break up with Patrick, it'll hurt my family. It won't just push him out of my life, it'll push him out of theirs.

I unenthusiastically pile potatoes on my plate. Eventually, I'll date someone new—someone who my parents will compare to Patrick, with whom they've never found a single flaw. If I have a new boyfriend next year, will he even be welcome at Thanksgiving? Or will my parents treat him like one of Robbie's girlfriends?

"You good?"

Patrick's voice is low, for only me to hear. His hand has found my knee, and I realize I'm frowning. Looking over, I find his warm brown eyes on me, gently inquisitive. I force my face into a weak smile.

I don't have to reply. Grandpa interrupts us from across the stuffing. "So, have you two started college applications yet?"

It's even harder keeping my smile upright now. "Not yet," I say lightly.

Mom chimes in, sounding innocent while she digs determinedly into the cranberry sauce. "They're due by the end of the year, though, right?"

I permit myself to purse my lips. Mom knows perfectly well when they're due. She's pushed me about them literally every week since the school year started. I swear, she pokes around on College Confidential whenever she's not checking Robbie's scores and standing on the Arizona Interscholastic Association website. While I've resisted her efforts, she knows I can't hide from this conversation in the middle of Thanksgiving dinner. Hence her latching on to Grandpa's question.

"Yup," I say unflappably. "Guess I'll have to start sometime next month."

Mom shoots me a look. I pretend I don't see it, stuffing some potatoes in my mouth to forestall further conversation. Objectively, I know my mom's concern is fair. It *is* time to work on college apps. I'm not avoiding the hard work of writing half a dozen essays about myself, although I'm not exactly looking forward to it, either. I'm hesitant because I don't know what I want next year to look like. Many of my friends and classmates are applying to specific art schools or engineering programs. They know what they want to do with their lives.

I don't. I don't have one guiding passion, like theater, computer science, or architecture. Not yet.

Mom changes her strategy cleverly. "How about you, Patrick?" she asks, casual and congenial as ever. "Surely *you* have a very organized college list."

Patrick laughs uncomfortably. "I'm still doing my research."

I stay silent, knowing Patrick's deflection is charitable. He knows exactly what he wants to do in college. He's probably finished half of his applications already. I'm a little grateful he's eased the pressure on me, and a little frustrated he's given me one more reason to appreciate him.

Mom doesn't drop it. "Pre-med, right?"

Patrick is unable to help himself. His instincts kick in. "Definitely," he says, nodding.

I shift in my seat. Mom's unknowingly stumbled onto a different pressure point of mine. It's been Patrick's plan since freshman year—pre-med, med school, the whole white-coated nine yards. I've never understood his conviction. Patrick's smart, so he does well in math and science, but he has to work twice as hard as he does in English and history. He wasn't going to be president of Model UN just for his likeability. He gaveled at every conference, and he reads about politics and international relations for fun. Each year, I wait for him to admit he's grown out of the plan he picked when he was fifteen, probably inspired by his surgeon mother. Each year, he doesn't, and he never will. Patrick is a committed committer.

Mom redirects her gaze. I know she's focused when she doesn't reprimand Robbie for reaching over fully half the table to serve himself more turkey. "Siena," she says, "don't you wish you had Patrick's certainty for something?"

I glare. I know I'll get no help from Dad, who's keeping his head down, cutting his turkey into progressively tinier pieces. Grandma's watching us like we're *Days of our Lives*, while I know Grandpa, who's following the conversation without interjecting, is complicit with Mom. *Okay*, I decide, *fine*. If she wants to have this discussion in front of guests, knowing they're keeping me hostage, then she can't get upset in front of guests when I don't give her what she wants.

"I agree," I say, sweet and sour as her cranberry sauce. "It *would* be nice."

Mom doesn't hesitate. "What about Model UN?"

My lips flatten. Like yesterday, I'm again realizing the reasons I've hung on to Model UN might not be worthwhile ones. I feel like I'm walking toward a fork in the road I'd never really considered reaching.

The idea doesn't scare me. Which is why I don't hesitate to lob this information like a grenade into this pseudo-fight with my mom. "I'm not sure how much longer I'll do Model UN, actually," I say casually.

"Siena!" my mom exclaims. I raise an eyebrow, and she remembers where she is. "We'll discuss this later."

Patrick dashes into the fray, defending me unnecessarily. "Siena's great at so many things. She's an excellent public speaker, and she loves history. She'll definitely get into a good college," he finishes confidently.

It's painfully sweet. I'm hit with a pang of affection at Patrick's description of me. He's not entirely wrong—I guess I like history and public speaking. I just also like reality TV, classic rock, and recreational volleyball. None of them are passions I want to found an entire future on.

"What part of the country do you want to go to, sweetie?" Grandma asks, her voice about fifty degrees warmer than Mom's. "Who cares what you study? Pick somewhere that excites you."

I give her a genuine smile, and for once, I really consider the question. Images form in my head of the frosty East Coast, of chilly Chicago, of the Pacific Northwest, until I find my reply. "I want to go somewhere near the beach," I say. "That feels like a nice change from the desert."

Instinctually, I start imagining the me who lives near the beach. Flip-flops every day, beach bag loaded with textbooks or novels to read on the sand. Learning to surf in the summer, learning to snowboard in the winter. *West Coast Siena.* It's nothing like the me I would find in the mirror right now—which is exactly what's exciting.

Mom is physically unable to not pounce on the idea. "A UC school maybe? UCLA? UC San Diego?"

"I'm not ready to commit just yet," I reply levelly.

"No one is making you commit, honey," Mom says. "We just want to help you."

Her patronization pushes me past my limit. I would have preferred further rigorous questioning. I decide to slam the door on the discussion. "Mom, I'll apply to college," I snap. "And when I'm there, I'll explore my options." Refusing her the opportunity to find her new argumentative angle, I pivot quickly. "Hey, let's all ask Robbie about his new workout regimen."

"The gains are amazing," Robbie says without a moment's pause.

Satisfied, I finish my potatoes while Robbie goes on about circuit training, leg day, and high-protein diets. It's not long until everyone's hiding their boredom under polite *oh yeahs* and *tell me mores*. Except me, and not just because I'm glad I'm out of Mom's line of fire. No one can deny Robbie is passionate about lifting. While it's easy to make fun of, I respect him for it.

I respect everyone who knows what they want out of their next five or fifteen years. It's just not me, and I'm fine with not having decided already. I'm not a nothing—I'm just a not-yet. I like the opportunities opening up for me. I could do anything, be anyone. I just need the chance to try things, the freedom to figure out what fits.

I focus on the food for the rest of dinner, ignoring the

nervous glances I'm getting from Patrick. I don't understand where they're coming from until I remember what I said to my mom. *I'm not ready to commit to anything. I'll explore my options.*

While I hadn't explicitly meant him, I hadn't *not* meant him, either. Regardless, I'm not taking back what I said. No matter what happens with him and me at the end of this trip.

Eleven

THE REST OF DINNER goes uneventfully. Mom doesn't mention college again, which is a small comfort. I know she's saving up her comments for when Patrick returns home.

After we finish eating, Patrick insists on helping with the dishes, and he and Robbie and I spend what feels like forever cleaning practically every plate my family owns. When we're done, the guys put on the Bond movie. With my feet curled under me on our perfectly worn gray couch, I half watch while I text everyone to invite them to the party tomorrow. It's late, and it's possible I doze off while *Bond, James Bond* expertly drives yet another fancy car.

On the way back to my room from brushing my teeth, I stop in front of Robbie's door. I push it open quietly. While my parents don't have a strict no-closed-door policy with Patrick and me, I also know they won't hesitate to enforce one if they think I'm abusing my freedom. I find Patrick lying on Robbie's bed, wearing sweats and a long-sleeve shirt, reading *Ruff Justice*.

I'm hit with the sickly sweet combination of affection

and guilt I'm getting increasingly familiar with. "You know you don't have to read that," I say immediately. If I do dump him, I really hope it's not when he's one hundred pages into canine crime fighting.

Patrick smiles, his expression openhearted enough it makes me almost regret coming in here. "I don't mind. Really," he says. He looks down at the book. "I'm definitely suspicious of Mr. Abernathy. He's the only character without a pet."

I say nothing, my own smile forced and wobbly. I press my palms to my pajama shorts.

While I'm silent, Patrick's expression shifts. He puts the book down, giving me a serious look. "Siena, can we talk real quick?"

My stomach clenches. *He knows.* "Um. Yeah," I say, except I'm completely, 100 percent lying. I'm not ready for this conversation. Starting to panic, I sit down in Robbie's desk chair. The cushion is worn to nearly nothing, the plastic frame poking into me uncomfortably.

"Are you really going to quit Model UN?" Patrick asks.

I open my mouth, anticipating every question except this one. "Oh. Um. I think so," I say, recollecting myself, feeling relieved but also confused. "I think I need a change. MUN was always more your thing than mine." I hear steadiness in my voice.

Patrick nods, saying nothing.

It's probably enough for me to wrap up the conversation pleasantly. Except now, I'm curious. "Does it . . . bother you?" I ask.

He frowns. "Not exactly. I just . . ." I wait while he

formulates his response, unexpectedly nervous. "Everyone knows you're part of MUN. Alicia's depending on you for conferences and stuff. I guess I just don't understand why you'd check out of something you committed to."

"They're not *depending* on me. I'm not very good," I say, forcing humor. Knowing I have to face the real points he's making, I continue more soberly. "I . . . don't really enjoy it anymore, and I don't see why I should make myself do it. It's just a club. It shouldn't matter to you—or anyone—if I'm in it. Unless"—I skirt his eyes—"what you're saying is you wouldn't like me if I don't do Model UN anymore."

Patrick's reply comes automatically, which is not exactly comforting. "I'll like you no matter what."

"Why?"

When Patrick looks up uncertainly, I meet his eyes. I know I've moved the conversation much past MUN.

Still, I repeat myself. "Why *do* you like me?"

His forehead furrows in confusion. "I just . . . do. I've always liked you, Siena."

I sigh a little, feeling proven right. He's already moved on from the *why* to the *when*. I wish he would admit where his resistance to me quitting MUN is coming from—admit he doesn't want me to change, ever, because then we might not fit together.

His expression has clouded, like he's realized he's said the wrong thing. "I want you to be happy," he adds, sounding sincere. "If that means quitting Model UN, then you should."

It frustrates me a little—enough to make me glad I didn't

leave the room with the conversation unspoken. "Great, well, I want us *both* to be happy."

Patrick's eyes narrow, not angrily, just intently. While I fuss with the drawstring of my shorts, he pauses, undoubtedly choosing his next words with care.

"I *am* happy," he says. It's loaded honesty. I don't reply, and he continues. "Aside from Model UN, what, um . . ." He pauses like he's preparing himself. "What else might you want to change?"

There's defeat in his voice, and his expression makes my heart crack. I pull my eyes gently from his to stare into the room, my mind registering how painfully humorous it is we're having this conversation amid Robbie's filthy furnishings. Even so, we're here now. I know what Patrick's asking, and I can't lie to him.

So I don't. "I'm not sure yet," I say.

He swallows. "Okay."

When he picks his book back up, something in me sinks. *This* is the worst I've felt since before he left this summer.

It takes me some moments to figure out why. He's not going to fight for me, not even going to try to convince me why we should be together. Maybe, I reason generously with myself, he's scared it wouldn't work. Or maybe he just doesn't care enough.

"Right. Well, goodnight," I say.

Then I wait. Patrick senses the intention in the pause. This would be the moment we should kiss goodnight.

Sure enough, Patrick leans forward.

Hesitation locks us momentarily in place. I don't know whose fault it is—I might tilt my head slightly, or Patrick might miss the angle—but whichever it is, his lips land on my cheek. Neither of us corrects it, and when he withdraws, I get the lingering feeling the non-kiss wasn't exactly accidental.

"Night, Siena." The wan smile he gives me isn't even the faintest shadow of the one I got from flirtatious Patrick earlier.

I stand, hot with something I haven't felt in every reevaluation of us—resentment. *A peck on the cheek?* This entire trip, we've hardly touched. It's largely because I've been trying to put distance between us, but honestly, it hasn't been that hard. Patrick hasn't even been trying.

The idea he doesn't care introduces something new into the equations I've been running since summer, formulating my restless percentages. Maybe Patrick doesn't want *me*. The only thing he wants is the routine our relationship gives him, the routine of *PatrickandSiena*. While it's not enough for me anymore, maybe he wants nothing more.

I carefully shut Robbie's door behind me. When I do, I'm surprised to find a tear stealing down my cheek.

Twelve

THE NEXT DAY, I'M not surprised when Patrick suggests we go to the public library.

I *am* incredulous at his decision, which is different from surprised. When we weren't going to the West Vista library after school, Patrick and I would head to the public library and work on homework in companionable silence. I'm amazed we've spent months learning new routines and figuring out how to enjoy our different lives, and now we only have a couple days in each other's company and *still* Patrick just wants to study in the library. He's acting like he's going to go to school with me on Monday, our West Vista lives unchanged.

We sit at our regular table. We organize our books and notebooks in their regular arrangement, Patrick's in one stack and mine fanned out on the side. I'm silently resentful of how easily I set them up, muscle memory kicking in. We start in on the homework we were each assigned over Thanksgiving.

I'd be on edge if everything were normal, but it's not,

which is making me more on edge. Patrick hasn't even mentioned our conversation last night, hasn't acted differently in any way. He's been nothing but pleasant and genial. It's like suffocating in cake frosting, and I'm over it. He doesn't want to know any more about the doubts and frustrations weighing on my mind. He just wants to go to the library, study side by side, and pretend nothing ever changes.

The worst part is, it's working. I've only been to the public library once or twice since the summer. Each time, I didn't stay long, finding everything too weird. It was like joining a tour group through a museum of my past life. Now, though, sitting with Patrick, the feeling has faded. The familiar routine is uncannily easy to fall into. Like the past three months never happened.

Patrick slides his highlighter toward me, the way we used to share the neon pens. On instinct, I reach for it.

Then I stop myself, curling my fingernails into my palm. I will *not* walk backward and blindfolded into old patterns. The point of this visit was to figure out what I want from the future, not to repeat the past. Being here isn't helpful.

I close my book. "I need to"—I come up with my explanation on the fly—"run some errands. For the party." I stand up, shoving my books into my backpack. "We'll need drinks for tonight, maybe some snacks."

Patrick starts to rise. "Oh, well," he says. He looks earnest, like he's trying, which I know is only because this deviation doesn't come naturally to him. "I'll go with you," he offers.

"No." I don't regret the way the word snaps out of me.

I'm kind of pissed he doesn't want to discuss last night, doesn't care what's going on under the surface as long as our Friday afternoons look the same. "You only have one full day here, and you shouldn't spend it at Trader Joe's," I say firmly. Patrick opens his mouth like he's going to object, but I cut him off. "You said you wanted to finish your homework at the library, and that's what you should do. You should do everything you want while you're here. I'll only be an hour, maybe two. It's not worth interrupting your day."

I shoulder my backpack, realizing part of me hopes he won't leave the discussion here. For a moment, I let myself believe he's going to insist he wants to be with me. Rather than repeating our standard school days of library homework, he'll point out he's here to spend time with his girlfriend.

I realize I'm waiting in his silence. "I'll see you back at your house, then?" he asks instead.

While I register my disappointment, I try to keep it off my face. Disappointment that he doesn't want to come with me is nothing but more muscle memory. I shrug on the other strap of my backpack. "See you there," I say, not meeting his eyes.

I walk out of the library. The change I feel is instantaneous. It's relief, even freedom. My steps feel lighter as I start off down the sidewalk.

It's ironic, I realize. My boyfriend traveled a thousand miles to see me, and here I am, needing space.

Thirteen

I PERUSE THE SNACKS slowly, stalling.

Upon leaving the library, I realized I needed a car, which left me on Joe's doorstep one fifteen-minute walk later. When he opened his front door and found me, he didn't bother to hide how his face fell. His exact words were *Now what?* I gave him my winningest smile. Like I suspected it would, it earned me the short drive over to Trader Joe's.

"I thought everyone was supposed to bring leftovers to this party," Joe says, following me down the aisle listlessly. "Do we really need"—he pulls two packages out of my cart—"peanut-butter pretzels and pancake bread? What even is pancake bread?"

I return them deliberately to the cart. "Yes," I say. "We do. And pancake bread is delicious."

He fixes me with a look while I pick up the white package I've been reading. "Okay," he replies. "Well, I don't think we need *granola*." He intercepts the bag I'm holding and returns it to the shelf.

I honestly hadn't even realized I was holding ancient-grains-and-nuts granola. Not really. I've been thinking, weighing the decision I'll have made this time tomorrow.

I spin to face Joe. "What would you do if you were me?" I ask him in the wild hope of having someone else solve my problem for me.

"Well." He considers. "I'd probably buy some lemonade and sparkling water."

I frown. "No. I mean, yes, let's get those," I say. "But I meant Patrick. Would you break up with him?" While one wobbly wheel rattles, I push the cart into the drinks aisle. The store is more crowded than I would have predicted, even for Black Friday. Joe and I circumvent moms with toddlers and older customers taking their time examining their options while the store's usual '80s rock plays indistinctly.

"I think he's nice, but I'm just not really attracted to him, you know?" Joe replies.

I swat his shoulder. "I'm serious," I say.

Stopping in front of the lemonade, Joe sighs. His expression sobers, his eyes drifting from mine. "I think if you have to keep asking yourself that question, then you already know the answer. I mean, Patrick's here to visit you and you're avoiding him in the snack aisle of Trader Joe's."

My heart sinks. Suddenly, my decision feels painfully clear. It's something I've been overlooking for months. In every question I've asked myself about Patrick and me, I've neglected the question of the question itself. It's not pleasant, but it's undeniable. I know what I need to do.

Wrestling with this, I grab a pack of sparkling water from one of the lower shelves. I'm shoving it under the cart when I hear a familiar voice. "Hey, guys."

I straighten up, finding people I know from school walking toward us. Reed Kim and Lacey Ramos, both seniors in the drama department. I've always known *of* Reed and Lacey since they're prominent in every school musical. I've only gotten to know Reed this year, though. He sits behind me in English. On the couple peer-review exercises for which we were partners, we both had fun.

He's pushing a shopping cart while Lacey follows. I'm not surprised to find he's wearing an unbuttoned brown vest over a plain white tee, with rips in the knees of his skinny jeans. Reed is a hipster, no question. He pulls off his loud stylings due to a combination of unabashed charisma and good looks. He has tawny skin, playful eyes, and black hair so straight it never really looks messy, even when it is.

"Hey," I say. "What's up?"

"Nothing much." Reed smiles, something he does a lot of. "Having a party tonight and grabbing some mixers." He reaches past me for the seltzer water and cranberry juice.

I immediately feel childish. Here I am, getting lemonade for my party while Reed picks out mixers for a *real* party with *real* drinks.

"You guys should come, if you're free," Reed says enthusiastically, looking to Joe and me.

"We're going to play a drinking-game version of

charades." Lacey glances up from her phone. "It's supposed to be hilarious."

I flush. "I wish," I say. "I . . . have an MUN party, though."

Reed shrugs. "No problem. Feel free to stop by after if you want."

My awkwardness soaring, I reply stiffly, "Thanks. I probably can't tonight, though."

I'm not refusing on my own account. Reed's party is the kind of plan I would be interested in, because it would be different. It could let *me* be different. I don't really imagine myself a hard partier, but something like this could be fun. Truthfully, I would go if it were any other weekend.

But Patrick wouldn't. Drama kids and drinking? Two things in which he would have no interest because they're not part of our routine. It's our paradox. The fact that it's outside our unchanging plans is exactly what's exciting to me.

Nevertheless, no matter what I've decided, I owe Patrick some courtesy. Since it's his last night here—and our last night ever—I won't force him.

If Reed notices my frustrated, forced delivery, he doesn't react. "Another night," he replies easily.

A real smile slips out of me. "Totally," I say, meaning it. Pushing my cart forward while Joe follows, I remind myself that breaking up with Patrick will mean doing the things *I* want to. I'll determine my life on my own without running every choice through the eternal catalogue of checkboxes my relationship has become. I'll make decisions for myself, not for me *and* someone else.

When I reach the end of the aisle, I hear Lacey laugh. I glance over my shoulder and find Reed holding up an artisanal root beer like he's about to recite poetry to it. I chuckle to myself. Reed is larger than life in a goofy way, the opposite kind of charismatic from Patrick, who carries an intellectual confidence.

Joe clears his throat next to me.

I look at him. He's watching me with very indicative eyes. "What?" I ask.

"You know what."

"*No,*" I say, stopping the cart. I ignore how guilty my defensiveness might look. "What?" I repeat.

Joe hesitates. "Seems like you have more than one reason to break up with Patrick," he says, his expression strained, like contemplating my love life is causing him great stress, possibly indigestion.

"I don't *like* Reed," I shoot back, feeling my eyes flit wider. "Not like that." He raises a disbelieving eyebrow. "Even if I did," I go on hotly, "I am *not* looking to jump right back into another relationship. I just want to go to a party," I say, softer. "It's different." I start wheeling the cart up to the checkout line.

"You know," Joe begins delicately, "if you really want to go to that party tonight, you could always just ask Patrick."

"He won't want to go," I say instantly.

"How do you know?" Joe presses.

"I just know." I hand the cart off to the cashier. "It doesn't matter though. Because you're right. It's time I stop deliberating." I wish the conviction in my voice matched my words. Still, I go on. "Tomorrow, I break up with him."

Joe's quiet for a moment. When he speaks, it's with gentle humor. "Do you want to rehearse your breakup speech again?"

I laugh, a little less miserable. "No," I say. "Just promise me you won't leave Patrick and me alone for very long tonight. It'll be . . . harder to pretend when it's just the two of us."

"I'll be your requested third wheel," he promises.

"Thanks," I say, then look over more seriously. "I mean it. You're a really good friend."

While Joe rolls his eyes, I catch him hiding a smile. He shoves his hands into the pockets of his black jeans, leaving his *You're welcome* unsaid.

I pay for my groceries, and we continue into the parking lot, the asphalt warm in the midday sun. Finally, I feel kind of okay. I can do this. With Joe, with our friends surrounding us, I can get through this night. Then, by this time tomorrow, it'll finally be over.

Even if it hurts to imagine, it's a relief.

Fourteen

IN WRESTLING WITH THE Patrick question, I went overboard with the groceries. We have pretzels and pancake bread, crispy chickpeas and "veggie" fries, and four flavors of sparkling water, including cranberry clementine, which reflects creativity I'm not sure I've ever seen in seltzer. It takes me and Joe threading bags on each of our arms then hefting them like weight lifters to get everything into the house. We spend the next hour setting up in the backyard.

When we finish and I return home to Patrick, it's pretty much time for the party. I find him in Robbie's room, folding his Thanksgiving clothes and placing them neatly into his open duffel. It's one of our differences, one I've noticed on family vacations. While I stuff everything into my luggage just hoping it fits, Patrick folds and organizes precisely. It's the care he shows with everything, preparing his life so it's functional and comprehensible.

"Hey," I say. "How was your day?"

He startles at the sound of my voice. It's weird proof of how in just a few months, we've gotten used to not having each other nearby. When he relaxes, his smile seems forced. "It was nice," he says. "I finished my homework at the library, then got tacos."

I don't need to ask to know where he went. I've gone to Sonora with his family on plenty of Sunday nights. "Sounds perfect," I say honestly. I genuinely wanted him to do everything he'd looked forward to in Phoenix. I'm glad he did.

He doesn't reply, leaving the silence between us while he places the loafers he wore last night into his bag—with the soles pressed together, so no space is unfilled. His eyes go to the dresser, where I notice his old West Vista High sweatshirt.

I grab it for him, surprised he still has it. I've worn this sweatshirt. One day when Patrick and I were caught in unexpected Phoenix rain walking home from school, he gave it to me. With me cozy in the green hoodie, he didn't stop grinning the whole way to my house, even while the rain soaked his shirt. I held on to the sweatshirt for a full week, not wanting to part from his smell.

Sadness steals swiftly into my chest. I have memories like this with nearly everything of Patrick's. The hairbrush he kept on his dresser in his old bedroom, the jacket he wore to the football team's lock-in fundraiser in the gym, the socks with succulents on them my mom got him for Christmas last year. I know his things as well as I know my own.

By tomorrow, they'll all be gone from my life.

With my decision made, I'm starting to feel a new reality settling onto me. Patrick was a huge part of the last three years of my life. Important years, full of milestones I'll never repeat—high school, growing up. He was my first boyfriend, and the memories I have with him will be ones I cherish forever. Just because I'm choosing to end it doesn't mean I'll forget his fingerprints on my life.

I hand him the sweatshirt, and it feels like giving up a part of myself.

"Thanks," he says casually. It's impossible to ignore how it seems like we're living in separate worlds. Instead of packing the sweatshirt away, he puts it on, then moves his bag from the bed to the floor. "Just figured I should start packing now in case we're out late."

I latch on to his words. Remembering what Joe suggested in the store, I decide I have nothing to lose. "Yeah, actually, Reed Kim is having a thing tonight, and he invited us to come by," I say. "If you're interested in going to a real party later."

Patrick straightens up. He looks at me, not even skeptical, just confused. "We *are* going to a real party later."

"I mean one with, like, drinks," I say delicately. Patrick and I don't drink. It's not a huge imposition or unusual choice, and it's not like it's prevented us from having fun at the occasional party we've gone to where half the attendees were raging. Because we started dating so young, before any of our classmates drank, neither of us ever broke out of the pattern we established with each other.

Patrick's expression is clouded with disbelief, like he literally can't imagine why I'd even suggest what I did. Maybe he really can't. I know the plan I'm proposing is far outside our norm. I know I'm swinging for the fences. It's precisely the point.

Which is why I'm not surprised when it's a swing and a miss. "I don't think so," he says, gentle and final.

I nod. Despite the fact I knew it was what he'd say, I can't help being disappointed anyway. I don't try not to be, either. Disappointment is easier to handle when it doesn't have forever dangling off of it. I fix on a smile. "Right," I reply. "Well, you ready?"

"It's just, we've hardly had five minutes on our own since I got here," Patrick explains. There's some strain in his voice.

I could try to deny what he's saying, spin the events of this trip to point out all the times we *have* been alone together. But that wouldn't be fair to him. He's been patient, but of course he's picked up on the distance I've purposefully kept between us.

"I know," I tell him, my expression sympathetic. "I'm sorry."

"It's all right." Ever kind, he rushes to reassure me. "I know there's been a lot to fit into these couple days. And, look, I really am looking forward to seeing everyone. I appreciate that you've planned this homecoming party."

This turns my smile genuine. I reach out my hand for him, and he takes it. Leaving the house, I focus on what the evening could be. What it *will* be. Just because tomorrow will be the end of an era in my life doesn't mean I have to be sad. I can make tonight one last fond memory, one worth commemorating my first relationship. My first love.

Fifteen

I CUT SLIVERS FROM three different pumpkin pies, their colors varying from dusty orange to warm brown. Carrying my plate with me, I walk to the edge of Joe's pool, where I slide my sandals off. I dip my feet into the water, enjoying the cool even though it's not hot outside.

Joe's backyard is unbelievably perfect for parties, like the set decorator for some teen movie designed the spacious patio, lighted pool, and stretches of fake grass where we put coolers earlier. When Patrick and I got here, we weren't the first ones. Our friends had started trickling in while Joe's computer played songs from Spotify, moody hip-hop or soul music choruses looped and chopped up with electronic beats.

The party is in full swing now. It's not saying much—the MUN crowd is ten or twelve people hanging out in groups under the patio lights. While Joe isn't in Model UN, he's hung out with my friends enough to be friends with them, too. Besides, Joe knows the whole school. He could slide into any social circle he wanted and no one would question it.

Patrick is with the newly reunited Marcus and Jenny, standing near the drinks set up on Joe's outdoor bar. When everyone laughs, I'm hit with a strange feeling of dislocation, the sense everything's stayed the same even though it obviously hasn't. Patrick has slotted back into the group seamlessly. He looks happy, relaxed around our friends.

It makes me smile, which gives me the sudden urge to cry.

Tomorrow will hurt us both. But the pain means the relationship we had mattered, I remind myself. I push the feelings down, holding in my tears. There will be time for that later. Right now is for one last good memory.

Patrick glances over mid-laugh and notices me watching. His expression softens. Holding his gaze, I fight how hard it is knowing what I'm going to do tomorrow while he has no idea. He doesn't know to savor the night, doesn't know to memorize the details like I am. The care and contentment I see in his brown eyes are the same I feel. The context is just completely different.

Over the music humming into the night and the gentle rippling of water around my feet, I can't hear what Patrick's saying to the group. I figure he's excusing himself, because he breaks off from our friends and heads my way.

He joins me on my end of the pool, standing next to me. With him nearby, it's hard not to feel like some fundamental law of the universe has reasserted itself. The Griffin-Reynolds effect. Nobody will win Nobel prizes for studying this one, though. Especially not in twelve hours from now.

Patrick stares out over the setting sun. The Phoenix sky is lit up with vivid orange and purple, the clouds an endless blanket of fiery color. "Arizona sunsets are the most incredible in the world," he says with a note of longing in his voice. "It's magical."

I look out over the sky with him. This time, I can't object—it *is* otherworldly. The enormity of the sky, the view uninterrupted in every direction until the mountains rise in the distance. I give myself a moment not to take it for granted. When Patrick and I are over, I realize, happy memories won't be all he's left me. When I need them, I'll have his ways of looking at the world. His positivity, his conscientiousness. "No one in the history of mankind has ever found Phoenix magical," I say, teasing only a little.

He looks at me. "Well, I have."

While I smile, he sits down next to me. He takes off his shoes and socks, then rolls up his jeans and puts his feet in the water. Leaning back on his elbows, he's silent. It's not stilted silence. It's comfortable, with enough room in it for me to reflect on the many quiet moments like this one we've shared in our years together.

"Do you remember our first kiss?" I ask him.

He laughs, glancing sideways and meeting my eyes. "I could never forget it."

I reach forward, trailing my fingertips in the water. It was a night like this one, under the crimson glow of the sunset. Looking back, I feel how much *younger* we were. The years that separate now from then sit solidly in my memory, reminding me of how much has changed. Even so, the similarities stand out. The hush of the evening, the feel of Patrick at my side.

We'd gone out to the firepit in his yard. I ignore the pang

I feel knowing I'll never return to that firepit. Never return to those feelings, either. Not with Patrick. With the water lapping my shins, I can conjure the crackling flames, the way we both waited and waited for each other to make the first move. It was our third date, but the first that had ended with some privacy, instead of in a car while my mom or Patrick's dropped one of us off at home.

Next to me, Patrick speaks, picking up the memory like we're reliving it in some shared way. "We stayed outside for over an hour, just . . . talking about nothing. I was focused on building up my confidence. I thought the date had gone really well, and I was desperate to kiss you, but . . ." Laughing a little, he sits up straight to rub his neck.

"But what?" I prompt him. I want to enjoy this memory, enjoy its sweet reminders of everything we had that was good.

"But I was nervous, Siena!" he exclaims, playfully indignant. He's smiling sheepishly, and I mirror his expression without thinking. Even with Joe's music playing, with the sounds of the neighborhood drifting over the yard—cars pulling into driveways and crickets in the gravel—the world suddenly seems far away. We're wrapped in memory, and I kind of love it.

"Why?" I ask, incredulous. "I was making it so obvious I wanted you to kiss me. And you'd already had your first kiss. I hadn't." I remember how I kept shifting, putting our bodies into contact. Our elbows, our thighs. How I leaned into him every time I laughed.

Patrick scoffs grandly. "I may have had *slightly* more

experience," he replies, "but I was definitely the more nervous one."

"How could you possibly have been nervous." I flatten the question into a statement.

Vulnerability catches the edges of Patrick's voice. "Because I liked you so much. You were so pretty and funny, and I had no idea why you'd agreed to go out with me. None of which has changed, by the way." He presses his palms to the knees of his jeans. "Sometimes, I still get nervous around you."

His admission shatters the memory. I study him. Is *that* why he hasn't really tried to kiss me? I struggle to formulate my questions. "You get nervous? Kissing me? You've probably kissed me hundreds of times."

His eyes drop to the water, then return to me.

"That doesn't change how badly I always want to," he says.

Something flutters in my stomach. No, not something. Hundreds of somethings. Full-on butterflies. The water casts light onto Patrick's face, the white lines of the reflection making his eyes sparkle in the dark.

"Okay," I say. "You *haven't* forgotten how to flirt."

I'm hiding everything I'm feeling behind the flimsy cover of humor. When he grins wide, I feel more butterflies open their wings.

He inches closer. Our legs and elbows touch. Even fifteen minutes earlier, I would've moved, would've gotten up to grab some cranberry clementine seltzer. I don't move, though. I don't want to. He's about to put his arm around me.

The past few days have reduced the distance separating us from miles to inches, and now he's about to erase even those, about to press his lips to mine.

I don't panic. In fact, I'm as calm as the night around us. I close my eyes, and I feel the warmth of a fire from three years ago on my face.

"Hey, you guys have to watch this video of Garret's dogs!" Joe's voice douses the moment. Opening my eyes, I see him and Garret walking in our direction.

In a pang of frustration, I remember Joe's doing exactly what I asked of him. Keeping Patrick and me from being alone. Reaching us, he and Garret sit on the pool chairs right behind Patrick and me.

I don't reply, caught up in the emotional aftershock of our almost-kiss. Patrick recovers faster. He gives me an apologetic glance before getting up to look at Garret's phone. "Show me," he says.

When I find my footing, where I land is—disappointed.

I'm disappointed I didn't kiss him.

I've felt disappointment plenty over Patrick's visit in predictable ways. Ways I've fought off during the past few months with the regularity of every one of Patrick's and my other routines. Ways I've learned to ignore like familiar aches and pains.

Not this way.

This disappointment is one I don't know what to do with.

Sixteen

HOURS LATER, I'M CURLED up on one of the pool chairs. The sun has set, night having fallen over the neighborhood in gray and black. The party's winding down. Patrick sits in front of me on the long reclining bed of the chair, talking to those who are left, Joe seated beside him. Three of our friends share the pool chair opposite ours. Other than them, everyone's gone home. Without the music, the night is quiet.

I'm too far back to be part of the conversation. I don't mind. With my eyes half-closed, I enjoy the evening cool while Patrick fields questions about his new school. It's not *fun*, exactly. It's nice. The night has the intimacy only open spaces do, and it's comforting.

Patrick's voice lulls me until I feel light, on the cusp of falling into sleep. "The food is great," he's saying. "And the music."

Someone asks him a question I don't hear. I close my eyes fully now, following the rhythm of his voice while only catching some of the content. His words have dropped to a low rumble, and he's describing mileage and trails, early morning views of the river . . .

I blink. Tilting my head up, I cut him off midsentence. "Wait, what were you just saying?"

Patrick faces me. His expression is easygoing, but unreadable. "Just how I've started hiking on Sunday mornings. Nothing too long yet, although I'm hoping to get up to ten miles."

I watch him, uncomprehending. "When did you start hiking?" He's never mentioned it to me. Moreover, it's not something I ever would have predicted of him. Patrick's not particularly outdoorsy. On those walks in the woods with my bird-watching grandpa, he'd wear the same scuffed Converse he wore to school, swatting bugs real or imaginary as we went.

"Sometime in October," he says. "It's not a big deal, though. Just for fun."

His shrug and smile are entirely relaxed. I don't reply, hoping I don't look as disjointed as I feel. He's not wrong, of course. Objectively, it's not a big deal. I've never particularly felt like policing what Patrick does with his time.

Yet for some reason, it's shaken me. While the conversation continues, Patrick answering some new question I don't catch, I work out why. When I imagine Patrick in hiking gear, it's incoherent in my mind, the seeing-your-teacher-at-the-supermarket effect. The Patrick I know doesn't hike. He doesn't even have a passing interest in lacing up heavy-soled shoes, slapping on sunscreen, and striding out into canyons and valleys.

Which is exactly it. I felt certain I knew Patrick, felt like I could predict his every thought and decision.

Now I don't know.

I'm forced to confront the possibility that Patrick can still surprise me. Which means . . . maybe we can still change while staying together. Maybe long distance itself will give me the room I need to discover myself.

The pool chair suddenly feels small and stiff behind me, like I need space to contend with this revelation. It's such a small shift in my mind, and yet it feels enormous. How many more surprises does he have in him? It's like realizing you've slotted wrong puzzle pieces together, leaving you with an incomplete picture.

I study his profile, faintly outlined in the distant light from the patio. Searching for clues in features I feel like I've known forever—his solid chin, the way his lips look like they're on the verge of smiling—I find none. My mind starts running new percentages, not the chances of whether I'll break up with him. When he got here, I'd assumed he was 100 percent the Patrick who had left. Now I'm wondering if he's not. If he's more like 90 percent, or 85.

Or maybe I just didn't entirely know the Patrick who left.

These thoughts keep me quiet as everyone starts talking about going home for curfews. Alicia stands up, poking her feet into her flip-flops under the chair. Then Garret and Joe. I don't move, still watching Patrick's every shift and flicker of expression.

While I'm lost in thought, water splashes my face.

Garret's head emerges from the surface of the pool, which

he's jumped into, fully clothed. He shakes water from his shoulder-length hair, grinning widely. "Come on in," he calls up to us. "The water's amazing."

Without hesitating, Alicia kicks off her shoes and deposits her phone on the grass, then dives in with him. It's a Model UN tradition—after conferences out of state, everyone would jump into the hotel pool fully clothed when the chaperones thought we were asleep. The effect now is immediate. Everyone starts shucking off jackets, emptying their pockets, and leaping in. Even Joe, who's never been to an MUN conference, flips spectacularly into the deep end.

I laugh a little, waiting with Patrick. We're the last ones on land. Lit by the pool lights, the turquoise water looks inviting, a thin line of steam rising from the surface into the cool evening.

Patrick faces me, his hair half-matted from everyone's splashing. He grins in anticipation—then pulls off his West Vista hoodie and dives in. I don't overthink it. Standing, I pull off my shoes. Patrick treads water in front of me, looking at me, his eyes sparkling with expectation, and I wonder if butterflies can swim.

I jump in. The shock of the water envelops me. At first, it's cold and electric, but by the time I come up for air, I can feel warmth spreading through my clothes. I swim over to Patrick, who's floating on his back, gazing up into the night sky. While our friends splash and shriek, he's quiet.

I draw in a breath, holding it deep in me to float next to him. I have every excuse to join our friends the way I would've wanted to earlier.

Right now, I don't want to. I look up the way Patrick is doing. Here in the city, haze keeps most of the stars from view, but there's still a scattering of them on the charcoal night.

"I miss this place so much," Patrick says quietly.

I don't speak for a moment. I don't joke, don't ask him why. With my clothes billowing around me, droplets of water on my face while we look up into the dark starlight, I understand him completely. "I hope you liked the party," I say.

He sinks down from his float and faces me. He's pushed his hair back from his forehead. It makes him look a little older, and more handsome, although it's not only the hair I'm admiring. Like a new frame around an image I've known for what feels like forever, it draws out new details from familiar features, making the light in Patrick's eyes seem luminous in new ways. "I really did," he says. "It was perfect."

I smile softly, treading water in front of him. His eyes drift from me toward where the horizon lies behind houses in the distance, a little of the light fleeing his expression. Out of compassion and curiosity, I find myself wanting to know where it went.

"I don't want to go home tomorrow," he says. I nearly don't hear his words over the gentle sounds of the water.

Suddenly, the night air feels colder on my face.

"I hate it in Austin," he continues, speaking like he's scared that what he's saying will swallow him up if he's any louder. "I . . . haven't found any friends, and I miss doing Model UN. I'm just waiting for my senior year to be over."

There's emotion choking his voice, but I can't tell if he's crying, not while his face is slick with water.

His confession hits me with sad shock. I knew he'd missed Phoenix, but I had no idea how unhappy he was in Austin. I flip through the same memories I've examined and reexamined while I evaluated our relationship, their edges frayed and corners dog-eared, remembering our conversations over the past three months. All he had to say about Austin were the positives—how his mom likes her job, how his house is next to amazing food, how nice the people are. I'm learning now it wasn't the whole story. Whether he was withholding his real feelings for my benefit or his own, I can only guess.

I've always known everything about Patrick, which meant I always knew everything to say to him. Tonight, glimpses of the Patrick I didn't know have felt like gifts. But this one feels like something stolen. I don't know how to talk to this Patrick. I don't know how to make him feel better.

I desperately want to, though.

I reach for his hand under the water. When his fingers entwine with mine, the smile he gives me doesn't reach his eyes.

"I'm not going to think about going back yet," he says. "Not while I'm still here. Still with you."

I can only hold his hand tighter, feeling the depth of the water between me and the firm ground below.

Seventeen

WE WALK HOME WET and shivering. Last I checked the clock on my phone, it was past ten. The late hour makes no difference—the wide road is as empty as when we walked it in the afternoon. There's one streetlight on each corner, leaving only us and a night sky full of questions I haven't yet answered.

I don't object when Patrick hands me his hoodie. I pull it on, wrapping myself in the soft fabric and the familiar scent. It's comforting, and I'm even appreciative of how it returns me to the memory of when I first wore this hoodie, in the rain with Patrick years ago.

Everything feels strangely the same, my clothes wet under the warm fabric, Patrick next to me, matching my stride like it's instinct. I'm used to resenting the sameness of everything. Right now, I don't. While the pieces are repetitive, somehow, it's not just what we're doing that's the same.

It's how I'm feeling. The day we walked home in the rain was magical, the special kind of magic conjured out of the ordinary. I'd walked home from school a thousand times.

That day with Patrick was proof that the thousand and first could be extraordinary. But I'd resigned myself to only ever feeling that particular joy in past tense. Pictures on a postcard, snow globes on a shelf.

Which is why tonight is fragile and wonderful. Because some of the same magic is following me in these familiar footsteps.

When we reach my house, the shared driveway of our unit is quiet, everyone's cars parked for the night. The windows are dark. As silently as I can, I unlock my door, not wanting to wake Robbie, who's asleep on the couch with his phone next to his face.

I place a hand on Patrick's chest, cautioning him to move slowly.

And I'm met with one more surprise. When my fingers touch the damp fabric of his shirt, sparks shoot through me. Patrick's eyes lock on mine. I pull my hand back, hardly recognizing the sensation. Earlier, I felt like the night sky visible in the city—a few scattered stars, barely shining. Now I feel like the sunset, lit up with fire.

Regaining control of myself, I press my finger to my lips and point with my chin to Robbie. Patrick nods his understanding, and we head into the darkened room. I don't need light to navigate everything perfectly. Nor does Patrick. We pass the credenza and the armchair nearest the couch without hitting hip bones on corners or stubbing toes.

Reaching my room, I fire off a quick text to my dad, letting him know I'm home. While my parents are asleep, if he woke up in the night and didn't find confirmation I was here, safe and sound, he would flip. When I see DELIVERED slide up under the message, I turn, finding Patrick waiting in my doorway.

Without speaking, he walks in, shutting the door softly behind him.

His eyes fixed on me, he steps closer. My mouth goes dry from the heady rush of this parallel-universe version of Patrick in front of me, at once unlike I've seen him and exactly like the boy I recognize. With our wet clothes still sticking to our skin, the silence in the room feels heavy. We stand there, just looking at each other. Then Patrick takes another step closer.

When he speaks, his voice is hushed, and somehow loud. "I really want to kiss you now, Siena."

I feel my breath hitch. It's half shiver from the cold—half something else.

"I've wanted to since I got here," he goes on, smiling sheepishly, pink rising under the freckles on his cheeks. "Not like that kiss in the airport with your mom watching, either. A real kiss. The kiss I've been fantasizing about for three months."

Everything in me wakes up at his words. *Patrick fantasizing?* I mean, of course he's fantasized, I guess. He's just never shared it with me. Hearing him mention it now is—exciting.

"Why haven't you?" I ask in a whisper suspended over a chasm.

His face softens with sincerity. "I wasn't sure *you* wanted to," he says. "Besides, it's not like you've given me much opportunity between going to Joe's house and running errands.

Which is fine!" he rushes to clarify. "I never want you to think you, like, owe me this because I'm not in town for long. But I guess I want you to know"—his expression now holds heat as well as warmth—"I've wanted to. I *do* want to."

His hand finds mine. Following years of instinct, my fingers entwine with his. I don't pull away.

I'd made my decision. I'd prepared myself for the morning, for tonight to be our last night. Yet now, looking over the edge in the confines of my childhood room, the drop looks different. The shadows slant wrong. The idea feels like falling, not flying.

I could kiss him right now and pretend it's one last kiss. One last memory to hold on to. But I would be lying. I'm not wetting my lips out of nostalgia. My stomach isn't swooping from sentimentality for what's ending. I *want* this. For no other reason than wanting.

"Then kiss me already," I say.

I'd imagined our relationship was firm, flat ground. I had no idea being with Patrick could feel like a leap of its own.

His lips flit halfway to a smile. My mind can't catch up to the explosion of anticipation in me when Patrick steps up, pulling me to his body. Suddenly, his mouth is on mine, and I'm gone, everywhere and only here. Gently, his hand—the one I'm not holding—finds my cheek. His lips are shockingly warm compared to the chill of his soaking clothes. It's sort of perfect, the study in contrasts. I sink into the kiss, chasing that warmth and letting it spread through me.

The way his lips caress mine, inviting and needing, is completely familiar—the echo of a thousand kisses—and yet there's something brand-new in it. Something born of distance and surprises.

It feels, impossibly, like a first kiss.

I let the sensation sweep over me, relearning the rhythm of our mouths. His chest pressed to mine, my arm holding him against me, I'm a total mess of newly awakened nerve endings, rushing heartbeats, the sweet squeeze I feel in my stomach. I'm no longer myself, just a jumble of happy pieces.

When Patrick pulls away, his gaze holds mine. The intensity in his eyes is unmistakable. He wants more.

"See you in the morning," he says instead. His lips curl into—*dear god, is he smirking?* He's scattered the pieces of me across the floor, and he's *smirking*? I'm indignant, or I would be if I could get ahold of myself.

He walks out, closing the door behind him, leaving me still dazed and wanting. I drop onto the edge of my bed—collapse, really—my mind exquisitely empty.

What just happened can't possibly be condensed into a percentage. It doesn't fit into my formulas. I don't know what I want anymore. However, I suspect it includes more kisses like that one.

Looking at my reflection in the mirror over my dresser, I laugh a little. I've stolen Patrick's West Vista High sweatshirt, like I did years ago. With his smell on it, along with Phoenix starlight and the chlorine from my wet hair, I feel like I'm wrapped in a new wonderful memory.

Once again, I have no intention of giving the hoodie back. Not when holding on to it feels like holding on to him.

Eighteen

PATRICK'S FLIGHT BEING ON Saturday, the morning finds us—where else?—in Rex's. It's an hour before Patrick needs to be at the airport, and normalcy is everywhere. It's in early sunlight streaming in the windows. It's in the scream of the cappuccino machine, in the glassy sheen of Patrick's almond croissant. It's in the give of the cushion of my usual seat.

This was the moment I was going to break up with him. I was going to turn the conversation to long distance. I would reassure him it wasn't him, just the difficulty of time zones, of travel logistics, of senior year. I had ready my library of clichés designed to console him. I'd even contemplated ending my speech with an upbeat *maybe if we end up in the same city for college* . . . I hadn't decided if I'd say it yet. Then I would send him off to the airport. It would be done.

I don't do those things. They were erased by last night's kiss and our conversation by the pool, by every revelation of Patrick's under the cover of dusk. Instead, while Patrick bites into his croissant, I sit still, our routine filling every pause and unspoken sentence.

Sitting to my right, like a silent third presence between us, is every doubt I had about our relationship. While last night changed things, having reasons to stay doesn't mean not having reasons to leave. Those haven't gone away. I still need to find myself instead of letting my boyfriend occupy my entire identity. But that's on me to do, not on him. If anything, the changes I've found in Patrick give me hope I can do the same. I just have to do it.

He finds my eyes hesitantly, no trace of the flirtatious Patrick who left my room after our kiss. I can't imagine even the ghost of his smirk right now. "So . . ." he says, "I think we should talk about us."

It's what I was going to say to him. It's an unneeded reminder of how indistinct we've become over the past three years. Even our relationship-discussion openers are the same.

I shift in my seat. It's like the reasons sitting next to me have started drumming their fingers on the table.

"When we decided to do long distance, I told you we could consider it a trial," he says. "I guess now I'm asking whether it's been a success. Do you . . ." He runs one finger over the ceramic edge of his croissant plate. "Do you want to keep going?"

The reply is out of my mouth before I even think it. "I do want to."

There it is. I've decided. Or something in me has. Despite my doubts, I've known deep down this whole morning what I was going to do. I knew it ever since his lips touched mine. Everything isn't fixed with Patrick. Every crack isn't mended. Even so, I want to hold the fragments together a little longer.

"Do you?" I ask, hearing the fragility in my voice. It's entirely possible this offers Patrick not relief, but disappointment. I recognize the voice whispering this particular poison in my ear—what if it were easier for him if we broke up? What if there's a girl in Austin who's caught his eye, or he hers, and who could make him happier?

"I do," he replies, and I'm knocked off-kilter by how happy it makes me. I nod, and he continues. "I was honestly having a tough time reading you these past few days." He gazes out the café windows. The sun lighting his face illuminates the sadness everywhere on his features. "I know you want to make some changes, and I . . . wondered if I was one of them," he goes on.

Even though I hear the somberness in his voice, what he's saying is reassuring. He *has* noticed some of what I've been feeling these past few months.

It gives me hope. When Patrick got here, I decided I would either break up with him or *not* break up with him. Not breaking up with him means more than just hanging on. It means fighting to make this work. No more second-guessing. No more percentages. No more waiting for the day we fall apart. Now that I've decided I'm staying with him, I need to find my way forward, and he's just given me a little more guiding light.

Looking into Patrick's eyes, I find them reflecting the moments I've loved in this visit. The times we laughed together, the times we were honest. What we have is real. I would regret throwing it away.

But the problems in our relationship are real, too. If I'm ready to fight for us, I need to start by facing what gave me reservations in the first place.

I take his hand. "Our relationship isn't going to be the same as it's always been," I start. "Not while you're a thousand miles away. I think that's a good thing." Saying everything I'm feeling is incredibly, wonderfully freeing. Instead of hiding my hopes and fears behind flirtatious jokes and uncertain pauses, I'm finally speaking my thoughts out loud. It's like suddenly running in open space. "But I don't want long distance to hold either of us back from throwing ourselves into the lives in front of us," I finish.

I'm figuring this out while I'm speaking. The main problem with our relationship is how stuck I feel in our routines, our intertwined identities. Long distance is an ironic opportunity. It's the chance to split seams I think need splitting.

But I'm remembering Patrick's confession in the pool. He hates his life in Austin, and I'm unsatisfied in my life here. While I want to continue our relationship, neither of us can just rely on it to put color into the gray parts of our worlds.

Which is what we've done, consciously or unconsciously. I'm Patrick's tether to his old life, an excuse to keep himself apart from his new one, while he's inscribed in every routine of my school and social life. I want to be part of whatever future Patrick finds for himself in Austin—and I want him to be part of mine here. We just need to start searching.

"I know Austin hasn't been ideal for you," I say. "I want you to try to find something to love there. I'm going to do the same here," I add encouragingly. "Figure out what my life looks like now. You . . . deserve to spend your days there not wishing you were here."

His expression clouds. Now the sunlight hitting him through the windows seems uncomfortably illuminating, invasive. The world's largest interrogation-room light. "Siena, I'm trying. You think I want to hate it there?" he asks. His voice sounds frayed.

"No, I know you don't," I say quickly. "Just, I love that you've started hiking. I think maybe if you tried more things like that, eventually"—the next part is the most fragile, the most deliberately optimistic—"you'd make a life there. Me, I want to find something like hiking is for you. MUN isn't it, but whatever it is, it's out there. I think if we both try to lead our own lives, we would eventually learn to love them."

Patrick pauses, working on this idea. He squints like he's trying to see what I'm saying. "You want us to stay together . . . while leading our own lives."

"Yes," I say, hearing my own conviction. If we're dating from a thousand miles' distance, we'll have room to try new things. We'll have room to grow. Our relationship won't feel stilted like it did this summer. I'm proud of myself for saying the things I should have said months ago.

"I think it's harder than you're making it sound," Patrick says slowly. "I like what I like. I can't change that."

I'm not resentful he's pushing back. In fact, I'm glad. It means we're really doing this, fighting to keep us going instead of settling for empty promises. "I'm not trying to change you," I insist. "I just don't want to hold you back from what's in front of you, either."

His fingers loosen around mine. Suspicion sharpens his gaze. "Do you, like, want to date other people? Like an open relationship? Is that what this is about?"

"No!" I flush, frustrated with myself for giving him that impression. "I just want us both to find other things in our lives, not only count down the days until we next see each other. I want us to be happy."

Patrick falls quiet, his eyes drifting to the table. When his gaze returns to me, he pushes his almond croissant away. Without a word, he gets up out of his chair. With the scrape of its legs on the tile, I feel pulled out of the private world of our conversation. The clinking of cups on saucers suddenly sounds louder, the rich scent of coffee suddenly heavier. Patrick walks up to the register, and I watch him order something.

When he returns, he's holding a bran muffin.

He sits down, grinning. "For you," he says, "I can try new things." I laugh a little, the sweetness of the gesture coloring my cheeks. "But," Patrick continues with flair, "I have a request to make in return."

I play along, looking intrigued. "Oh?"

"If you're going to quit MUN and pick up another

activity," he starts more softly, "I want to know about it. Everything. I just . . . don't want our changes to push us further apart. Austin to Arizona is far enough."

I nod, moved. "Deal. I want to know if you're not happy there, too," I say, remembering his confession in the pool. "We'll both tell each other more."

Patrick smiles. "Deal."

Looking triumphant, he takes a large bite of the muffin. I watch him chew. Then swallow. He makes a face, setting the muffin down.

"I do already know what I want, though," he says, his eyes fixed right on me.

Nineteen

I USED TO THINK breaking up with Patrick would be the seismic shift I needed to start finding my new self. With him remaining in my life for the foreseeable future, I need to make other changes, fast.

Patrick leaves on Saturday, and on Sunday, I email Alicia and quit Model UN.

I kept waiting for my momentum to run out, for myself to hastily delete the draft email. When I didn't, I started to feel, for the first time in weeks or even months, genuinely excited. Confident. I'm going to take advantage of long distance to try new things in hopes of ending my quarter-life crisis. This year, I'll find the new Siena—Siena who has a long distance boyfriend but is her own person.

On Monday, when I leave the lunch line with my pizza in hand, I realize I have no idea what I'm going to do for the rest of lunch. I stare helplessly out into the quad, over the familiar yet unwelcoming geography of the social landscape. Last year, I had lunch with Patrick every day, sometimes with Alicia and Garret and the rest of Model UN, but more often just the two of us. This year, I've gravitated to the Model UN table out of convenience and routine.

Today, though, I know joining them won't work. Alicia was understandably not happy when I dropped MUN a month out from our conference, and I wasn't surprised she had no interest in hearing *why* I needed a change—our friendship wasn't as real as hers and Patrick's. I have no doubt the MUN crowd is discussing conference details right now. They won't want me there.

Which is fine. I want a fresh start anyway. Now is the perfect opportunity.

I walk into the quad, squinting under the silver clouds illuminated by the sun, searching for something to draw my eye. Summoning my courage, I head in the direction of the first open seat I see, near some people I know from my Spanish class. *I don't have to impress them with sparkling wit*, I remind myself. Starting fresh just means *starting*.

But when I'm steps from the table, someone else takes the spot. Thrown, I instinctively veer off, like it was my intention the whole time.

Sometimes, high school feels like a place where you can be whoever you want as long as it's who you already were. When everyone here has known you since kindergarten, the *you* they expect is only the product of unconscious choices from when you were seven, or ten, or fifteen. The contours of a mold you didn't know you were carving. Despite my wanting to shape myself into someone new, it's difficult, lonely—even sort of scary.

I deliberately slow my steps, continuing to look

nonchalantly for open seats. This part, I know, is temporary—it's transitional. I just need to find my new club, my new group, my new whatever. I consider flipping open last year's yearbook and pointing with my eyes closed to something random. Even if it doesn't work out, it would be new.

Passing the low concrete wall near the school office, I notice Joe sitting with some of his popular athlete friends. Joe is a lunchtime floater of his own volition, switching among his several groups—which was me and MUN sometimes, but only when our number was up in his rotation.

Right now, however, I'm desperate. Joe is my best friend. I can sit with him if I need to. Which I do.

Refusing to question my decision, I head over and drop onto the concrete wall next to him. Joe, mid-bite of his school pizza, looks slightly surprised to see me, but only smiles instead of questioning my sudden presence.

I glance past him to the rest of the group, who don't look bothered by the fact that I just sat down without invitation. *I don't need inviting*, I remind myself. There's nothing keeping me from sitting here. In fact, there's nothing keeping me from being just like them. I imagine joining everyone at football games and huge parties. Posting hilarious videos on social media. Getting invites instead of ignoring the lack of them, then, eventually, doing the inviting. *Cool-girl Siena.*

Ha. Easier said than done.

They continue their conversation while I lean forward, trying to look casual. I don't really know them, but on the upside, they don't know me, either, which means they don't see me as just Patrick's girlfriend.

On the downside, however, it seems to mean they have no interest in interacting with me whatsoever. My pizza uneaten on the paper plate in my hand, I feel nervousness sapping my appetite while I sit embarrassingly silent. They're talking about some show I've never heard of.

This was a mistake, I admit to myself, while their conversation flies on past me. With each second I sit here woodenly, I feel more unmoored, more lost than ever.

I'm on the verge of leaving when I remember Patrick. If I wanted, I could return to Model UN, to stability, to knowing what each day looks like. It's tempting. Patrick doesn't have those options. In Austin, he's facing nothing except not-yet-friends and unfamiliar lunch tables.

Which makes me feel even more discouraged when I find myself pulling out my phone. With sweaty hands, I slide open my screen and tap my top texting conversation, where I tell my boyfriend I just got out for lunch. It feels like surrender.

Today was supposed to be the start of me living my independent life. Instead, I'm leaning on Patrick. While I might have quit Model UN, I'm realizing how suffocatingly little idea I have of how to replace it. Of how I'll reexplore my life the way I told myself, and told Patrick, I wanted to. Finding the new Siena is starting to feel incredibly daunting.

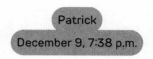
Reason number 249 why LDRs suck.
Having to watch the new Netflix rom-
coms on my own.

LDRs?

Long distance relationships. What else
could I have possibly meant?

Legendary Dinosaur Rebellions?

Ah yes, I understand perfectly your
confusion. However, dinosaur rebellions
are not the cause of my pathetic solo
Netflixing.

Hold on. I'm getting my computer.
I'll watch with you.

Now there's an idea. Let's Duo Rom-com.

Less Depressing, Right?

What are you up to?

Heading out for a hike. You?

Student Government is holding a winter carnival. Joe and I are going. Apparently the balloon-animal guy bailed, and the senior officers watched a single YouTube video and will be filling in.

Request something difficult for me.

Obviously. Like what?

A self-portrait.

Wow. Yes.

Please take pictures of every single dog you see on your hike.

Like I need to be told.

Ladies Dig Robbie.

Yeah, right before Ladies Dump Robbie.

Hey. Lad Deserves Respect.

Bravo.

So Mr. Curtis said something interesting in English today.

The school lit mag is requesting submissions.

Whoa! Like, he recommended you submit?

Haha. No. I've gotten, like, one A in there this year. He just said it was open for people to submit.

That's really cool. So you're thinking you might send something in?

I mean, now that I have more free time without MUN. Maybe. I went to a meeting, and I'm not sure I love it. But . . . it just feels like something I could try. I'm going to write something this weekend.

Yeah? Can I read it?

I'd be offended if you didn't!

Wait, you're not going to write about me, are you?

Oh, did I not make it clear I was going to write about every embarrassing thing you've ever done?

Won't be a very long piece then.

The world needs to know about the time you texted the MUN group chat asking if anyone was horny instead of hungry.

First, that was autocorrect. Second, how dare you.

This is the danger of LDRs. You can never leave your past behind even in a new city.

I would never want to.

Hey, any chance you're horny?

Patrick!
What? Oh, I meant hungry.

You sure?

Why? Have anything in mind?

A couple things. Interested?

Definitely.

Are we doing this?

If by "this" you mean sexting, then yes.

December 22, 10:57 p.m.

Hey. Lately Definitely Reallymissingyou.

Pretty sure that's cheating. But I'll allow it.
I really miss you, too.

New Year's

Twenty

THE MORNING OF MY flight, I'm wide-eyed under my covers with my phone clutched in my hand, fully panicking. I watch the clock change from 5:59 to six. It's official—I've lost the fight to get some sleep.

Since four in the morning, when I woke up jittery in the dark, I've tried everything. I read some of *Ethan Frome*, which I need to annotate for English. I literally counted sheep. I stared up, studying the precise color of the paint on my ceiling. No luck. There was no putting out of my head what happened last night.

While I shift and rustle under the covers, my phone lights up. Figuring it's Patrick in his central time zone, I reach over for the phone, not resenting the distraction.

Instead, I'm surprised to find it's Joe, sending the "Haha" reaction to the last message in our thread, which I sent him in the middle of the night when I was bored. It's his current favorite GIF, hairless cats in a bath.

Curious, I write him quickly. Joe's usually a late sleeper on the weekend.

Why are you up?

While I wait, I fixate on my background photo of Patrick and me from prom so intently that we start to look like just blobs of color. Until last night, I was nothing but excited to visit Patrick and use the plane tickets that were my parents' Christmas gift to me so I could stay with his family for New Year's.

The past month hasn't gone exactly like I'd imagined. While things with Patrick have been great—our conversations have been easy, fun, even flirty—I haven't found something I love to replace MUN. I wrote for the lit magazine and went to a few meetings, even started picturing myself filling those nice leatherbound notebooks with smudged handwriting or one day seeing my name printed on shiny covers. *Writer Siena.*

It just didn't feel *right*. It didn't feel like me. I haven't quit and probably won't, but it's not going to be the beginning of the new me.

Instead, I've wound up confronting the unnerving error in the logic of my not-break-up speech to Patrick. I thought with long distance providing me the room to explore, I would explore. It turns out, though, exploring isn't easy. There's no guidebook, no map. Which . . . is kind of the point of exploring, I guess. Regardless, I've mostly found myself facing how much I *haven't* done.

Last night put me over the edge. Robbie walked into my room while I was packing for my flight, and now I'm stuck with questions I really don't want to be asking.

Joe's reply lights up my screen.

I'm having a crisis.

Under the covers, I respond instantly.

Perfect. Me too.

Perfect. Can you come over?

On my way.

I leap out of bed. Simultaneously, I pull on my sweat-pants and step over my suitcase laid open in the middle of the floor. On my way out, I grab a sweatshirt while slipping on my Vans, crushing the backs under my heels.

Moving quickly, I walk down the hall. The entire front half of our place smells like coffee, and sure enough, I find my dad at the kitchen table with his Grand Canyon mug. He smiles when I come into the front room.

"Excited for your trip?" he asks.

"Yeah," I say hurriedly, stepping around the Christmas tree, which is a little too large for the space. "But first I need to run to Joe's real quick." I grab my keys off the front table, heading purposefully for the door.

I hear Dad set his mug down. It's not hard to imagine the consternation in his expression. "Siena, we have to leave for the airport in thirty minutes."

I face him, thinking fast. "I know. I'm already packed and ready. I just need to . . . pick something up." I race over the syllables, knowing it sounds like bullshit but hoping I can put it past him. I read in psych class if you give someone a reason for something, they're more likely to let you do what you want, even if the reason makes no sense.

It doesn't work. *Thanks for nothing, CP psych.* Dad's nose wrinkles. "Whatever it is," he says skeptically, "we can pick it up on the way."

Instead of risking one more brush with my dad's bullshit detector, I change my strategy, swinging open the front door. "That's okay," I call breezily over my shoulder. "I'll just jog over there."

I know I've won when I don't hear him stand up to follow me. "If you're not back in thirty," he replies, "I'm driving over to Joe's."

"Sounds good!" I swing the door closed behind me.

Ignoring the bitter cold of Phoenix winter, I bounce down the steps. When I hit the driveway, I start jogging, hoping blood flow will help me fend off hypothermia. Here, forty-eight degrees is practically arctic. My breath forms frosty puffs in front of me while I run. It's the Friday of the dead week between Christmas and New Year's, so the street is unusually sleepy, noiseless except for the chirping of morning birds. It's dark out, but sunrise has turned the base of the sky blue and orange. Normally, I would enjoy the chill. Today, though, I sprint the whole way to Joe's house, squinting in the painfully dry air.

I make it in record time. Standing outside his front door, I text him, telling him I'm here. He opens the door immediately.

Looking drawn, his Coachella shirt wrinkled from poor sleep, he lets me in. "Wait, don't you need to go to the airport or something?" he says in greeting.

"Not"—I huff—"yet. We have twenty minutes."

Joe nods with military urgency, then beckons me upstairs. His room is just off the landing, and I follow him in.

The second his door shuts, I say, "You go first."

"Okay. I have a huge crush on Lacey Ramos," he announces with a conspiratorial air, which makes me laugh.

"Yeah, bro, I know," I say. I've known for weeks. He's been finding ways to bring her up in casual conversation, and I've noticed his eyes lingering on the back of her head in biology.

Joe processes this for a moment, then barrels on. "Well, I kind of asked her out. And I—I don't know if she said yes or not. And I've spent the entire night overanalyzing."

I frown, not unamused. "What do you mean you *don't know*? And what do you mean *kind of*?"

Wordless, Joe unlocks his phone and solemnly hands it over. On-screen is his conversation with Lacey. I read the recent messages, in which Joe mentions a benefit show featuring a few local bands. When I reach the final exchange, I understand the problem. Joe's invited Lacey—*kind of*.

You want to come? Bring your friends
if you want! Or we could go just us.

Yeah!

Regretfully, I look up. "Oh, Joe . . ."

My friend puts his head in his hands.

I can't resist. "I thought you were good with girls!" I chide.

"Siena! Fifteen minutes!" he says desperately. "Move on to the helpful part of this conversation!"

"Okay, first we'll see if she shows up to this concert by herself or with friends. But I don't think you need to read into it if she *does* show up with friends." I rush through my advice, conscious of the time. "In the future you do need to ask her more directly. When school starts, I'll see if I can hang out with her and get a sense of how she feels about you."

Joe nods slowly, listening. His shoulders relax, his expression finally looking less intense. "You'd do that? You'd talk to her for me?"

"Yeah, Joe," I say, more sincerely. "I promise I will."

Heaving a sigh of relief, he sits down on his bed. "Great," he replies. "Okay, your turn. What's your crisis?"

I blurt my question out. "Are you a virgin?"

Joe's eyes widen. Understandably—we've never really discussed the physical parts of our romantic lives. It's not that he's a guy and I'm a girl. I just don't want to visualize my closest childhood friend in that way, and on my part, I just don't share those details with friends—because they're not just my details. It feels like sharing Patrick's private life behind his back. But this isn't about Patrick. Not really.

"Your crisis is you're wondering if I'm a virgin," Joe summarizes slowly. "I'm almost afraid to ask why."

"I know. It looks bad," I say. "But I'm seeing Patrick in just a few hours, and last night, Robbie came into my room asking if I could lend him money so he could buy . . ." I close my eyes, realizing in a flash of clarity why my mom got really into the meditation app on her phone. "Condoms," I force out.

I let the impact of this revelation reverberate into the room. Unexpectedly, however, Joe's expression remains impassive. He watches me with tired eyes, his mouth flat.

"*Condoms*, Joe," I repeat, sure he didn't hear me. Or perhaps his comprehension is foggy.

"So?" Joe asks.

My hands fly up. "*So!* My *kid* brother has apparently been having *sex*—" I practically shout, then swiftly realize I've just shouted *sex* in Joe's house at six in the morning. His parents are probably sleeping—or I hope they're sleeping. I lower my voice to the lowest whisper I can muster without sacrificing the seriousness I need to convey. "Has been having sex since the beginning of the year. He's a *sophomore!*"

"Okay . . ." He pauses like he's waiting for the other half of the story.

Which is ridiculous. It's like I just told him I won the lottery and he's waiting for me to say I saw a UFO afterward. Exasperated, I sigh, hearing vulnerability steal into the sound. "Has everyone been having sex this whole time and I never knew?"

"I'm not sure what you mean by *everyone* or *this whole time,* but . . ." Joe leans back on his desk, looking remorseful for what he's going to say next. "No, I'm not a virgin."

I drop onto the edge of his bed, feeling small. "When?"

"I'm not sure it's relevant," he says carefully. "It's not like I'm constantly doing it. Besides"—he shifts on his feet, watching me with delicate curiosity—"I kind of figured you and Patrick had?"

"Well, we haven't." I hope he knows the frustration in my voice isn't frustration with him. I had the whole night to work out why learning about Robbie got to me. I'm not ashamed Patrick and I haven't. When we first discussed sex when we were fifteen, it felt important to me to wait until the right moment.

But I'm not fifteen anymore. I don't know that I care about the *right* moment. I don't know what the right moment even means.

"You know it doesn't matter, right?" Joe asks, his expression sympathetic. He hasn't moved from his desk, the early morning sunlight now starting to light up his window. "There's no timeline you have to keep up with."

"Don't you think it's kind of weird, though?" I hear how miserable I sound. I know I'm being ridiculous, but I can't seem to shut up the little voice now whispering in my ear, threading questions through some of my favorite memories with Patrick. *Why wasn't "the right moment" when we when we went to Garret's sleepover after prom last year? Or when we stayed in hotels for Model UN conferences?* "We've been together for *three years*," I say, "yet I'm a virgin, while my fifteen-year-old brother isn't. And now, with my relationship conducted from a thousand miles away, I'm just going to keep falling further and further behind."

Of course, it's not *really* my brother's level of experience putting this urgency into me. I guess it was just one more jolting reminder of a question I haven't thought about while my boyfriend isn't in the same state as me. Patrick's and my texts have gotten—well, hotter on occasion over the past few weeks, and maybe I'm wondering if we could build up to something new.

Joe moves to his desk chair. Scooting with his feet, he rolls over toward me until he's right in front of me. "You're not falling behind. I mean, what even is virginity? You guys have, like"—he falters for half a second—"done other stuff, right?"

"Yes," I say a little impatiently. "I have seen and interacted with Patrick's penis."

Joe can't help laughing. I fix him with a stern look. Instead of recognizing the gravity of the situation, which had me hustling over here in forty-degree weather, he's laughing like a seventh-grader because I said *penis*.

"Joe," I reprimand him. "Be serious."

He flops back in his desk chair, wiping tears from his eyes. "I can't be serious while you're talking about *interacting with penises*"—he can't even finish the sentence without starting to smile—"like you sat down and had a long conversation with one. Or like you played a little chess with one in the park."

Glowering, I grab his pillow from the head of his bed and chuck it at him.

He catches it to his chest easily, then raises his free hand in surrender. "Okay, I'm sorry," he says. His mouth still wobbles a little, which I'm forced to permit. I'm out of pillows. "My point is, it doesn't matter. You guys haven't had sex. Who cares?"

"I care!" I say, frustrated he's not understanding. "I'm ready to do *more* interacting with—"

"If you finish that sentence, I'm going to have to ask you to leave," Joe says.

I'm forced to recognize the ridiculousness of what I'm saying. I smile a little, which makes me feel better. "I'm just saying, I wonder if I'd have had sex by now if I weren't in a long distance relationship."

"Well," Joe says slowly, "you're about to see Patrick. In fact, you're about to stay overnight with Patrick. For several days." His eyes have caught a leading glint, and he crosses his arms. "If you want to do it, you could. Like, tonight."

This silences me. I look to the floor, wrestling with the suggestion. What Joe's saying is excitingly, stressfully, exactly right. I *do* want to. Theoretically. *I'm* ready, personally. But the last time I saw Patrick, I was on the verge of breaking up with him. We need more time to reestablish our relationship, to fan the new flame between us. Having sex right now would be like choking that fire with too much tinder.

Or would it?

If I'd *been* with Patrick for the past month, maybe we

would've reached that point together. I try to imagine how the things we talked about over text could have become reality if we were together in person. We might have found the *right moment*—or we might have not cared how right the moments we had were. If we do it now, it could even strengthen our relationship, bringing us closer together despite the distance.

"But you don't have to, Siena," Joe says gently, no doubt noticing my slumped shoulders. "I know it feels like forever before you'll be with him again, but it's not. Looking back, it won't make a difference to you if you have sex now, or in two months, or in six months, or whenever."

"Objectively, I know that," I say emphatically, still feeling wound up. While I fuss with the drawstring on my sweatpants, I check my phone. I have five minutes to run home before my dad ends up honking outside Joe's house or ringing the doorbell three or four times. I stand up, releasing my stress into a quick sigh. "Thanks, Joe," I say sincerely. "I guess I'll have my flight to think this over."

Joe stands with me, returning his pillow to the bed. "You know, you could just talk to Patrick about this," he says.

I roll my eyes playfully. "Please. You're way too rational while I'm trying to freak out." I flash him a grin. "You should try to go back to sleep," I go on. "I'll walk myself out."

Not protesting, he flops onto his comforter, arms behind his head. "Say hi to Patrick." I head for his door. When I reach for the handle, I hear him speak behind me. "Oh, and Siena? If you and Patrick do end up *interacting*, have fun."

When I face him from the doorway, I find him with eyebrows raised, grinning. I shake my head judgmentally, grinning in return.

Closing his door behind me, I make my way silently through the house. I haven't reached the sidewalk by the time worry descends over me once more. The flight to Austin is only two hours. I won't have long before I'm with Patrick. Then, once I get there, I won't have long before I'm without him.

I thought I knew exactly what I wanted from this visit—to get to know the new Patrick and rebuild our relationship. Now, though, there's this whole new question. I need to decide whether I want to take the next step with him. It's like finding a differential equation in the middle of a timed writing.

I pick up my pace, starting to run, the soles of my sneakers hitting the concrete still the only sound in the neighborhood. Drawing the cold into my lungs, I follow the familiar streets back to my house, to my packed luggage. My chest feels tight, my head full of the realization starting to form.

Long distance means each trip is never just about one thing. It needs to be about everything, stuffed full of what everyone else gets to do every day. We'll just have to find a way to fit a month into seventy-two hours.

Twenty-One

EVEN AUSTIN'S AIRPORT IS cool. It's smaller than Phoenix's, but the stereotypical parts—the stainless-steel window frames, the shiny tile floor—can't extinguish the place's undeniable uniqueness. While I walk from my gate toward ground transportation, I pass rows of homey, eclectic restaurant stalls, the smell of barbeque wafting over the walkway. Every sign boasts the city's personality, its nightlife, its music. I lose count of how many guitars I see, slung over travelers' shoulders, in signage, even statues.

In the terminal, a man with long hair sits on a portable amp and strums the handsome purple guitar in his hands, echoing something melodious and syncopated into the space. For a second, images flash into my head—myself practicing with a guitar or in front of a mic, channeling impressions and emotions into song. Vinyl records covering my floor, obscure bands on my shirts. *Songwriter Siena.*

Walking from my gate, I immerse myself in my destination. I already have the impression Austin is a city dialed up to ten, while Phoenix is content at a three. There's electricity here, and not only the power-lines kind. With how dramatically my surroundings have shifted, it's hard to imagine I was home only hours ago.

They were not comfortable hours. I spent every minute of the flight working over the sex issue. In my seat, with the cheap fabric of the cushion under me, my earphones wrapped unused in my sweatshirt pocket while cold compressed air dried out my skin, I soul-searched. Gazing out my window, watching the beige flats of the country pass under me, I recognized that I am, obviously, deeply curious about having sex.

Now, in a way, I feel like Patrick and I are back at the beginning of our relationship. I'm excited to get to know us all over again, to find out what's new about Patrick and for him to discover what's new about me. I just don't want the expectation of sex to rush these reintroductions. On paper, we've been together for three years. In my head, though, we're kind of only on our second date, if a weekend-long one.

Somewhere over Texas, I decided I would erase the question from my mind. I've gone three years without having sex with my boyfriend. It won't kill me to go a couple more months. Besides, I rationalized, I don't even know if I'll want to have sex with Patrick if the moment comes. Sex in general? Sure. Sex with this particular boyfriend at this particular time? I won't know until I'm facing the chance. It was only a month ago I was just warming up to kissing him again.

I walk outside, leaving baggage claim behind me. Winter weather in Texas is similar to Phoenix. The pale blue of the sky is nearly white in the midday sun. Even so, it's not exactly cold, and everything has an earthy scent I find intensely invigorating.

Pulling my suitcase, I continue to the wide drive-through where Patrick texted me he'd be waiting. I find him immediately, wearing sunglasses I don't recognize, standing next to a car I only recognize from the photos he texted me when he got it, and in a snug-fitting quarter-zip jacket I *do* recognize but never took notice of.

The sight stops me for a second, my suitcase rolling into my heels. Because Patrick looks . . . *hot*.

His hair is just long enough to look windswept, his neck and face tanner than I've ever seen them. I know it's from all the hiking he's been doing, even in the winter. I was glad he'd taken up hiking just because it was a new hobby. Now I'm glad for a whole new reason.

The effect is instantaneous. Every one of my rationalizations about sex, not rushing, and focusing on rediscovering our relationship vanishes from my head, drifting into the open Texas sky.

In the same moment, Patrick sees me. He doesn't move forward, but a grin slowly spreads across his face and he lowers his sunglasses.

Remembering I'm stalled on the sidewalk, having nearly forgotten my own name at the sight of him, I start walking. I don't run into his arms. I stop a foot away, enjoying the charged space separating us. I wait, wetting my lips, letting my eyes roam over him while his roam over me.

Finally, slowly, he leans down and intently presses his lips to mine. His hands pull my waist to him.

The sky is swallowed up. The electricity is no longer around me—it *is* me. I let my body fold into his, let my hands find the back of his head, and I'm overcome with his familiar smell. While the taste of his lips is familiar, it's a familiarity hidden under the shock of everything new. It's proof, devastating and delicious, that our kiss on the final night of Patrick's visit was no fluke.

Just thinking about the visit makes me want to laugh because it reminds me of the last time we kissed in an airport.

When we pull apart, Patrick's eyes fix on me. "Now, that's better," he says definitively, and I know he's also remembering our stilted peck in front of my mom.

He reaches for my luggage—which I surely would've forgotten on the sidewalk in my dazed stupor. The effect of the kiss is only just starting to wear off, and I don't know whether to be exhilarated . . . or frustrated.

Frustrated because I just wasted the last two hours of my life.

My deliberations at thirty thousand feet were worthless. I didn't need to spend minutes and mileage wondering if sex would put pressure on our fragile, renewed relationship. It's only pressure if I feel like it's pressure. Which I don't. I feel like it's exactly right. If Patrick were to ask me now if I wanted to lose my virginity in the back of his new car, I know what I would say.

I reach for Patrick's passenger door, letting myself relax. Deciding whether I wanted to have sex on this visit was the hard part—the turbulence. Knowing I do feels like touching down on the runway.

Twenty-Two

PATRICK DRIVES US OUT onto the open highway. Postcards paint Texas in flat stretches of sunbaked desert, but Patrick has explained it's not the way the state really is. Looking out the window while we enter the city, I see what he means. Austin in winter is brown lawns and bare trees. In summer, I imagine the place is covered in green.

The city's charm is everywhere. We pass horses pulling carriages, vintage stores with cowboy flair, modern hotels and food halls. I'm amazed how exactly it fits Patrick's descriptions, which have gotten more favorable over the past few weeks. Its skyscrapers sit side by side with its artsy cool, neither sacrificed to the other. Cutting through the middle is the river, reflecting the sky like a long, winding mirror.

Patrick drives over a bridge, and I watch the water pass under us. He continues for a couple blocks until finally, he pulls down a narrow street.

Once more, I find myself comparing what I'm seeing to the place I left just this morning. Patrick's new neighborhood is entirely different. I feel the insistent tug of envy in my stomach. There's no terra-cotta tile here, no beige plaster. The driveways don't sprawl like they have nothing better to do. The houses are vibrant colors and different styles, some rustic farmhouses and others modern with solar panels and water-conscious landscaping.

Halfway up the street, Patrick pulls the car into a gravel driveway. The house in front of us is a renovated bungalow, red with white trim and a wide grass lawn.

I love it instantly. Seeing the photos Patrick sent is one thing, but in person is another. The house is different from everything around it, and it feels out of place for Texas, like it belongs on the beach. I imagine Patrick here, and it fits new context to everything he's told me over the past few months. I can frame every video call we've had, every time he's mentioned walking home, with this.

"Here we are," he says. Spontaneously he leans over the center console, and I pull my eyes from the house, lining my lips up with his—which linger for the smallest moment, like he's enjoying having me this close. I'm enjoying it, too. Very much. When he kisses me, I feel in the quick heat how much he wanted to for the whole drive in.

When he gets out, he grabs my suitcase and leads me up the porch steps. Before he can unlock the door, Patrick's mom swings it open from the inside. "Siena!" she says, holding her arms open.

I smile spontaneously, not having expected how nice seeing Mel would be. Her haircut hasn't changed, short with bangs, nor her orchid hand lotion, which I smell instantly. I step into her hug.

"We're all so happy you're here," she says into my shoulder. Mel is surprisingly petite given Patrick's slightly upward-of-average height.

"Me too," I say, hoping she hears how much I mean it. "I love the new house."

"Come see the inside," Mel says.

When I follow her over the threshold, I'm disoriented for a moment, like I've stepped into a parallel universe. I know all this furniture, the gray couch with yellow pillows, the shaggy navy rug, the wooden coffee table. It's everything from Patrick's old house, laid out in perfect symmetry to how I remember it. Patrick's cat, Roger, even sits on his usual couch cushion, where he magnanimously receives my enthusiastic head nuzzles. The only differences are the new dining table, chosen to fit the smaller space, and the new drapes hanging over the longer windows. Despite the similarities, everything feels somehow new, like changing the context has revitalized the familiar—lightening new corners, sharpening new details.

"Make sure you look at the coffee table," Mel urges me, sounding eager.

I double-check the piece of furniture, wondering if I was mistaken and it's new. If it is, it's identical to the one on which I've placed countless cans of LaCroix while eating hummus and making small talk with Patrick's parents.

Then I recognize the magazine cover on the dark wood.

It's the issue of the West Vista literary magazine where my story was published.

"You have to sign it for us," Mel says proudly, with poorly concealed insistence.

I laugh, not knowing what to say. Honestly, the request leaves me slightly embarrassed. It's how Mel is, I've learned in three years, intensely supportive with a streak I can only call crushingly sentimental. I would not be surprised if Patrick's soccer medals from first-grade AYSO have remained hanging over her computer even after the move to Austin. She's a wonderful cheerleader, and she's undoubtedly where Patrick gets his drive, as well as the unfailing and inclusive leadership I've seen him demonstrate in MUN.

Nevertheless, it leaves me stuck in moments like now. I don't know how to explain to her that writing one story for the magazine doesn't mean I'm embarking on the start of some long, focused literary career.

"Mom," Patrick says, no doubt picking up on my discomfort. "Don't put her on the spot."

"I'm not." Mel waves him off, characteristically unable to take no for an answer. "Siena, I had no idea you were a writer. All this time, you've never once mentioned it."

"I wouldn't say I'm a writer," I reply, blushing, the words leaping out of me on something like instinct. "I just—did it for fun."

"Well, I'm not joking about you signing it," Mel says with caramel-coated firmness.

I stand there stiffly. The idea of *signing* my work feels

vaguely ridiculous. I guess I'll scrawl *Siena Griffin* in the same standard cursive I used on the form for my library card.

Patrick rescues me. "Later, Mom. Siena and I have a schedule to keep," he says, and I'm grateful he's picked up her assertiveness as well. He looks to me. "We can drop your bag off, then get going."

I follow him farther into the house. What he's said has caught my curiosity. "A *schedule*?" I repeat, raising my eyebrow.

"We only have three days together and a *lot* to fit in. I plan to make the most of every second." He shoots me a glance that makes my insides heat. It leaves me wondering if he's considering the same thing I am.

Until he ducks out of the hallway and deposits my bag in front of . . . the Reynolds' guest bed. I recognize the rest of the guest room's furniture, the small vase of sticks on the white end table, the folded quilt draped over the comforter.

My small spark of hope I'd be staying in Patrick's room dies. I'd wondered whether the special circumstances of my visit would provide an exception to the general pattern, which is Mel's unwavering intensity about what Patrick's doing under her roof. Whenever we wanted to do something involving less clothing, my house was the safer spot. While we've never slept in the same bed together, I recognize— from the dim feeling in my chest—that I was sort of hoping this trip would be the time.

Before long distance, *firsts* never concerned me. They were inevitable stops on one long, uncrowded highway. I'd had each of mine with Patrick relatively early in high school, but with no forced timing, no rush. Seeing each other pretty much every day made it easy. Now I'm conscious of every first I won't be having while I'm back in Phoenix and my boyfriend is . . . here.

This visit is our only opportunity. Not just for sex, either. There's literally sleeping together, or taking a road trip just the two of us. We've never even said *I love you*, which I know is somewhat unusual, but when we were fifteen, we didn't want to rush to say those three important words. I remember the conversation we had about it—we weren't going to be one of those couples who did just because we liked the idea. Those words felt to me like forever, which privately, I didn't know if I wanted to set in stone quite yet.

We said we would wait until we felt ready. But now, when we do feel ready, I definitely don't want it to be over text.

Which changes what would be a matter of spontaneity into a moving target. I never expected we would have to schedule our *I love you*s. It's a new reality I decidedly don't like.

Patrick's voice pulls me from my thoughts. "Everything okay?" His tone says he thinks it is.

He has no idea what I was working over in my head— and that, I decide, is perfectly okay. I hold on to his positivity. This visit *is* full of promise. We have three days, we have each other, and we have a schedule. I smile at him. "Give me ten minutes to change out of my airplane clothes. I want to make the most of this trip, too."

While the excitement in my words is genuine, even as I'm

saying them, I feel the weight of expectation starting to pile on to me. Making the most of every second *sounds* nice. In practice, it's less of an ideal and more of a pressure.

I *don't* want to waste a single second with him. When I packed my bag, I was expecting, essentially, a vacation. I was envisioning local restaurants, walks over the river, holding hands. Not counting minutes to calculate how many happy memories I could convert them into. While this visit might be many things, I'm realizing a vacation isn't one of them. Vacations are relaxing. Fitting everything I want into a little over a weekend is hard work.

Especially when with Patrick, I'm realizing just how much more I'm starting to want.

Twenty-Three

BEFORE LONG DISTANCE, PATRICK and I would make sure to organize dates every so often. Not just Saturdays at Rex's. Occasions, plans we could look forward to enjoying just the two of us.

This, however, is a new record. Patrick's decided we're cramming a month's worth of missed dates into one *day*.

He informs me of this plan while we're walking into what I intuit is date number one—a late breakfast at Patrick's new favorite café. I hardly react to his words because I'm too busy falling in love in with the place. It's industrial, sleeker than the homey simplicity of Rex's, with unpainted concrete floors, exposed ducts, and indoor plants. The other patrons look like college students on winter break and business-people refueling during the workday. I see laptops open on music production software, unfinished screenplays, long Spotify playlists.

We eat our pastries, then grab hot chocolate to go. From the café, it's not far into downtown Austin, where we sit on a bench in the park outside the impressive capitol building, clutching our warm drinks in cold fingers. While we finish our hot chocolate, we dog-watch. The morning sun, almost directly overhead, matches exactly how I'm feeling. It's the start of the day, and the start of something new.

Next Patrick loads us into his car and drives us to South Congress. *SoCo*, he calls it, and I don't miss the easy way the localism rolls off his tongue. We park on one side of the expansive street under the old-school marquee for a leather-goods store. Patrick leads us up and down the sidewalk, letting me wander into whatever stores catch my eye.

It's overwhelming in the coolest way, everywhere a collection of cactus prints, polished cowhide, and rose-colored crystals. Every store is different, yet they weave together into a tapestry of the city's esoteric and vibrant energy.

Surrounded by inspiration, I kaleidoscope, finding new versions of me in every direction. The store windows reflect *Designer Siena*, sketching out dazzling creations in Photoshop, swelling with pride seeing them on smartly cut clothing. *Chef Siena* stands focused over the counter of the outdoor farmers market–style pizza oven, handling sauce and spices with practiced efficiency. Everywhere, *Entrepreneur Siena* balances budgets and meets with investors, building dreams into brick and mortar.

I love this city.

I promptly get Patrick to try on cowboy boots and purchase a KEEP AUSTIN WEIRD shirt. When we've walked until my feet start to hurt, Patrick pulls us into the line for what he—and obviously everyone else in Austin—considers the best tacos in Austin. I don't mind the wait. We watch the street, absorbing the city and the smells drifting from the restaurants while Patrick explains to me the legacy of Texas breakfast tacos.

When we finally get our food, our table crowded with containers of queso and salsa and plastic baskets of chips, I don't hesitate. I bite into my fried avocado taco.

"Good?" Patrick asks, grinning like he already knows.

"Incredible," I declare, except it comes out more like *incumble* past melted cheese and soft, chewy tortilla. I swallow, then continue. "I can't believe I was in Phoenix this morning with no idea how radically this taco would change my life." It's large, closer to a deconstructed burrito. I inhale it in just a couple bites anyway, then turn to my second taco.

"Don't forget the queso," Patrick reminds me.

"I could never," I reply, indignant.

Patrick finishes his first taco, then lifts his second out of his basket. He examines it with reverence for a moment. "It's possible I judged this city too harshly," he says.

Wiping my fingers on my napkin, I smile. Personally, I don't know how it's possible to judge this place harshly, but then, I guess I'm not the one who moved here in my final year of high school. "Well," I venture, "I think the city suits you."

Patrick chokes a little on his bite of eggs and hot sauce. Washing it down with soda, he tries to recover. "Yeah? How so?" There's the hint of something pleased in his voice. He's not just curious—he wants me to elaborate.

I warm to the task. "You fit in here. It makes you . . . I don't know." I stare into the restaurant while I search for words. I'm remembering the half dozen times just today Patrick made me laugh unexpectedly, or he pointed out something interesting, or his smile woke up those persistent butterflies. "Brighter somehow. Maybe I sound silly," I go on, suddenly a little self-conscious, but not in a bad way.

"You don't," he says softly. He sets his taco down, looking earnest in a way that's so characteristically Patrick. It's unexpectedly nice to see. "I'm glad," he continues. "I've been trying to look for the good here, and, well, there's definitely a lot to find. And showing you is even better."

It is exactly the right thing to say. The past few months have been full of good memories, but this, I decide, might be my favorite one. "Is this what you do *every* weekend?" I ask, sort of impressed.

"Well," Patrick says, "I generally go on fewer dates."

I laugh, then pull an interrogating expression. "*Fewer* dates?"

"Only one or two a weekend, tops," he replies without hesitating.

I throw a chip at his chest. "Really, though," I say, "you must be having to fend off the ladies left and right." I keep my wording playful to hide the semi-seriousness of the question and the sudden pang it makes me feel.

"You know you're the only one I want," Patrick reassures me.

His reply is sweet. Perfect, even. But it isn't totally

reassuring, because he didn't deny what I've suggested. I file the information away, a piece of the new Patrick. Back home we were thoroughly enmeshed in each other's lives. *PatrickandSiena.* Everyone knew we were an us, not a him and me. Here, though, I'm face-to-face with the question of how other girls see him—with his windswept hair, his new tan. Not that I have any reason to distrust him. It's just a reality that's brand-new to us.

One of many.

I determinedly chase the feelings off. "I kind of feel like we're on a first date," I say. Patrick's expression falls, and I rush to clarify. "In a good way! So much is new in our lives, and I get to relearn what your days are like. It's kind of fun. We're getting to know each other all over again."

Patrick looks neither convinced nor comforted. He chews slowly, then gives me a small smile. "I'm happy if you are," he says.

Before I have the chance to reply, three girls pause near our table. "Patrick!" one says enthusiastically. She's on the right, her dark hair falling over her shoulders, her shirt featuring the name of what I'm guessing is some band. She's smiling in a genuinely friendly sort of way. "Is this the girlfriend?" she asks, her gaze swiveling to me.

Patrick startles. They're his friends from school, I figure. He says nothing for a second, and watching him, I get the sense he's struggling to reconcile these two parts of his world colliding. The other girls watch him with eager curiosity. Except I guess they're not watching him. They're watching *us.*

I give our visitors a closer look. They're cool in the way everything is in this city, put-together portraits of black jeans, sleekly simple makeup, geometric jewelry, and understated boots. Frankly, their effortless style is not the image of the people Patrick hung out with in Phoenix. I wonder if this is just the way Patrick's entire new school looks or if he's fallen in with a more popular crowd.

Patrick finds his voice. "Uh, yeah." He blinks, the Patrick I know returning, his discomposure fleeing. He smiles, and his eyes find me. "Yeah, sorry, this is Siena. Siena, this is"— his gaze sweeps from me, left to right—"Vic, Sam, and Carly."

I nod like the names mean something to me. They don't. "Um, hi," I say, nothing else coming to me.

The girl in the middle, who I guess is Sam, smiles welcomingly and with a hint of something conspiratorial, like we're in on the same joke. "We've heard *so* much about you," she says. "Patrick's been counting down the days until your visit. It's honestly been adorable."

"Wait," Carly cuts in with what sounds like scandalized realization. "We're not crashing your day of a dozen makeup dates, right?"

Patrick laughs politely. "Sort of," he admits. I look from the girls to him, trying to decode what's going on behind those brown eyes, and to unravel my own bittersweet emotions. It's obviously flattering—and reassuring—knowing Patrick talks about me enough for these girls to know exactly who I am and what Patrick and I are doing today.

Even so, I'm . . . uneasy. I genuinely trust Patrick, but I can't help feeling like I'm in the dark. Why is it they know everything they do, and yet I've never heard their names?

Vic glances to her friends, then back to Patrick. "We shouldn't interrupt you guys," she says.

I put on a smile, some instinct in me wanting to even out the strange imbalance here. Mustering into my voice every ounce of the confidence I've practiced in MUN, I speak over the noise of the restaurant. "Oh, it's fine. It's great to finally meet you all," I say, like I've known of them for months.

If Patrick notices the light edge in my voice or my use of the word *finally*, he doesn't react.

"No, we'll leave you be," Vic says quickly. Moving to leave, she pauses. She places one hand on the table. Peach nail polish, I notice, with an impressive symbol painted on her ring finger, the swirly one from the start of written music. "But because I doubt Patrick's told you as part of his agenda to keep you all to himself while you're here—you're *both* invited to my New Year's Eve party."

"Vic..." Patrick says like he's had this conversation before. It's not exactly uncomfortable resistance, though. There's an inside-joke ring to it. Once more, I don't mind. It's just a curious flash of the life I don't see.

"I know, I know," Vic preempts him. "You don't have to stay long. Just drop by. We'd love to get to hang out with you for real," she says the last part to me, and I decide I'm flattered. Whatever their connection to Patrick, these girls seem genuinely nice, and it's kind of them to invite me into their world. Not just their world—his, too. A party would be the perfect way to experience it.

Patrick's voice cuts through my building excitement. "Maybe," he says gently. "We'll see." His tone is temperate, but I know Patrick, and what he's really saying is *no, thank you*.

My chest deflates. If we weren't long distance, we would definitely be going to someone's New Year's party back in Phoenix—something small, with our MUN friends. Just because we're in Austin, where I don't know his friends yet, doesn't seem like reason enough to skip this.

"Yeah, yeah. We know what that means," Vic says, rolling her eyes. Her gaze darts to me, and we share a commiserative glance. It feels nice, how easily we fall into this secret understanding. "Well, regardless, Siena," she goes on, "it's great to meet you. Patrick really adores you, which I'm sure you know already."

I smile at her words, my frustration with Patrick dimming just a little. "I'll see if I can convince him to come to the party," I tell the girls.

"Good luck!" Sam says with the same knowing grin. They wave and walk off, already onto their next conversation.

I face Patrick, who's tidying our trash for the servers. Fully moving on from his friends' invitation, he checks the time on his phone. "Okay, we should head out to the next date," he says. He looks up and smiles at me, and it's the sort of smile that stops everything—for a second—quieting unmade plans and little surprises. "We still have a lot to make up," he informs me, a low note of promise in his voice.

"Let's go, then," I say, standing. We walk out of the

restaurant, tracing the path Vic, Sam, and Carly took from our table.

My mind starts to make a list while we head out. I want to go to this party with Patrick. Like everything exciting the next few days might hold, it's also one more thing to fit in. I should feel lucky there's so much I want to do with Patrick, and I do.

Even so, I can't ignore how the list keeps getting longer and longer while our time together trickles down every minute.

Twenty-Four

LEAVING THE RESTAURANT, WE head down the sidewalk back the direction we came. It's only gotten more crowded, the pavement congested with shoppers popping in and out of stores while the line for tacos has grown. We say nothing for a few moments in the companionable post-queso lull. Patrick looks relaxed, his footsteps upbeat. He's a naturally fast walker.

"Your friends seem nice," I say when we're waiting at the crosswalk. I pause for a second and wonder if Patrick notices. "Why haven't you ever mentioned them?"

He looks surprised, his brow furrowing. "No reason," he replies with a kind of forced ease. It's not evasiveness, not discomfort. He's just curious why I'm asking, and it's disrupted the moment. When the light changes, we step off the curb.

"I want to hear about them," I say gently, making sure I don't sound like I'm interrogating. Which I'm not. I'm glad he has friends he can neglect to mention to me. "I want to hear about all your friends, actually."

Patrick ponders until we reach the other corner. "When we talk, I'm kind of focused on you, on us. Even on our friends back home," he says. "Wouldn't it be boring to hear about the lives of people you don't even know?"

"But they're part of *your* life," I point out. It's perfectly Patrick, really, to not share those details just because he's worried they'll bore me. "I want to know what your days look like, Patrick. I want to feel like I'm still part of your world, even when I'm not there."

He gives me a long, curious look. "Okay, well," he starts, "Carly's working on a group project with Ross, which is kind of awkward because of his whole thing with Vic. Not to mention, Danny Escobedo is in the group, too." He's loading insinuation and implication into his voice. "Is that the kind of thing you want to know?" he asks.

"Yes!" I say, amused and slightly annoyed. "I do. But I . . . might need a little context."

Patrick laughs. Then his smile softens, or maybe it fades. "I guess I didn't think you were interested."

"I am," I say. We pass an old-fashioned candy shop, then a storefront with vintage cameras in the window. Patrick's admission makes me feel slightly guilty. While he could have volunteered more details, I also could have asked for them. It's just not something I'm used to, a sharp difference from years of conversations founded on shared experiences. I guess I shouldn't be surprised to find myself still learning the new patterns of our relationship now.

I make a mental note to ask more. Starting now.

"How did you become friends with those girls?" I ask.

He smiles. He knows what I'm doing, and he's willing to work with me on it. "They're all in Young Dems Club."

"Young Dems Club?" I repeat, putting together this new information.

"I've gone to a couple meetings now. It's sort of becoming my replacement for Model UN," Patrick replies. "I know local politics and international relations are really different. Still, I like it a lot. You know, registering people to vote, canvassing."

I want to feel nothing but enthusiasm for him, want to fondly imagine him with his clipboard and stack of campaign stickers, gamely wandering the neighborhood and collecting voter details. Instead, I find myself feeling a little hurt that he didn't tell me this sooner. Wasn't this what we discussed in Rex's? Keeping each other in the loop?

It makes me want to pry. To dissect the feeling. I don't, though. Because with the tight timeline of this trip, I don't want to waste the hours we have on nitpicky issues of communication. He's telling me now. That's what's important.

I force enthusiasm into my voice. "That sounds really cool." It's not hard to say. After all, it's not untrue. I've long known Patrick flourishes when it comes to politics and government, connecting people and pushing issues he believes in. Past my fading hurt, I'm proud of him, if not without some small stab of jealousy for everything he's found for himself while I'm still searching.

Patrick smiles. We stop on the sidewalk, and I realize where we're standing. There's a dirt path leading into an enclosed clearing. I hear live music drifting over the sounds of the street.

I look at Patrick. The intention in his eyes is unmistakable. "What is this?" I start to smile. "Date number . . . four?"

"Honestly," Patrick says, half-sheepish and half-brash, "I've lost count."

With my hand in his, he pulls me deeper in, until a large stage decorated with strung light bulbs emerges where the band I heard from the sidewalk plays. I take everything in, lost in the wonder of this place. The leafless trees stretch over the space scattered with picnic tables and people. In front of the stage, a crowd dances while others listen from their seats on one edge of the clearing under a towering oak that reaches high into the sunlit sky. I understand why Patrick brought me here. It's full of the magic of hidden places, and I love it.

"I was thinking *this* date would make up for our three-year anniversary," he says softly.

I pull my gaze from our surroundings to the boy next to me. His eyes sparkle in the lights, hopefulness illuminating every corner of his expression.

It surprises me. Not the idea we would celebrate our anniversary, which was technically two weeks ago, but that the celebration would look like this. This date is like nothing we've ever done together. For our other two anniversaries, we went to the fancy Italian restaurant near Patrick's house. The first time we went, I was excited. The second time, I foresaw it becoming one more tradition, one more repetition that would only end if I ended it.

I press my shoulder gently to his. "This is so much better than La Vecchia," I say. "You know, I never liked their ravioli that much."

Patrick withdraws from me a little. "You didn't?" he asks. "I never knew that."

I wish he'd laughed off my comment like a harmless joke on our younger selves. Not quite defensive and not quite comfortable, I shrug. "You never asked," I say, a little recklessly.

He pulls far enough from me now for me to watch his expression twist. When he opens his mouth to reply, I cut him off.

"It's fine. Really," I say hurriedly. "We're here now. Let's listen to the band." I don't want to dredge up the past, discontentment I'm happy to forget. Not while we're here, under these lights, immersed in these sounds. I lead Patrick by the hand into the crowd, where I wrap his arms around me from behind.

We sway together, his chin to my cheek. Pressed to him, it's suddenly very easy not to dwell on the past, and impossible not to feel other things. The music envelops us, rough and romantic, slow and sweet—the kind of music that's easy to sink into. The bass thrums up through my feet, the bluesy vocals drifting over the daytime breeze.

I'm very conscious of the place where my backside aligns with Patrick's body. The contact is newly charged, enough to jump-start unfamiliar tingles in my chest and fingertips. I'm not sure if it's because of all the changes between us— the ways this day has felt less like returning to someone and more like rediscovering them—or if it's because of my plans for this trip. *Specific* plans.

When the song shifts, I follow it like a cue, turning in Patrick's embrace to face him.

He looks down at me, his gaze heated like mine.

While the chorus washes over us, I press my lips to his, and it's a kiss like a low, aching melody. I put as much of my intention as I can it into it, letting him know there's something new growing between us. When I pull away, his gaze is half-lidded. He opens his eyes, and I know he feels it, too.

"I'm asking now," he says. "Do you like *this*?"

His question isn't accusatory or resentful. He genuinely wants to correct past wrongs. And while *like* is one word for it, it's far from the only word I'd use to describe this perfect moment. They could write songs with the rest.

"Yes," I tell him. "I love it."

Twenty-Five

WHEN WE FINALLY HEAD back to Patrick's, I'm the happiest kind of exhausted. The day was perfect. Like I was living out the highlights of someone else's camera roll. We left the concert sweaty and excited, our feet starting to hurt. It didn't matter. From there, we watched the sunset over the river, then got barbeque, then finally donuts.

It was a day full of new experiences. Even so, some of my favorite parts weren't even the memories we made but the ones Patrick shared with me from his past few months in Texas. He described the group of friends he has lunch with, the teachers he likes best, the hikes he takes. It was like our conversation earlier had opened a gate, letting me into the new life he's found here. In return, I told him how I've spent free time hanging out with Joe and how I felt having the school read my story in the lit journal.

I had to ignore how insubstantial my new life sounds next to his. Even so, it was nice to tell Patrick everything, nice to hear about his life, too. Better, even. It made me feel close to him. Maybe Patrick has me reaching for hiking metaphors, but it felt like I'd spent so long wandering in the wilderness, and now I'm starting to find the path. Everything about our renewed relationship feels stronger, in ways familiar and foreign. Which only reinforces my new objective for this visit.

When we get inside, I follow Patrick to his bedroom.

It's the same furniture from his old room, the same MUN gavels on display, the same extendable desk lamp. The same framed poster of his favorite documentary, which is on the US healthcare system and which I've seen three times.

The similarities make the differences so much more striking. The textbooks we no longer share sitting on his desk. The collage of photos on his bulletin board. Pictures of us, our friends, even just some Phoenix postcards—saguaros in the sunset.

Patrick is quiet while I walk farther into the room, getting used to his new space. Taking in the details the photos he's sent me didn't capture. The laundry hamper, the closet, the Sierra Club poster on the back of his door. I'm studying the photos on the bulletin board more closely—the horribly lit one from homecoming where I'm wearing green—when Mel walks by. "Door open," she singsongs, pushing the cracked door open wider on her way past.

Patrick rolls his eyes behind her back. "Sorry," he says to me.

"It's fine," I reply, hiding how my heart sinks. I have no idea how we'll get the privacy we'll need for what I want. The question won't go quiet. I focus on Patrick's kind eyes, his half smile. "I had a lot of fun today." I say it like a suggestion, not a sign-off.

Patrick's smile goes from half to three-quarters. Probably even five-sixths. "Me too."

His words sound inviting, too. I step nearer to him, liking their direction. Today has my feet sore, my back stiff, my legs aching. Right now, I feel none of those things. Not with him so close to me. "It was really wonderful to hear about your life here. The new things you've tried. I . . ." I hesitate, feeling my cheeks heat. I'm not used to having these kinds of conversations with Patrick. But while he's trying new things, I will, too. "I wondered if you wanted to try . . . other things. *Certain* other things."

Patrick straightens, suddenly more alert than our hours of walking should have left him. His expression isn't exactly unsure, just cautious. "What, um, do you mean, specifically?"

"Sex," I whisper. *So much for being coy.* Speaking the word out loud feels strange, if excitingly so. It makes me wonder how many individual times in my life I've even said the word.

Patrick doesn't look startled. He understood what I meant. He's just too much of a gentleman-slash-feminist to presume without me confirming explicitly. It fills me with warmth, finished off with a dash of relief. "Now?" he asks.

I nod to the open bedroom door, laughing. The sounds of the TV, Patrick's dad watching sports, echo down the hallway. "Well, not *right* now," I say. "But . . . before I leave."

Surprise flits into his eyes—which, I realize, hurts a little.

The idea presently occupying my every waking moment is one he hasn't even considered.

"What happened to waiting for the right moment?" Patrick's question is earnest, and understandable.

"I—" I exhale, finding the changes I've thought about recently ready on my tongue. "I know it's what we said when we were younger. But we've been keeping the 'right moment' on the horizon for years. I don't know if I . . . care about it now." When Patrick looks like he's considering my words, I continue on. "But if you do, I completely understand. I'm completely okay to wait if you want to."

He smiles softly, and there's no whisper of doubt in his voice when he speaks. "No, I . . . I feel the same. I just . . ." Color rises in his cheeks now. He shifts, straightening the hem of his sweatshirt. "I really do. I just don't know how . . ."

My brow furrows. Surely he's not *that* clueless. Not that I consider myself an expert, but I feel like I have a handle on the basics. "Patrick, I'm pretty confident we'll figure it out," I say delicately.

Which earns me a look of mortification. "I mean how logistically," he rushes to correct my unfortunate misunderstanding. "Not, um, physically. I have—a good idea of how physically," he finishes with his face fire-engine red.

It's incredibly cute. I smile, starting to reply. Right then, unfortunately, Mel appears in the doorway. "You two need anything?" she asks.

Patrick closes his eyes in evident pain before turning to face her. "No. We're good," he replies patiently.

Her gaze darts from me to Patrick like she knows exactly what's going on. I have to give her mom-intuition credit. "Okay," she says slowly, matching the levelness of Patrick's voice. She starts to step out of the doorway, then doubles back. "Oh," she begins, and I can't decide if she's returned out of genuine forgetfulness or some clever ploy to spend more time monitoring us. "Patrick, have you submitted all your apps yet? I know they're due in a couple days."

"Yes," Patrick places a little restlessness on the syllable. "I submitted the last one yesterday."

Still, Mel doesn't leave.

"What about PLME?" she asks.

Despite my desire for her to leave, Mel's question flags my curiosity. *PLME?* I don't recognize the acronym. Patrick and I have talked about where we're applying to college, but not in any coordinated way or even in a whole lot of detail. Still, PLME doesn't square with the names of colleges he's mentioned—in fact, with no *U* or *C* in the name, it doesn't even sound like a college.

"Yup," Patrick replies slowly, with sarcastic patience. "I submitted everything."

"Good," Mel says. Without a moment's pause, she finds her next line of inquiry. Her eyes shift to me. "How about you, Siena? Did you get your apps in?" Her voice is somewhere between pushiness and genuine motherly concern.

"Don't interrogate her, Mom," Patrick preempts me protectively, as if I haven't had this kind of prying conversation with Mel plenty of times.

"I'm not!" Mel protests innocently. "I just want to make sure you two don't have to worry about this while you're together this weekend."

I'm pretty certain *worrying* isn't what she wants to make sure we won't do this weekend. Nevertheless, I smile graciously. "I turned them in last week. Don't worry about us," I say, a little firmly.

"Of course you did." Mel looks pleased. It doesn't change my slight irritation at how obviously she's intruding. Before leaving, she pointedly pushes the door open one inch wider.

When her footsteps fade down the hall, Patrick faces me. "Where were we?" he asks. His question hums with the promise of our unfinished conversation.

Wherever we were, though, I'm no longer there. Mel's question has caught my mind like a sweater snagged on a corner. "What's PLME?"

"Oh." Patrick looks somewhat surprised but handles it gracefully. "I told you I was applying to Brown," he says, the statement holding the hint of a question.

I relax. He did. While it's not like I expected him to check every plan with me, I worried for a second I'd stumbled onto something else he hadn't shared, like Young Dems or his new friends. Honestly, this time, I might have been truly hurt. "Right," I say, wondering if my relief is evident. "What's PLME, though? Some kind of program?"

Patrick's face lights up. "The Program in Liberal Medical Education," he says enthusiastically. "So, you know I'm going to do pre-med."

I nod. Despite how Patrick really has been trying new things, it's not like I expected him to change the college plan he's had for years.

"Well," he goes on, sounding like he can hardly contain himself. "Brown has this really cool program where you apply, and if you're admitted, you're not just admitted to the undergraduate college, you're also admitted to the med school."

My eyes fly wide. *Med school?* It feels wildly premature. Usually people have four years of classes in diverse subjects before making this decision. "Whoa," I say—not the impressed kind of *whoa*, the unnerved kind. "You're applying to med school? Already?"

"I know," Patrick says, missing my emphasis entirely. "It's a really exclusive program, so I probably won't get in, but it would be incredible."

"You're *that* sure you want to be a doctor?" I ask. "It sounds like a huge commitment."

His brow furrows. I understand his reaction. I've never spoken my hesitation about his unchanging focus on med school. Just, I can't help wondering if, now that he's opening himself up to new things, he might start seeing past the decision he made when he was fifteen. He can't really know what he wants to commit his entire life to now.

"I'm sure," he says, hardly giving it thought.

"But what about politics or government?" I ask, unable to stop myself. It's like I've opened up some reservoir of long-held questions, even doubts, and now they're rushing forth in ways I can't predict or control.

What I'm feeling isn't just formless hesitation, either. I have a suspicion about what's going on here. Mel loves the idea of Patrick following in her footsteps. She's never made it a secret. Which has left me wondering how much of Patrick's medical aspirations come from him and how much come from wanting to make her happy. Patrick is unfailingly kind, uniquely generous. I'm afraid sometimes the goodness in his heart forces everything else out. If he did discover his passions lie elsewhere, I'm worried he'd never speak up.

He shrugs, looking very much like I *haven't* disturbed some existential hornet's nest in him. "I like politics," he says. "I'm sure I'll continue to volunteer in some way or other. But I want to be a doctor, Siena."

"I know you do *now*," I say, disliking how desperate I sound. I'm practically scolding. I'd regret it if I wasn't sure I was right. "What if you change your mind in a year or two? Don't you want to keep your options open?"

Something unreadable crosses Patrick's face. He steps closer, and I feel his fingers intertwine with mine. "I'm not like that." His voice is soft in a strained sort of way, like he's handling his words with care. "When I know something, I know."

His eyes fix on me, and I realize what he's really saying.

I'm opening my mouth to reply, not entirely sure what I'll say, when Mel's voice cuts into the room, pushing between Patrick and me like a repelling magnet. "Patrick? Time for bed, okay?" She sounds distant, like she's calling from her own doorway.

Now Patrick's expression is very readable. He looks like he wants to vanish into a hole. "Okay!" he shouts back. He lowers his voice for me only. "You should probably go. But"—his eyes soften—"I'm *going* to find us some privacy while you're here." He leans down, pressing his lips to mine with promise.

I smile, my thoughts too scattered for me to respond. I settle for squeezing his hand. Leaving his room, I walk quietly down the hallway into mine, the guest room.

While I'm getting ready for bed, putting my phone to charge on the familiar nightstand, grabbing my pajamas from my suitcase near the bookshelf displaying photos of Patrick's grandparents, my mind remains restless. *I'm not like that.* In the small room, Patrick's words feel like they're everywhere. I've always suspected Patrick was committed to pre-med for the wrong reasons. Now, suddenly, I'm wondering if our relationship is no different. If it's also something he's committed to out of old plans and a desire not to disappoint. Not to hurt anyone—hurt me. How can I possibly know if he wants *me* or just wants to hold on to the decision he made when he was fifteen?

I climb under the covers, wishing the question would let me sleep and knowing it won't.

Twenty-Six

I'M WOKEN UP THE next morning by someone shaking my shoulder. Groggily, I glance out the window. It's dark outside, no hint of sunrise lighting up the sky. Grimacing my way out of sleep, I find Patrick standing over me, fully dressed. He's somehow bright-eyed. He even looks like he washed his face. "What time is it?" I mumble.

"It's just before six," he says cheerfully.

I squeeze my eyes shut. "It's too early," I say, knowing if I were capable of more coherent expression, I would have continued, *If I had one dollar for every time I wanted to be up before sunrise, I would have no dollars, Patrick.*

"Not if you want to see the sunrise on a hike," he counters gently.

My eyes fly back open. Taking in what he's wearing, I realize they're clothes I've never seen before. Lightweight athletic wear and hiking boots. "We're going hiking?" I ask, feeling the first flickers of something other than extreme reluctance to get up this early.

"That depends," Patrick replies. "Do you have shoes with decent treads?"

"Yes," I say. I'm wide awake now, energized. What Patrick's offering me isn't just fresh sunlight over dusty trails. It's the opportunity to experience this new part of his life. I'm excited he's invited me in—not to mention excited to see *Hiking Patrick*.

On second thought, I guess I would have *one* dollar.

"Then get dressed," he says. When he leans down to kiss me, I put my hand on his chest, stopping him.

"Not fair," I say. "You've brushed your teeth and I haven't."

His eyes travel down to where the comforter has revealed I'm not wearing a bra under my thin T-shirt. I feel my whole body blush.

"Yeah," Patrick says. "It's really unfair."

"Get out of here," I whisper roughly. "We have the sunrise to catch."

Patrick smiles, like he knows what his words have done. Without replying, he leaves the room. I spring out of bed and pull on the leggings I wore to the airport and the one pair of tennis shoes I brought. They're made more for running than hiking, but I won't miss the chance to do this with him. In the bathroom connected to my bedroom, I rush to get ready—including, obviously, brushing my teeth. When I walk into the kitchen, Patrick is filling up two of those environmental water bottles he likes. He hands me a banana on our way to the door. Then we're off.

We drive twenty minutes in the dark. Reaching the

trailhead, which is a little outside the city in some kind of nature park, I find we're not the first ones here, despite the early hour. There are a couple cars parked along the road, but I don't see any people. I step out of the passenger side, breathing in the winter woodsy smell of the outdoors.

There's no trace of the city out here. I'm not used to the density of the wilderness—the trees everywhere, some upright, some fallen, sticking out in surprising diagonals over the carpet of dead leaves. The only sound is the rustling of the branches, punctuated by the distinctive grating chirp of the grackles, the bird Patrick pointed out yesterday that's everywhere in Austin. The early hour has drifted to the back of my mind. It's perfectly tranquil here.

"Hey," Patrick speaks up, "after this, what do you think about FaceTiming Alicia and Garret?"

The question pulls me out of the hushed seclusion I've been enjoying. I frown, facing Patrick, who's looking out toward the trailhead with less of the wonder I just felt. It makes sense, considering he's probably been here dozens of times. Even so, with the picturesque woods surrounding us, I can't understand how his mind is on FaceTiming people back in Phoenix.

"I'd sort of rather spend time seeing your life here. Seeing the city," I say delicately. I've enjoyed meeting his friends, visiting his local spots. I guess learning about the ways he's chosen to live his life here feels like learning about the new Patrick, the boyfriend I'm inexplicably falling for more and more every day. "Isn't there more you could show me?"

Patrick's expression now matches mine. His voice holds the faintest hint of frustration. "Not every part of my life is nonstop excitement. Most of the time I'm just doing homework, or in my room." He shifts his backpack, not meeting my eyes. "Besides, I miss my friends."

I scrutinize him, really not understanding the imperative here. He's presumably *missed his friends* on days when his long distance *girlfriend* wasn't visiting him. Over us, the sky is starting to gray with the prelude to sunrise. "Sure, but I'm only here for a couple days," I say. "Can't you just call them after I leave? You don't need me to be with you to talk to them."

"I *want* you with me." When he sighs, I hear some vulnerability in the sound. "When it's just me, it's—it's different. I'm the one on the outside. With you here, it would be more like it used to. You know, just us with our friends. Not me on my own."

I soften, not unsympathetic. I understand his point. Still, with everything we're hoping to fit in, everything we can only do *here*, I can't convince myself FaceTiming old friends is a priority. Heading for the trailhead, I walk slowly, my sneakers crunching on the dirt. In response to our presence, birds scatter, flapping up through the leafless trees. Patrick joins me. "We hung out with them when you were in Phoenix," I remind him. "What if we spent time with your new friends here? I really want to meet them."

"Garret and Alicia are *our* friends, not just mine. You don't even know anyone here," he points out with a quickness that's unlike him. I shoot him a glance, finding him staring straight forward. A one on most people's irritation scale is a five or six on Patrick's, which is where we are now. We're walking side by side, not hand in hand.

"It's my *one* chance to meet them," I say. "Don't you want your girlfriend to know your friends and your friends to know your girlfriend?"

Patrick's steps have quickened. I find I'm stretching my stride to keep up with him. "They're not my real friends, Siena. I've known them for four months, and I'll be leaving for college soon."

I hide how what he's saying stings, squeezing something sour into paper-cut insecurities. "They can still be your real friends even if you only met them this year," I say, holding in the rest of what I'm thinking. Besides Joe, I'm still searching for new friends and new spaces for myself back in Phoenix. I don't want to believe they won't be meaningful even if I find them only this year.

"I just don't see why missing Phoenix is such a crime," Patrick replies. The sentence holds a bitterness bigger than this conversation.

It makes me stop sharp, feet from the trailhead. In step with me, Patrick pauses immediately, watching me. My gut twists. There's no right answer in this debate. Which means there's no compromise, just a winner and a loser after a long fight. I don't want to miss out on seeing the sunrise, like Patrick planned, because we're having a fight.

"I don't want to fight," Patrick says grudgingly, seemingly

reading my mind. He's not backing down, only putting this on pause.

I'm relieved, even if it's the kind of patched-up relief of a momentary half solution. "Me neither," I reply hastily. Even the dusty ground under my feet feels firmer, the morning more expansive. "We can fight over the phone when I'm back in Phoenix," I offer with a conciliatory smile.

He laughs, and I grin wider, reaching for his hand. "I can just call our friends later, when you've gone home," he says. "It's no problem."

I recognize how unsurprising it is that Patrick is the one to give up what he wants. Nevertheless, I don't object. I'm glad we've forestalled the fight, salvaging our chance to catch my first Texas sunrise. "Thank you," I say, the lightness in me matching the hue of the morning sky. "Really. Now let's do this hike."

"Let's." Patrick's voice is solid.

We reach the trailhead. Then, just like that, we step past the wooden marker, onto the path into the wilderness—into this new part of Patrick's life. I know we'll return to what his Phoenix comment meant later. I'm not pretending we won't have the discussion, debate, fight, whatever.

It just doesn't have to be right now. Right now is for sharing the good.

Twenty-Seven

WE LEAVE OUR FIGHT at the base of the trail. Chasing the pink glow of the rising sun, we climb the path up the gentle incline.

As I follow Patrick, I continue observing the nature everywhere around us, loving how lost I feel out here even while I know we're not. We're not far from the river, and the smell of the water drifts over us past the naked trees. With sunrise coming, more birds have begun to wake up. Their songs underscore the papery sound of leaves and wood chips under our feet.

Conversation comes easily, about everything and nothing. We caught up on each other's lives yesterday, and now our discussion is the kind of mundane I hadn't realized I'd missed—random observations, old jokes. We've picked up like the past month never happened, like we never spent any time apart.

The reminders we have come sudden and surprising. The new cut of Patrick's muscles when he takes a long stride. The way he expertly navigates the terrain. Each one is a persistent hint of the time we've spent separated, the parts of Patrick I haven't gotten to know as well as I want to yet.

I wonder if it's possible to be infatuated with your boyfriend of three years. No, I don't *wonder*. I have the proof in how, even with the beautiful scenery surrounding us, my eyes stray *very* often to Patrick's ass.

I lose track of the minutes we're hiking. Overhead, the sky offers vague indication, shifting from gray to shades of dark yellow. My legs, still recovering from yesterday, strain when the trail steepens. Not in a way I mind—it's the gratifying sort of ache.

Then we reach the top.

I'm winded from the climb, but the view steals the breath from my lungs completely. The sky is pink and golden all the way to the horizon. I walk to the edge, wanting to see as far as I can. We're the only ones up here, looking out on this view, sharing this moment. It's at once intimate and expansive.

While the sun rises above us, trees give way to a city on the cusp of waking below us. It's New Year's Eve, I remember in a bright jolt. With traveling yesterday and waking up in what I consider the middle of the night today, I'd lost track of the date. We'd planned this trip so we could spend the holiday together, but with everything else going on in my head, I'd forgotten.

I find myself swept up in the rightness of it. Today's the final day of the year, one celebrated not for the previous year's endings but for tomorrow's beginnings. It's a day of looking forward, of resolutions and hopes and plans. Of change and possibility. Here, feeling the warmth from the last dawn of the year, I think of my own resolutions, some of which I hope to accomplish in the next two days.

With my gaze fixed so steadily on everything in front of me, I startle a little when I feel Patrick's hand on my hip. Finding him beside me, I sweep my arm around his waist, pulling us close as we watch the last of the sun's ascent.

"So," Patrick begins when the sky has turned pastel blue. "I've been doing some thinking, and I may have figured out how we could have some time alone . . ." Only someone who knows him the way I do could pick up the slight unevenness in his voice, breathy with the hope his statement holds.

I look at him over my shoulder. "Oh yeah?"

Patrick meets my gaze. "My parents are going to a New Year's Eve dinner with friends, then watching the sunset on the river. They should be gone for a couple hours." My stomach cartwheels at his words. While I was planning to convince him to take me to Vic's party, this is much more enticing. "I had dinner reservations for us. We could cancel, though, and just have something at my house. That way we'd have more time for . . . whatever you want to do." He pauses, eyeing me with new inquisitiveness. "And I do mean whatever," he goes on. "Just because you mentioned it yesterday doesn't mean I'm going to hold you to it. Obviously, I'm— very eager to, with you. But if you want to wait, or—"

He's rambling, and it's adorable. I cut him off with a kiss.

"Cancel the dinner reservation, Patrick," I say. For a

moment, this morning's fight and last night's doubts steal into my conviction. Maybe now isn't the *ideal* time, I concede. But it's the *only* time. What's more, this is something I really want.

My resolve redoubled, I level meaning into my look. Meaning he doesn't miss.

He nods, the expression on his face decisive and disbelieving in equal parts. "I'll do it as soon as we have service," he says softly.

When we reached the summit, I didn't think it could possibly feel more intimate, more like our very own perfect place. I was wrong. With the early sunlight wrapping us in its warmth, I step away from Patrick. After I've given the gorgeous view one final glance, I face the other direction, looking down the trail where we came from. I inscribe into my mind every detail, the texture of the dry trees, our footsteps in the dust. Because I don't just want to remember the sunrise. I want to remember everything. Everything I'll forever pair with how I feel right now.

Patrick waits like he understands what I'm doing. After a few minutes, we agree without speaking that we're ready to leave.

Starting our descent, I notice my calves searing. Patrick follows me, navigating nimbly, I know, from how little sound his shoes make scratching on the dirt. I expected hiking up would be the hard part, and I sorely miscalculated. Hiking down is harder. Muscles I don't use much protest when we hit the steep part of the trail. It's easy to distract myself from the pain, though—my mind is elsewhere. On tonight. Sex with Patrick will be the perfect start to the new year. Light spreads through me like the new day, excitement and nervous energy and—

I slip.

My shoes slide on the dry sand, my balance deserting me. With our downhill momentum pushing me, I'm unable to keep myself from tipping forward. Then I'm falling. I lose my footing completely, the world slanting sideways. Gravity wrenches me downward face first, and on instinct, I fling my hands out to break my fall.

I hit the ground hard, my wrist absorbing the impact as I smack into the earth.

Twenty-Eight

I'M STUNNED AT FIRST, feeling nothing when I land. I know I fell hard and pain is coming, though. I roll over, conscious of Patrick running down the hill where I stumbled. Embarrassment works its way into my disorientation. I probably look ridiculous splayed out in the dirt. Not to mention the way I probably looked falling, like one of those YouTube videos you feel bad for laughing at.

"Oh my god." Patrick reaches my side. "Are you okay?"

I rise shakily into a sitting position, feeling out my feet, my legs, my back. There are scrapes on my palms and probably my knees, although I managed not to rip holes in my leggings. "I think so," I say.

"What happened?" Patrick asks. He kneels at my side, worry in his eyes.

"My foot slipped on the loose rocks," I admit, my cheeks heating out of a combination of chagrin and adrenaline from my fall.

He glances down, his eyes narrowing. "Siena!" he says a

little harshly. "Your shoes have practically no treads. You told me you had appropriate footwear." When his eyes return to me, I'm surprised to find them accusatory.

"I thought I did! It's not like I've fallen down a mountain in these shoes before," I offer with a half smile.

"Not funny," he says stonily. "We didn't have to do this if you didn't have the right gear."

"I wanted to do this," I reply more firmly, flattening the waver in my voice. "It was our one chance to do this before I go back to Phoenix for who knows how long."

Patrick still looks displeased. "Let me see your hand."

I surrender my left hand, knowing it's the one he means. While it's bleeding more freely now, the blood dampening the dirt on my palm in gunky black streaks, it's just a scrape. However, when Patrick gently takes my wrist, I gasp. All of a sudden, I'm aware of pain stabbing out from within my wrist, white fire under my skin. I withdraw from him instantly, jerking my hand close to my chest.

Concern shadows over Patrick's face. "Was it me? I barely touched it."

"I don't think so," I say. "It just hurts, like, constantly."

He studies my wrist, his demeanor calm yet focused. "It looks swollen," he observes. I follow his eyeline. He's right, my entire wrist is puffy and pink. For the first time since I fell, real worry knots in me. Whatever happened to my wrist when I landed, it's probably not good.

Patrick's sudden movement distracts me from the new pain. Shrugging off his backpack, he unzips the front pouch and pulls out our water bottles, which he places on the ground. Then he takes out a forest-green pouch I don't recognize. I peer in when he zips it open to reveal first aid supplies. Past the throbbing ache in my arm, I smile a little. Of course ever-responsible Patrick has an entire first aid kit with him wherever he hikes.

"Elevate your wrist," he orders me with controlled urgency, "and take one of these."

He shakes an Advil into my uninjured hand, then passes me my water bottle. I do what he says. Swallowing down the pill, I start to feel steadier. *The Advil's going to work*, I reassure myself. In fact, I can feel the pain lessening even now. By the end of this hike, I won't even feel it. "I'm fine, really," I say. "Let's head back. We have the whole rest of the day, and I'm not going to let a bruised wrist slow us down."

Confident, I make a fist with my left hand. The effect is not the one I'd hoped for. Pain shoots sharper down my forearm.

I fight to cover the reaction, but Patrick's watching too closely. He catches me wince. "You might have broken it," he says seriously.

"I think I'd know if I'd broken my wrist," I shoot back, not caring how snarky I sound.

It earns me no points with Patrick, who gives me a flat look. "This isn't just a bruise," he continues, kind but humorless. "It could be a bad sprain or a hairline fracture, or worse. You don't want to do more damage by exerting it."

Willfully ignoring him, I get to my feet, pushing myself

up with my right hand. I'll just walk this off. Stretching my legs, I'm relieved to find nothing else hurts. My knees only smart a little, like I've skinned them.

Still, the throbbing in my wrist intensifies, and my eyes sting with frustration. I can *not* have broken my wrist. Not on this trip. I've never broken a bone in my entire life, not even when Sarah Choi kicked my thumb with the soccer ball I was reaching for in seventh-grade PE. I don't have time for this kind of injury, not when tonight—

I shut down this line of thought. It'll be fine. The only first I'll have on this trip won't be breaking a bone.

"Hey." Patrick's voice is tender. He places his hand comfortingly on my back. "It's going to be okay."

I swallow down my tears. Thinking positive helps with recovery, right? I'm pretty sure I read that somewhere. "Totally," I say. "Let me just rest for a second, and I'll be good as new."

Patrick's still scrutinizing me. "I have bandages. Would you let me wrap it before we keep going? Or"—his face lights up with inspiration—"you could wait here while I go down and get help."

"That will *not* be necessary," I reply immediately. "Unless you'd like to speed things up by having me die of embarrassment."

Patrick persists over my humor. "At least let me wrap it."

I nod grudgingly, not loving the idea but knowing I need to give Patrick something. The problem is, while he's well-intentioned, the more time we spend on this, the longer I can't ignore it.

Reluctantly, I let Patrick lead me to a rock speckled with small dead leaves. I sit, elevating my arm the way he advised as he pulls bandages and Neosporin from his first aid kit. First, he cleans the cuts on my palm, then he starts to wrap my wrist. While it still hurts, I can immediately feel how immobilizing the joint is helping. I watch him smoothly loop bandages around my wrist and my hand, his head bowed with focus on his task. He's collected, confident.

It works some magic on me. My breathing slows, the knot in my chest loosening. My pain dulling into the background, the nature surrounding us returns into focus—the quiet chorus of brittle wood and birdsong I noticed on the way up.

He looks up for a moment and catches me looking at him. The wobbly smile he gives me has me feeling like I'm flat on my back again. Filtering in past the trees, the new day's sunlight illuminates his eyes, sending streaks of gold into his brown irises. Somehow, I'm only noticing how perfectly his hair is mussed, swept from his forehead and curling slightly over his ear.

"Hi," he says.

"Hi," I say. I fall into the feeling of gratitude that I'm here with Patrick, that Patrick is here with me. That I can feel this total adoration for this boy even while my wrist is on fire. He fastens the bandage, then neatly repacks his supplies and slides his first aid kit into his backpack.

I watch him, lost in my daze. *It's got to mean something*, I hear myself think. The fact that this is my favorite moment of the trip thus far—not tacos or even sunrises, but this, *just* because Patrick made it okay—must mean something. It does a little to loosen the pressure I've dwelled on since I woke up yesterday, the stressful effort of fitting every moment I want into this trip. Because Patrick's shown he's capable of turning every moment into one worth wanting.

"Take as much time as you need," he says. "Because once we get to the car, we're going straight to the emergency room."

His words shatter the moment, the pain in my wrist roaring back. "You're *joking*," I say.

"Well, it's New Year's Eve, so most urgent cares will be closed," he replies reasonably. "The emergency room is our only option."

My eyes widen. He's serious. "The *hospital*? Don't you think you're overreacting?" The edge in my voice says, *You're definitely overreacting.* "We have plans for today, remember? For *tonight*? I'm not letting this get in the way."

I'm not imagining it—for a moment, Patrick does look disappointed, even stricken, at the reference to our plans, the ones we made just minutes ago. Then his expression evens, with the sureness of a unilateral decision. "It won't get in the way . . . *if* a doctor says you didn't break anything."

I don't reply. I can't. I'm furious—furious at Patrick, at myself, at my stupid shoes. The emotion comes on faster and more consuming than the pain did when it first exploded into my wrist, and now the anger is everywhere, hazing the corners of my vision, stoppering up my words.

"I just want to make sure you're okay," Patrick continues, his voice gentler.

It does next to nothing to calm me, like spritzing a squirt bottle on a raging fire. Still, it's enough for me to push my next words out. "Fine. Let's get this over with." I start marching down the trail, watching my feet with resentful care. The path narrows down to an obligation I have to finish, one pissed-off step in front of the next. "I hope you know. This"—I hold up my wrist, wincing when I do—"changes nothing for me. We're still having sex tonight."

Patrick laughs lightly behind me.

"I'm being serious," I insist.

He walks up next to me, moving over the terrain with skill I choose to ignore. With one hand loosely finding the small of my back, he presses a kiss to the side of my forehead. "Okay, Siena," he says.

I fume the rest of the way to the car.

Twenty-Nine

HOURS LATER, WE HAVEN'T left the hospital.

We *have* left the waiting room, which is something. With the plastic cushion of the cheap chair there unyielding under me, I probably shifted my posture once every thirty seconds. I memorized every meaningless detail of the patterns in the white wallpaper while Patrick waited patiently, not reading his phone. Over us was the clock, which was close enough for me to hear the faint motion of the second hand.

We spent our first hour here waiting in the drab room until finally a harried-looking doctor evaluated my grip. She then sent me off to get X-rays, which took several more hours. Afterward, the technician sent me back to the hard, plastic chairs while Patrick and I waited for the *first* doctor to review my images.

Over the course of the morning stretching into afternoon, I sat, hoping the nurses would call my name while Patrick fetched depressing hospital sandwiches, then coffee, then magazines. I couldn't muster smiles whenever he would return, not even when he'd found my favorite canned latte. No coffee could make up for spending my second-to-last day in Austin in the hospital.

Unsurprisingly, New Year's Eve in the ER is far from empty. With my composure frayed down to nothing, I've watched myself get bumped behind other patients over and over. I don't blame them, with how *not* an emergency my injury is. Instead, the nurses have called back women going into labor and people bleeding from visible wounds.

Finally, after we'd spent the better part of the day here, I heard my name.

We're now sitting in the exam room, which has everything in common with our purgatory for the past six hours now, right down to the wallpaper. Waiting for the doctor, I'm perched on the paper covering the examination table. Patrick sits in the one chair in the room, reading *The Atlantic*, knowing I need some space. My mood has only darkened since we got here, especially because the nurses gave me more painkillers, an ice pack, and a splint, and now my wrist hardly hurts when I'm not using it.

I check the clock on my phone. It's nearly five. "Your parents are leaving for dinner by now," I inform Patrick, my voice coldly casual.

He closes the magazine and looks up at me. "Trust me. I'm aware."

Our window is closing with each minute we're trapped here. And for what? "We could just leave," I offer.

Patrick's expression flattens. "Siena, the doctor said it could be broken."

"So I'll see a doctor tomorrow," I protest, my voice pitching up. *"After."* I raise my eyebrows, making my emphasis unmistakable.

Patrick pauses for a moment. I watch him intently. Our window might be closing, but I start to feel the light of hope shining through it. He's really considering what I'm suggesting. He knows we *have* gotten nothing done in nearly the entire day. We *could* leave right now. I'm halfway to exhilarated when he replies.

"You know," he begins delicately, "we don't have to have sex today."

While I realize the doctor could be standing right outside, hearing this entire conversation, I'm too pissed off to be embarrassed. "Actually, this is our only chance," I hiss, reckless now, feeling hope yanked out from under me. "Unless your parents plan on going into work tomorrow, on one of the most popular national holidays in the world."

Patrick dims with resignation. "Yeah, we won't get to tomorrow," he concedes. "But that's okay. I'm happy to wait however long we need to."

I scowl. Even though it's obviously the right thing to say, I'm in no mood for nice-guy Patrick right now. I know I'm reacting unfairly—pain and frustration and hours in the ER have pushed me to my limits. I'm not the best version of myself. Still, I can't stop the insecurity his words raise in me. "Do you not want to?" I ask compulsively. "Is that why you've forced us to spend the entire day here? You could have told me you didn't want to. You didn't have to turn this"—I hold up my splinted wrist, wincing when I do—"into an out."

To Patrick's credit, he doesn't get defensive or angry. He watches me with the same care I've seen from him all day. I return his stare, noticing how his even temperament deflates some of the pressure in my chest.

"I want to," he says in a way that leaves no doubt he means it. "I—I've wanted to for a while. I just didn't want to pressure you while you were waiting for the right moment." He looks unsure of himself, leaning forward in his chair and curling the magazine in his hands.

I register my surprise. *He's wanted to for a while?* "There's a difference between asking and pressuring me," I say slowly. "We've been together for a long time. It's natural for things to change—we just have to communicate when they do. They did for me. You can say when something changes. You can tell me when you want things."

Patrick's hands stop on the magazine. He straightens up again. The shadow in his expression says he understands we're talking about more than just this issue. "Okay," he says slowly. "I want to have sex with you."

I have no idea how he gets through the sentence so smoothly—not the way a virgin should.

"But I don't want you to be in pain or uncomfortable when we do," he continues.

"Well—"

"I mean," he cuts me off with a hint of droll humor,

"from your wrist." When I don't reply right away, he uses the opportunity, imploring reasonableness returning to his voice. "We can just wait."

I frown. Whatever ground his considerate and annoyingly logical responses were gaining, it's gone now. I don't *want* to wait, not when waiting doesn't just mean a few days, until the next evening his parents are out, the next movie night on one of our couches. It means months. Months we'll lose just because of something stupid like my wrist hurting a little.

Even so, while today's gone disastrously, I'm not going to make it worse. "Let's not argue about this," I say on a sigh.

"Agreed." Patrick's shoulders relax. "Let's table it. My parents will be out for an hour at least. We have time to wait for the doctor."

I've heard Patrick negotiate, heard him propose MUN resolutions and help formulate our plans for conferences. He does it well—and honestly, I've long had a soft spot for it. "Fine," I say, less exasperated than I want to be.

My concession makes him smile. He stands, laying his magazine carefully on his chair. "I'm going to get something to drink. Want anything?"

"Yeah. Sure," I say. "Pick me something I like." It's not a hard request. Patrick knows me well enough he could order for me no matter where we were and I know I'd enjoy whatever he chose.

In a small moment of self-recognition, I realize this is precisely the kind of observation I would have found frustrating in August. I don't now. Falling for new sides of Patrick has helped me love the familiarity of us.

I wish I were entirely grateful. Instead, part of me dwells perversely on when I had so much of a good thing I could forget how good it was. Now, I'm constantly faced with the reality of having something I really want, waiting to have it ripped from me when I fly back home.

Patrick brushes a kiss to my forehead, then heads to the door. With his hand on the knob, he nods to my wrist. "Have you told your mom yet?"

"No," I say, incredulous. "I don't need to worry them." The idea is vaguely off-putting, inflating something I would really rather ignore.

It steals a little of Patrick's new good mood. "Call them," he insists. "Your parents deserve to know when their daughter's in the emergency room."

He walks out, and I stare at the closed door behind him. Leaning back on the examination bed, I'm unable to push my discouragement away. Patrick's making a much bigger deal of this than he needs to. There's no way I'm calling my mom over a sprained wrist. No way I'm giving up on my plans, either. We'll get out of here in time for our privacy window. Not even hours in the emergency room will keep me from making the most of this visit.

Thirty

THE VERY NEXT SECOND, my phone rings. Checking the screen, I groan. It's my mom. I pick up, glad I'm not in the noisy waiting room.

"Hey, Mom," I say, forcing my voice to be casual and not at all like I'm in a hospital.

"Patrick just texted me," my mom replies, flying past the pleasantries. "You're in the emergency room?" Her tone is shrill. I can imagine her standing over the kitchen table, where she works on the weekend. Whenever she's stressed or on important calls, she gets up out of her chair, circling the table like a predator.

I have to laugh. I should have predicted Patrick would text her. He's incorrigible, but okay, it's kind of cute. "I'm fine," I say, wondering in a flash how often I've repeated those words over the past seven hours. "I slipped and sprained my wrist or something. It's seriously nothing. I wouldn't even be here if Patrick weren't being incredibly annoying."

Mom pauses for a millisecond. I hear her sit down, the

chair creaking under her. "You . . . sprained your wrist? That's all?" Her voice no longer sounds worried, only confused.

"Yes, exactly," I say, with a rush of relief that I have Mom on my side. "I mean, Patrick's afraid I broke it," I go on, "but I doubt it. Like I said, annoying."

"It's kind of sweet, though, isn't it?" Mom asks. There's typing on the other end of the line, and I know she's returned to work emails, her phone pressed into the crook of her chin. "He really loves you."

Her offhand assurance reminds me of the words Patrick and I *haven't* said to each other, despite how long we've lasted and how good our relationship has recently been. It's not my favorite subject in the world.

I stare into the room, my eyes finding the clock. I start to reply, and . . . I stop. The second hand flicks forward. Realization settles over me like the sunrise on our hike, soft yet suddenly everywhere. My mom is exactly right. Patrick *does* love me. Even though he's never said it, I know he does.

I blink in the overly bright lights of the exam room, not hearing what my mom is saying into my ear. I love Patrick, too. Because he dragged me here despite having his own plans, his own hopes for the day—hopes this ER visit ruined. He hasn't left my side, either, except to pick me out a drink I know I'll like.

Just then, I hear a knock on the door. "Mom, I have to go," I say. I hang up as the door opens. Dr. Sreekumar, the young woman who examined me earlier, walks in.

I fold my hands in my lap, my mind still on Patrick. Newly energized, I feel flushed, like I could run the whole way back up the trail we hiked without even being winded.

"Hi, Siena," Dr. Sreekumar says. "The good news is your wrist isn't broken."

"Fantastic," I say. "Great news. Thank you so much." I start getting up immediately. I'm not stupid. I know nobody ever says *the good news* unless they're going to follow up with bad news. But honestly, I'm not interested in bad news today.

"However," she says.

I sit back down slowly, pretending I was just shifting instead of making a dash for the exit. I catch the doctor smother a smile, like she was on to me.

"It's a moderate sprain, and there is some damage to the ligament," she continues. "I want you to wear the splint for a week and keep up icing, elevating, and resting the joint until the pain is gone. Do you have any questions?"

"Can I still have sex?"

The question flies out of me. Instantly, the flush in my face changes from pleased vitality into straight-up mortification. What I've asked is definitely not what Dr. Sreekumar was expecting.

Yet, like a true professional, she doesn't blink. She only nods once, like she hears this question often. Which, I don't know, maybe she does. "As long as you don't do anything to aggravate the injury," she says smoothly. "If you feel pain in your wrist, you should stop."

My embarrassment instantly fades under the relief of

having her permission. Permission I plan to repeat to Patrick verbatim when he inevitably needs to hear it. With the compound joy of this result and my feelings for Patrick filling me up, new images of the night start forming in my head. Doubtful hopes come into exhilarating focus. Patrick's new house, the lights dark when we walk in. His bedroom, familiar and unfamiliar at once.

I'm no doubt grinning goofily when I notice Dr. Sreekumar eyeing me. It's then I realize I'm probably giving off huge virgin energy. "Have you discussed how to protect yourself from STDs?" she inquires politely, confirming my suspicions.

"Oh. No. I mean, yes," I say, coming off extremely not-cool. "Like, we'll get, you know, like, condoms."

The doctor nods, smiling kindly. "Well, it was nice meeting you, Siena," she says. "Go easy on your wrist, and it sounds like you have some fun plans for New Year's Eve."

"I really do," I reply, my enthusiasm obvious in my voice.

It makes Dr. Sreekumar laugh. "Then we won't keep you."

I need no further encouragement. Jumping up from the exam table, I follow her into the hallway, then diverge, heading for the waiting room. Quickening my steps, I check my phone. Our window isn't closed, but it's closing. We'll have to hurry.

My pulse picks up with stress and excitement. I walk into the waiting room, where I'm checking out with the nurse in front when I hear Patrick's voice.

"Hey," he says, and I spin, finding him holding cans of sparkling water. "They were out of—"

I cut him off with a kiss.

"It's not broken," I say, "and we still have forty-five minutes."

Thirty-One

WE REACH PATRICK'S HOUSE with twenty-nine minutes to spare. I walk up his front steps, giddy with excitement and a little nervous. It's dark out now, like it was when we left for the hike this morning. The day I envisioned then was different from the one we've had—I imagined lunch on some sunny patio, the smells of frying food drifting over us, the quirky colors and eclectic antiquity of Austin's storefronts. It hardly matters to me now. When I linger on Patrick's porch, my butterflies are fluttering at full strength.

I look at Patrick and find him grinning widely. While the day *hasn't* gone as planned, we can salvage this.

Except when Patrick opens the front door, my heart sinks. My butterflies drop dead.

We hear the unmistakable chatter of voices, the clinking of glasses. In the living room, Patrick's parents sit looking fully comfortable on the gray couch, like they're in the middle of a long evening in.

"You're back," Mel says, setting her half-full wineglass

on the coffee table. I recognize the charm on the stem, the Hawaii-themed set Patrick's parents have had forever. "Siena, how's your wrist?" she asks, sympathy wrapping her voice like a heavy quilt.

"Oh," I say, fighting to focus past my disappointment. "It's fine."

Patrick jumps in, sounding uncharacteristically sharp. "What happened to your dinner with the Rossis?" With how easygoing he was earlier today, I'm distantly glad he seems genuinely put out.

"We left early," Mel explains. "When you texted that Siena was hurt, well, we just had to come home and check on her. Do you need anything, hon?"

I cut Patrick a glare communicating, *Seriously?* He does not meet my eyes, which is probably smart. "I'm really fine," I tell Mel, the sentence coming out rigid. "You two should go out, enjoy your evening," I continue, the cheerfulness in my voice feeling like it's pulling the corners of my mouth up into a smile.

"Believe me," Patrick's dad speaks up. "We're not missing anything." Greg is reclined with his feet up on the matching gray ottoman. He rubs his beard, eyeing his wine with satisfaction past his glasses.

"Greg." Mel elbows her husband, chiding. "The Rossis are nice."

Greg rolls his eyes.

"Okay, well," Patrick interjects woodenly. "We're going to hang out in my room."

Mel waves us off, and I follow Patrick down the hall, disheartened. I can't help resenting every light on in the house, every laugh from Patrick's parents. This was the one part of the day that was supposed to go the way I'd hoped. Now it's flattened into this unrecognizable shape, just like everything else.

When we're in Patrick's room, we close the door as much as we possibly can while obeying Mel's rule. Then I round on him. "You *told* them?" I hiss.

"Why wouldn't I tell them?" he says, the strain not gone from his voice. "They were going to find out when they saw you with your wrist in a splint."

"That would have been *after* their night out." I glare, not wanting to risk him missing the implication of what I'm saying. "*After* we'd had sex." While I'm whispering, I have half a mind not to. If my voice carries past the cracked door, well, what's the harm? Mel can't keep us from having sex any more than she already is.

Patrick's shoulders sag dejectedly. "I really didn't think they'd come home early. I'm sorry, Siena. But . . ."

"But what?" I snap. I feel my composure shaking, my face heating. This debate is veering into fight territory—heading down the conversational one-way street in front of which I've posted a DO NOT ENTER sign. Still, the open door keeps my voice a controlled, fierce whisper.

His eyes skirt mine like he knows what he's going to say will provoke me. Which it probably will. "You *are* hurt," he says delicately. "It wouldn't be the worst thing in the world if we just took it easy tonight. We can watch the ball drop in Times Square, order something on DoorDash."

I have no interest in *taking it easy*. To me, this injury doesn't exist for the next forty-eight hours. "No," I say firmly, my voice changing to a calm I hope leaves no room for discussion. "I know you're just suggesting those things because you want me to rest. But I can *take it easy* when I'm home in Phoenix." Patrick winces, hearing the spite in my repetition of his words. I preempt his rebuttal. "Patrick. It's my body. I get to decide if I rest it or not."

My point works on Patrick instantly. His gaze rises to mine. "Okay. Fair. What do you propose we do, then?" He sounds resigned, the way he did at MUN conferences when he knew his proposal wasn't going to pass. "Sprained wrist or not, our previous plan is just not going to be doable." He waves to the door right as Mel's laugh drifts down the hall.

I chew my lip. I'm disappointed, but faintly, I'm glad we're not fighting.

This relief pushes open new possibilities in my head. There were other things I'd wanted to do. Tonight doesn't have to be a total waste.

"What about your friends' party?" I say, the new potential of this plan hitting me like a rush.

Patrick looks doubtful, concern in his eyes warring with the point I just made.

I go on, gentler. "Would you want to go if my wrist weren't hurt?"

His expression settles. "It does sound more fun than

watching the ball on TV with my parents," he admits, starting to smile.

"Well, I feel great," I say genuinely. "I promise if I get tired, I'll tell you and we'll come right home."

Patrick's eyes flutter closed in momentary exasperation. When they open, he puts on a lightly annoyed smile. "You know, since you quit Model UN, have you considered trying debate team?"

I grin, lighting up with some of what I felt when we pulled into Patrick's driveway. While I'm still disappointed, I'm determined to hold on to this glittering new consolation prize. "Maybe I will," I say. I let my head start to fill with unfinished sketches of memories I hope I'll make in the next few hours, new glimpses into Patrick's life and this wonderful city illuminated by the special and unpredictable magic of New Year's Eve.

"Well, let's go, then," Patrick says.

I push open the door, and it feels like reopening the night's possibilities.

Thirty-Two

THE PARTY IS IN Vic's condo. While modern high-rises weren't something I envisioned when I thought of Austin, downtown is scattered with them, their mirrored sides sparkling in the night sky.

We rode the elevator in jittery, happy silence. When we reached Vic's, her condo's wide windows drew my eyes immediately. Her place overlooks the city, a soaring view of the lights reflecting in shimmering strands on the Colorado River. In the darkness, fireworks explode below us. They're everywhere, pattern-less, an endless roll of sparks crackling into cascades of glitter over the landscape.

I stand with Patrick near the window, chatting with some of the guys he's introduced me to. I really like his friends so far. They're easy to talk to and welcoming, not only of Patrick—who Michael, Chad, and Yi-Ping act like they've known forever, despite having met him only four months ago—but also of me.

My wrist aching a little, I separate from the conversation

circle and head to find a cold Coke in the ice-filled sink. I hold the can to my wrist, sighing in relief as the chill numbs the pain.

"Well done, by the way."

I recognize the voice I hear next to me. Vic has come up to the counter, where she's pouring herself another drink. She's wearing a black dress, undoubtedly from the kind of boutique Anthropologie and Free People pretend to be.

"Thank you," I say with no small note of satisfaction. "He's incredibly stubborn. It wasn't easy."

Vic grins. "Oh, I believe you. The way he raves about you, though . . ." She sips from her plastic cup, her dark eyebrows flitting up. "I knew you were our only hope of getting him to come out tonight."

I don't reply, embarrassed in a nice way. My eyes stray to the firework-lit windows, where Patrick's clapped a hand on Chad's shoulder. They're animatedly discussing something. Although I can't hear what, when I left, they were spitballing fundraising ideas for Young Dems. What lights Patrick's eyes isn't just the reflected color of the explosions outside—it's passion.

Watching him with his friends, his *new* friends, it's obvious how much everyone likes having him around. Like Vic said, they really were hoping he'd come out tonight. I felt it when we walked in. Everyone we passed hugged him, or stopped their conversations to greet him, or wanted to confirm plans with him.

For me, the newly introduced girlfriend, it was the fun

kind of intimidating. I knew I'd meet Patrick's friends. I just didn't know there'd be so many to meet.

Underneath my quiet pride, though, I notice the return of the ache I felt yesterday. Standing here with my cool soda in this dazzling condo, I recognize it for what it is. Patrick's done exactly what I hoped he and I would with the freedom of long distance. He's found friends. While he might not consider them "real," it's impossible to share his description watching him surrounded by this much love. He's found clubs and hiking routes. He's even found popularity.

While I . . . haven't. I'm the one who wanted to use the opportunities of long distance, who wanted to remake and rediscover myself with this newfound freedom. Yet I have only lonelier days and unfulfilling pursuits to show for myself, while Patrick has this. *Is there something wrong with me?* a little voice whispers in my head.

I chase it away, determined to enjoy the night. When I rejoin Patrick and Chad, their conversation has dramatically changed course from fundraising to the movie *Fast Five*, which, I learn in their recounting, a group of them watched together last weekend. I follow the discussion like a passenger in a boat someone else is steering, watching the scenery, the everyday details of Patrick's life.

When Chad walks off to get the Taco Bell someone's just brought in, I raise an eyebrow at Patrick.

He meets my eyes, his expression entirely unselfconscious. "What?" he asks.

I restrain myself from looking skeptical. He's serious, I know he is. I would make fun of him for false modesty, except with Patrick, the modesty is never false. "You didn't tell me you were popular," I say simply instead.

Patrick scoffs. "Yeah, because I'm not." He sips his Sprite, still frowning like I've just asked him a complicated chemistry question.

"You totally are," I inform him. While it's not like Patrick was unpopular in Phoenix, here he's got a glow about him. What's more, it's reaching me, some quiet magnetism under my skin. I don't know if it's because of the changes in Patrick or whether he just fits in Austin. This city welcomes the passionate, no matter their pursuit, whereas Phoenix, or at least my school, cares more about the usual combination of athleticism and wealth. I move closer, dropping my head on his shoulder for a second. "When are you going to admit you like it better here?" I'm asking with no resentment, pride winning out over my flickers of jealousy. I like that he's proving to himself how change can be a positive.

The thought vanishes when Patrick's expression twists. "Siena, it's not better here," he replies, heaviness settling into his voice.

"But you have these great friends, this amazing city." I gesture out the window, where, for the moment, the fireworks have subsided, leaving the depth of the night showing off the downtown sprawl. "You've found hiking and Young Dems."

"Sure," Patrick says, sounding reticent. "There's a lot I've

learned to like here. But that doesn't mean I've stopped missing home. Phoenix, I mean," he clarifies, his eyes clouding
over for a moment while he realizes what he's said.

"I know," I reply, placating. When I gaze out into the
room, though, the modern space vibrant with the energy
of everyone enjoying themselves, I find I can't drop it. Not
when it's obvious how good Patrick's new life is. When he
has no idea how much I've wanted to work this reinven-
tion in myself, and failed. "I guess I'm just saying it's okay to
admit you're happy here."

I see so clearly how Patrick has deviated from his plans
for the first time, only to be shown that when you let yourself loose from your expectations, it's possible for wonderful
things to happen. Like—

Like when I decided not to break up with him. It's striking, how perfectly the same our experiences have been in
that way. If I'd ended our relationship when I'd planned to, I
wouldn't be here, falling in love with him.

"It sounds like you want me to say I'm happier without
you, but I don't know why." Patrick's voice is combative now,
or as combative as he's capable of.

My head jerks up. I study his expression, which is unusually empty of clues. He's suddenly a wall I can't wrap my arms
around. "No," I say quickly, stunned how fast this conversation veered in the wrong direction. I wanted to point out the
good, not prod a sore spot. "I obviously don't want you to be
happier without me, but you don't have to be *miserable* without me."

He meets my confused gaze levelly. "Why are you press-ing this?"

My mouth opens and closes. The direct question catches me off guard, and the silence fills with my unspoken answer—the one I won't say because I know it'll cause a fight. It's the ugliest sort of suspicion, the kind you can never get rid of on your own, only hide out of sight. Deep down, I want to know Patrick is with me for *me*, not just because I'm familiar. What if I'm not just part of his routines—what if I *am* the routine? I don't want to think Patrick lives his life just being comfortable with what he has, never seeking change. But if he can embrace his new life over his old, it means he's *not* afraid of change.

It means he's embraced me because he *wants* to be with me.

I say none of those things. "I'm not pressing," I reply, pushing my fear to its familiar corner of my mind. Exhaling, I shake off the tension of the moment. Patrick is right. I'm being unfair. I have my own fears, my own insecurities, but they're not his fault. He's entitled to his feelings. "I'm sorry," I go on, meaning it. "We don't have to talk about this."

Patrick looks a little relieved, and maybe a little remorse-ful himself. "It's okay," he says. "Really. I'm glad we're here."

I'm conscious of the pounding pain in my wrist, cutting through the now warming Coke can. I pull my Advil out of my purse and swallow one down. While Patrick watches me, he doesn't comment, respecting what I told him in his room.

The volume of the music rises sharply, someone swapping out the previous playlist for dancefloor beats I feel vibrating through the floorboards. It draws everyone to the center of the room, where people push away furniture and start to dance. The echoes of our conversation fade under the pulsing rhythms.

"Do you want to dance?" he asks, nodding in their direction encouragingly. It's obvious he's making an effort to recover the fun of tonight, which is very endearing and very Patrick, and my heart swells. *He* should've *been popular in Phoenix,* some petty, proud voice in me says. *Because he's the nicest guy in history.*

Grateful for the invitation, I glance at the crowd, at everyone jumping up and down singing at the top of their lungs. It doesn't *not* look like fun. It just looks like chaos. My eyes stray, snagging on a stairway on the other side of the room.

Something sparks in me. I don't need to be jealous Patrick has found what I haven't. I need to chase what excites me, what makes me happy. I need to do what I promised Patrick and myself I would—make the most of every new opportunity.

I grab his hand with my uninjured one. "I have a better idea," I say.

Pulling him through the crowd, I have to slip past elbows and drinks held high, dangerous possibility sloshing near their brims. It's slightly harrowing until we reach the opposite wall. Patrick follows me up the sleek staircase.

On the second floor, the music still thrums, but quieter. The condo is impeccably stylish, with long windows lining the hallway. I try the first door, finding just what I need. It's perfect. Empty. Dark.

I know exactly what I want to do right now. How I want to end this year and usher in the next.

With Patrick's hand in mine, I lead him into the bedroom.

Thirty-Three

I SHUT THE DOOR softly. In what feels like the same motion, I'm facing Patrick, wrapping my arms around him. The music downstairs melts away. With the lights of the skyline providing the only illumination, this quiet corner of the universe is just where I want to be.

I kiss Patrick, and he kisses me. In the urgency of his mouth on mine, I feel how he's understood exactly what I have in mind, and he's with me. His hands find my sides, then move lower, pulling my waist forward with hunger matching mine. Our lips connect with insistence, fighting with the desire to prolong what's happening right now. He feels solid pressed to me, the familiar planes of his chest now places I can't wait to explore.

In the many, many times we've made out, it was never like this. Never with such a clear direction. Kissing was the destination. Now it's only one stop on the way.

I feel sparks deep in the pit of my stomach when Patrick walks me backward, leading us both toward the bed. I let myself fall onto the covers, the comforter pleasantly cool under me. Patrick waits, his dark irises drinking me in, until with my uninjured hand, I pull him down, closer. His smell is everywhere, warm, intoxicating in a way I don't remember. The shared privacy of the moment is nearly overwhelming. My heart pounds in my chest.

Patrick's kisses come faster now, moving from my lips to my neck. It's intensely obvious how much he wants this. Wants me. I make it obvious how much I want him, too.

Because I really do. For so many reasons—because I'm ready, because it's our window of opportunity, and because I love Patrick. The thought feels like riding an elevator into the clouds, heart-expanding and head-spinning. Even though saying those words out loud still feels sort of intimidatingly huge, I want to experience this closeness with him.

He lifts up my shirt, then shucks off his own. We come back together, his hands on me. I like this prelude, when I'm exposed only to him. I want to feel his skin on mine, without interruption. I reach for the clasp of my bra, and—

"Fuck!"

Patrick draws back instantly when I cry out.

Sharp ribbons of pain have cut into my wrist from the twisting motion of undoing the hooks. I wince, cradling my wrist with my other hand.

Patrick's concern is immediate. "Are you okay?" he asks.

I don't meet his eyes, not wanting to find the fire has left them. "Yeah," I say, breathing through the pain. "Just—give me a minute."

He sits back onto his ankles. The silence in the room suddenly feels present in a way it hadn't, like pressure.

This irritating injury will *not* win out. I focus on Patrick's chest—a part of him I haven't seen in months—and how good he looks. How much I want to touch him everywhere. Lightly tracing a line down his stomach, I give my fingertips permission to explore. I lean forward to kiss him, letting the good feelings he's giving me drown out the pain. Instinct pulling me, I reach out my other hand.

Stinging white heat shoots down my wrist. I hiss, knowing my hopes for the night have been shattered. Collapsing back onto the bed, I let out a quiet scream of frustration.

"Siena, let's just wait," Patrick says. His voice is newly decisive, the undercurrent of concern in his words leaving no room for questions. "I don't want our first time to be something you're fighting through."

I refuse to meet his compassionate stare. Screw this perfect bedroom, this glittering skyline. I'm smoldering with the disappointment of how the night I wanted has slipped out of reach. Literally. If I reached for it, my wrist would hurt.

I sigh, knowing Patrick's right. This isn't how it should be. But admitting that to myself makes my eyes prick with tears, warping the lights shining outside into watery blobs. "This was our *only* chance, though," I say, giving in to my frustration. It picks up momentum fast, unraveling out of me. "If we weren't long distance, we could just do this next week. Instead—what, we're going to have to plan sex into these already plan-packed weekends? What if I'm on my period, or you're not in the mood? Or I've broken my fucking wrist?"

I press my head into the pillow, rigid with agitation. My face feels hot. *Why didn't I just look where I was walking this morning?* I'm so mad I have to close my eyes.

His movements rustling the comforter, I hear Patrick crawl closer. "Hey, what's this really about?" he asks gently above me.

The question pries my eyes open. "Nothing," I say guardedly. When he looks unconvinced, I inhale, my chest feeling wound up. "Can we just not get into it? There's no reason to ruin this night *more* by fighting." I grasp on with wild intensity to this resolve I've held since this morning, fighting the undeniable fact that these sharp corners keep coming up in our conversations. This, I can control. I can't stop my wrist from hurting, but I can keep things from getting worse.

"Well, maybe we *should* fight," Patrick says combatively.

Not sure whether I'm hallucinating, I look up from the pillow, my eyes widening. It is possibly the most un-Patrick sentence I've ever heard.

"I'm serious," he continues. "This is a relationship, which means we have to be honest with each other. We can't just pretend we're not upset because the timing is inconvenient. We're here together. Let's work it out." He pulls on his shirt without hesitating.

"Fine," I snap. "Let's fight. Why not?" What he's saying simultaneously makes perfect sense and really pisses me off.

I pull on *my* shirt, matching his movement like we're in some confrontation contest. "Do you even want to be with me? Or am I just your last tether to the home you left?"

I'm surprised how quickly the question leapt out of me, like it was stuck there, just under the surface, grating against everything I've faced today.

Patrick is stunned speechless for a moment. Then it's like his mind unlocks, his expression twisting with incredulity. "Of *course* I want to be with you," he says with emotion in each word.

I shake my head, knowing he's giving me the easy answer, the obligatory one. I just wonder if it no longer fits, like I'm his coziest middle-school sweatshirt, the sleeves and hem ending short of where they're supposed to. Holding my wrist in my other hand, I permit myself to feel the pain, then finally I let out everything I've been holding in. "Patrick, you're building a great life here, and you barely even realize it," I say. "I'm worried you're trying too hard to hold on to home. The Phoenix postcards you have up, wanting to FaceTime our friends." I swallow. In the sterile quiet of the room, it's getting harder to speak this fear out loud. "Is that all I am? A way to hold on? A way to keep you from having to start over completely? But just—*look*." I nod in the direction of the party downstairs. "Look what you have here. You don't need me as, like, your security blanket."

I finish my speech, feeling halfway to exhausted.

But not only exhausted, I realize. The strange new pressure in the room has subsided. The silence sounds more like quiet. I hadn't expected what a huge relief it would be to get every fear and insecurity off of my chest.

Patrick's expression darkens, though.

"You think I'm with you because it's *easier*?" he asks in a low murmur.

I say nothing, knowing he's not finished. His question wasn't a question—it was the start of what he has to say.

"*Nothing* about this is easier," he continues. I can't help wincing at his emphasis. "I don't enjoy not having a date on the weekend or to dances. I wonder every day whether you're forgetting me. Whether you think I'm worth long distance. I live my life split in two places, feeling like I'm not really in either." His voice is raw, naked with emotion. "I'm so far from you, and I just want to feel like I'm part of your world. You're not a tether to home, Siena. Home is a tether to you."

I stare at him. My mouth opens a little, empty of sound. Patrick has always excelled at making speeches, wielding rhetoric however he needs to convince or inspire. While I've been in the audience of the speeches, I've never been the subject. His declaration leaves me spinning, my reactions an indistinct swirl, until one sharpens into focus.

It's a spark of joy. I'm *glad* I brought this up. I'm glad we're airing our fears and resentments, just so I can see this side of him. If I worried he wouldn't fight for me on our last visit, that's vanished now, disproven—destroyed—by the intensity of his stare, the passion in his voice.

"You *are* part of my world," I say, and *oh wow*. There are actual tears clutching my throat. "A really important part."

Patrick smiles softly. It's small, yet thrilling, like daylight silvering the edges of dark clouds. Or like sunrise.

"Well, I do like it here," he concedes gently. "But I also miss you. I miss you so much it hurts. Making a hundred new friends wouldn't change that."

I lean in close, pressing a spontaneous, gentle kiss to his lips. "I miss you, too." It feels good saying the simplest thing, the most honest. Like I've spent hours doing homework not noticing my shoulders are hunched, only to release them. The lightness descending over me is one I'd sort of forgotten existed. "I think that's why I put so much pressure on this trip to be perfect," I go on.

Patrick takes my un-splinted hand in his. "It *is* perfect. No matter how much we get to do," he reassures me, his conviction clear.

I smile softly. "You're right."

"Maybe it was a bad idea to try to fit an entire month into a few days," he says with hesitant humor, working to lighten the mood. "It's too much pressure. Let's just . . . be together."

I exhale, letting out in one long breath every hope, every idealized version of this visit, every fantasized chapter of this weekend fairy tale. It's extraordinarily freeing. Instead of carefully calculating minutes, when I look into tomorrow, I see only Patrick. It's enough.

I free my hand from his, then smooth down the bedspread where I was lying. The night narrows into my surroundings, the sounds of my leg brushing the comforter, the squares of moonlight the windows draw on the floor, the faint music downstairs. We don't have to be here, I realize. While I'm glad I got to meet Patrick's friends, I only suggested going to this party when I was intent on wringing something out of every second of this visit.

"I think I'm ready to admit my wrist really hurts," I say.

Patrick laughs a little. "Let's go home."

I stand, and when I offer Patrick my right hand, he takes it without hesitation. We head downstairs, where the countdown to midnight is just beginning. The walls echo with Patrick's new classmates chanting down the numbers. From the outskirts of the group, we join them. Knowing we're leaving simply because we feel like it charges the experience in a new way. We have no responsibility to tonight. We're not here for the party. We're here for *us*. With the countdown nearing its end, I don't focus on my many plans. I focus on right now.

When the year turns over, Patrick kisses me. I lose myself in it, swept up.

This new year might not have us physically together, but it'll be this—stolen moments worth so much.

Thirty-Four

THE NEXT DAY, I relent. We do nothing except FaceTime Garret, Alicia, and Joe and watch Netflix while I ice my wrist. While things are definitely different between Garret, Alicia, and me since I quit MUN, reconnecting with them is nicer than I expected.

It's nothing we couldn't have done in different cities. Even so, I don't mind. It's nice to sit curled into Patrick's side on the couch, to rest my head on his shoulder and breathe in the smell of him. There's no pressure in it, no plans we're rushing to fit in. In a way, it feels like a regular afternoon—not the last day we'll see each other for months. Which is what I need right now. With the winter sunlight warming the room, the blanket covering our laps, I can trick myself into forgetting long distance.

Until the next morning.

I wake up in the guest bedroom with my bags packed, my boarding pass loaded on my phone, feeling sadder than I expected. After hugs, plural, from Mel and cereal for breakfast, we're out the door. The crisp morning feels not unlike when we went hiking, yet the context couldn't be more different.

Patrick drives me to the airport, his demeanor pale and stiff. I'm silent the whole way, the only sound filling the car the soft hum of the road under us, while out the window I watch the receding shape of the city I'm leaving behind. The details of every street I'd found so exciting just days ago now feel like reminders of what I'm ripping myself away from. Neither of us seems able to say anything, and I know why. The only thing we're thinking is too hard to say—that this is goodbye for what feels like a long time. As long as we're silent, we can halfway pretend we're fine.

When Patrick parks and unloads my suitcase onto the concrete drive, I can't pretend at all anymore. I'm miserable.

It's not like this is the first time we've parted. Nevertheless, with every second winding down until I leave, the sadness pressing on my chest is like nothing I've felt before.

Knowing exactly the way today will go is its own kind of curse. I envision with painful specificity going through security, getting to my gate. Opening my text thread with Patrick instead of just talking to him. Living the horrible inversion of the day I got here, my favorite minutes becoming heart-wrenching when played backward.

Patrick stands in front of me while cars pass us on one side. This is when we say goodbye, when I get on the plane that will take me far away from him for too long. It'd be easier if we knew when we would see each other again, but with school and our trips dependent on our parents, I know our next visit won't be sooner than spring break. Three and a half months feels like forever. The thought is ridiculous, but so, so real.

"Maybe we can talk tonight?" Patrick suggests with somber hope.

I smile, which makes everything worse somehow. Tears spring into my eyes, catching me off guard. I'm stunned. I've never cried over a boy before. Never. Now the tears won't stop. My expression crumples, my composure collapsing like someone's pulled out the foundation.

Past watery eyelashes, I see worry flood Patrick's face. He reaches out, one comforting hand finding my arm. "What is it?" he asks. "Is it your wrist?"

A laugh breaks through my tears. "No," I say. "It's that I love you."

I don't even put thought into the declaration. It comes easily, out of some deep, protected place within me. This wasn't how I envisioned doing this, in the middle of this drab loading zone, with no time to dwell on the significance of it.

Still, I wouldn't dream of taking it back. I have this weird sensation of how much each word contains, like the one sentence echoes with sunrises and sunsets, endings and new years, explorations and cozy days in.

It looks like it hits Patrick with similar force. His entire expression changes, worry shifting in a split second into elation. A grin spreads unstoppably across his face. "I—love you, too," he says, the words seeming to leap out of him. Like they were waiting there.

It's taken us three years to get here, and now I finally know why. Never before have I felt like this. Not when we first kissed and I thought about him all night after, not when he asked me to prom in front of all our friends, not when he helped me cram for a history test until one in the morning. We had only scraped the surface of the feeling between us. Now it fills me.

My tears haven't stopped, but I'm grinning, too. We probably look like overdramatic teenagers to the other travelers pulling up. I don't care. I close the distance between us, and Patrick kisses me, holding my face in his hands. We grin into each other's mouths, happiness cutting through our heartache for just a moment, then combining with it.

In a way, this grief is a gift. It reminds me how much I love what I'm giving up for the next few months.

It's hard to believe that distance has made me fall in love with my own boyfriend. But the upside-down logic of it no longer surprises me. Somehow, separation has pulled us closer than ever.

We part. I know I have to head in. My lip wobbles, and I'm pretty sure Patrick's eyes are wet.

"It won't be too long," he says.

It's a lie, but I nod anyway. A week would have been too long, and we're looking at months—by far the longest we've been apart.

"We'll be together before we know it," I reply. It's the echo of what he said the night before he moved. It's so much sadder now, and so much sweeter.

I give him one final long hug. When I walk away from him, I force myself not to look over my shoulder. If I do, I feel certain I'll miss my flight. Entering the airport, the ache in my chest doesn't lessen. It sticks like emotional shrapnel in my heart while I follow the signs to security.

Everyone always warned me long distance was hard. Until now, I thought they were wrong. Long distance for me was freedom, growth, new experiences in a new city. With the memory of Patrick's lips fading on mine, I understand everything they meant. Long distance hurts. It really hurts.

I walk through security, my tears not stopping.

Thirty-Five

SADNESS LINGERS WITH ME when I return to school after winter break. For the first time since we started long distance, I just wish I had Patrick here with me, his hand to hold, his smile to look forward to. Instead, I just have his name on my phone, painfully insufficient.

I take my time packing up my things from English after the lunch bell has rung. I'm not really looking forward to the next half hour I'll spend making conversation with acquaintances I hope to turn into friends, tagging along with Joe, or helping the MUN crowd prepare for the conference I'm not going to. It's dreary outside, perfect for my mood. I pull on Patrick's West Vista sweatshirt, which today is weather-appropriate and emotionally necessary.

While I zip up my backpack, however, I notice Reed Kim waiting by my desk. Like usual, he's in skinny jeans, high-top Vans, and a shirt for what I'm guessing is some obscure hipster band. *Not* like usual, he looks a little uncomfortable.

"Okay, this is going to sound weirdly invasive," he says, "but you're good friends with Joe Crawford, right?"

My heart sinks. Is this my fate? To only be known by association with the various guys in my life? "Yeah, I am," I say.

Reed hesitates, stubbing one toe of his checkerboard Vans into the carpet. "Do you think he's into Lacey Ramos?" he asks hastily.

I straighten up. Reed's timing is uncanny. Today I'd planned to talk to Lacey the way I promised Joe I would.

Even so, I don't want to share Joe's private information with Reed Kim. "I'm, um, not sure," I say, dropping my pencil into my backpack's front pouch. While people file past us to the door close enough to have overheard, nobody seems to care. "And if I were, I'm not really into spreading gossip."

Reed winces, looking pained. "Shit, no, I'm not gossiping. It's—okay, look." He leans closer. "Lacey's my best friend. She's *really* into Joe, but she doesn't want to make a move if he's not feeling it."

I soften, understanding instantly Reed's stiff demeanor. He's in the worst of best-friend positions, deputized into romantic investigation. I stand, slinging my backpack over my shoulder. "I need to buy lunch," I say. "You getting anything?"

"Sure," Reed replies. "Yeah, I'll get in line with you."

We walk out, Reed following me. Our English class is near the cafeteria, where we line up for one of the windows. The outdoor space is packed, loud chatter surrounding us. I'm forced to fight off how overwhelming it is, how the clamor of everyone else is its own reminder of how lonely I feel.

Facing Reed, who's studying the short menu of pizza or sandwich, I continue our conversation. "Did Lacey ask you to ask me about Joe?"

His eyes flit to me. "Siena, do you think I'd *choose* to meddle in this? She begged me to ask you."

I study him, once more sympathetic, not to mention sort of endeared by his effort to help Lacey. I don't know Reed very well, but I've liked everything I've seen of him in our English class. I reach the front of the line, where I order two sides of tater tots.

Reed raises an eyebrow.

"Don't raise an eyebrow at my double tots," I say.

"It's not judgment," he replies. "It's reverence."

I laugh. It's the first time today the pain in my chest lightens. Reed steps up to his window and, sure enough, orders two tots.

While we're waiting for our food, a guy I don't recognize claps Reed on the shoulder. "Show on Saturday?" he asks.

Reed's expression changes entirely, lighting up the way I'm used to seeing him. *Lighting* isn't even the right word— he's charged with old-Hollywood charm, a Korean Clark Gable. "Of course." He grins. "You coming?"

"Yeah, man," our interloper replies. "Definitely."

He leaves, and once more it's just Reed, looking unselfconscious, and me, curious. "Is there a winter play or something?" I ask.

"Improv match," he replies.

"What's an improv match?"

Every spark of Reed's enthusiasm returns. "You have to come," he says, looking like he can't believe his luck. "Short answer, we square off against another improv team in a bunch of comedy games for a live audience. Longer answer—it's so much more. Improv is never the same thing twice. Every moment onstage is dynamic, like it's constantly changing. Come. Bring Joe." He winks. "Lacey is performing, too."

The mention of Joe and Lacey makes me roll my eyes. But his description of improv—*it's never the same thing twice*—has struck a spark of interest in me. "I might," I tell him honestly.

We receive our trays, piled high with tots. Now is the moment we part and I find where I'm going to have lunch today while fighting the urge to text Patrick the whole time. Even while I'm missing him, though, I have to live the life in front of me.

Reed reaches for one of his tots. Something impulsive grabs hold of me. "Can I sit with you guys? Maybe I can provide Lacey with some Joe insight," I say, projecting casualness instead of the fragility I feel.

Reed doesn't blink. He doesn't look skeptical or surprised by the idea of an intruder into his lunch group. He grins. "Definitely."

Flushed with gratitude, I follow him to the planters in front of the drama room, feeling like I might finally be on to something.

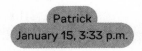

Hey, I love you.

I love you too.

I hope you're prepared for me to say that a lot now.

Oh, I'm prepared.

Good. Because I do. Love you. I love you.

Wait, you're saying you love me?

Oh, was I unclear? I LOVE YOU.

I love you and I miss you.

76 days.

February 10, 3:33 p.m.

Hey, how was the improv thing?

Good, actually! They structure their shows like matches against other teams. It was fun to watch.

. . . Just to watch?

Well, Reed and Lacey want me to come
to a practice/rehearsal next week. I'm
thinking about it.

Senior spring. Might as well try it, right?

My thinking exactly.

Oh my god, I forgot to tell you. Joe asked
Lacey out FINALLY.

Aw, tell Joe I'm happy for him.

Tell him yourself. I'm with him right now.
Let's FaceTime.

February 28, 8:56 p.m.

32 days.

Can't wait.

March 3, 3:21 p.m.

How was your day?

It was fine. Vic is pissed at me because I hung out with Ross.

Vic is never actually pissed at you.

Ha. Well, not for long, anyway. But I feel for Ross. Carly won, like, all the friends in the breakup.

And you're the only one to take pity on him.

He's nice!

You're nice.

March 8, 4:15 p.m.

I GOT IN!!!! UCSB!!!

Siena!!! I'm not surprised. You're amazing. Call me???

March 10, 4:15 p.m.

What are you up to?

~ 235 ~

Nothing really. Why?

I wish I could touch you. Kiss you.

Long-Deprived Romeo?

Loves Dirty Requests . . .

March 17, 5:01 p.m.

Hey, sorry I missed your call. Had a Dems
meeting. Can we talk tomorrow?

Ah. Can't tomorrow. What about this
weekend?

If we do it in the morning?

I'm having brunch with the family on
Saturday. How is this so hard?

I know. We'll find a time. I could come
home from Carly's birthday early Saturday
night?

No. Don't do that.

Sunday afternoon?

Lacey got Joe to invite improv over for a
pool thing.

Okay. Something will work out.

We need, like, a standing date so this
doesn't keep happening.

You're right. How about Saturday
afternoon? Instead of Rex's, we'll talk,
and we'll never plan anything else for that
time.

Deal. Ugh long distance.

Hey, we can do this. Love Despite
Reasons.

Love Despite Reasons.

Spring Break

Thirty-Six

I WALK UP MY front steps, laughing so hard I'm crying. It's evening, not chilly enough that I need a sweatshirt. Spring in Phoenix welcomes warmer nights and pleasantly hot days, the prelude to our dusty summers. Reed and I got dinner, then ice cream, and on the walk home he's been doing the most perfect impression of our English teacher.

"You have to stop," I tell him through my tears. "Let me breathe."

Reed frowns, putting on intellectual curiosity. "Could you expand on that statement? Use descriptive language," he instructs, channeling Mr. Curtis.

When I shove him lightly, he catches my arm for hardly a moment, until he holds his hands up in surrender.

I shake my head with joking consternation, my cheeks hurting from smiling. Since I joined improv, my new friendship with Reed, Lacey, and the rest of the team has finally started to feel like what I was searching for. It's something I can call mine. Really mine. *Siena's*, not *SienaandPatrick's*.

What it's led to hasn't just been me embarrassing myself in skits after school. In fact, everything has begun to fit into place over the past couple months. I've been going to Reed's house to hang out with the team and bringing Joe from time to time, which gave him the opportunity to ask Lacey out. I've had lunch every day with my new group of friends. What's more, I genuinely enjoy improv. It has the performative element of Model UN in exactly the opposite context. The freedom to fail, to not make sense, to just have fun—it's endlessly liberating. I feel like I'm uncovering the piece of me I was missing.

Now, with Patrick coming into town next week, I can't wait to introduce him to my new life the way he brought me into his.

Recovering my breath, I unlock my front door. "I need some water," I say. "Want to come in?"

Reed's eyebrows rise a little. "Sure," he says in his own voice, not Mr. Curtis's.

I don't know why he's surprised by the invitation. Maybe it's because we don't often hang out here, what with how Reed's house is the epicenter of the improv team's social life.

I head into the kitchen, enjoying the quiet of the apartment. Robbie is out, luckily, and my parents have gone to a movie for date night. I reach into the fridge. "You want some?" I call to Reed while I grab the pitcher of water.

"Yeah, thanks," he replies, dropping onto the couch.

I pour two glasses and walk them over to the coasters on the coffee table, which feature photos of Yosemite from when my family went when I was in fifth grade. "We could watch something," I suggest between sips.

"*TNG?*" he asks. Lacey has gotten us really into *Star Trek: The Next Generation*, and we follow Picard, Geordi, Troi, and goofily suave Riker's travels into "space, the final frontier" every weekend.

I turn on the TV, settling into the couch cushions. We're not five minutes into the episode when Reed starts fidgeting in his seat, shifting his leg so his knee barely touches mine. I figure he doesn't even notice. The well-worn pillows of our couch tend to sink, sloping people toward each other. I refocus on the *Enterprise*'s ominous encounters with the Borg.

Outside, the sun has set. The room is growing darker. We're quiet, but it's a nice, cozy quiet. I don't get up to turn on the lights, enjoying the movie-theater feel of the living room.

"Okay," Reed speaks up. "I feel like I know that guy."

"Who?" I smile, squinting. "The Borg? Like you recognize the actor from something else?"

"No, like he lives in Phoenix," Reed says.

I laugh. "He does *not* live in Phoenix."

"Hey, lots of cool people live in Phoenix." Reed pulls out his phone, where he swiftly swipes to IMDb. I know it's to check the actor's name so we can social-media stalk him.

The crisp light of the screen cuts into the pleasant darkness, distracting from the high-stakes Borg conflict happening on-screen. "You don't know him. Turn that off," I say. Playfully, I grab for Reed's phone, laughing as he moves it out of reach. I struggle for the illuminated iPhone, the saggy couch cushions doing me no favors.

When my face is near Reed's, he kisses me.

Stunned, I don't react for a moment. Then I do. I pull back sharply. For good measure, I promptly scoot all the way to the other end of the couch.

"Okay, that wasn't the reaction I was hoping for," Reed says into the dark, with gentle yet unmistakable disappointment. "I'm sorry. I thought . . ."

I don't reply, unmoving. The kiss wasn't long or forceful, only the lightest connection of lips and faintest suggestion of Reed's scent. While the show plays, the dialogue emptily indistinct to me now, I wrack my mind for explanations of what's happening. Why would Reed think I wanted to *kiss* him?

The realization hits me horribly.

"I have a *boyfriend*," I blurt.

I can't believe he doesn't know. *Everyone* at school knows about Patrick and me. Admittedly, I don't mention him often because I'm trying to be my own person. But I never imagined I needed to. Surely Reed knew.

Except the mortified look on his face says he didn't.

"You . . ." He falters. "Shit. Seriously? Who?"

"Patrick Reynolds," I say, heart pounding with frustration, guilt, the confusion of the moment. I have to focus on the information just to get the words out. "We're long distance."

Reed slumps forward on the couch, hanging his head in his hands. "Then why did you go on a date with me?" he asks.

He doesn't sound plaintive, only puzzled.

I reach forward, pausing the show. We don't need Patrick Stewart's stately voice interrupting this conversation. "I didn't!" I say, panic stirring in me. When he looks up, incredulous, the light from the TV coloring his face, I put together what he's thinking. He asked me out to dinner and then ice cream. He walked me home, I invited him in, and . . .

Oh god, I accidentally went on a date with him.

"I see how it looked like a date. It wasn't, though," I say weakly.

"Right. Because you have a boyfriend," he repeats, his gaze going distant like he's processing the information. His eyes flit back to me, full of real remorse. "Siena, I'm *so* sorry. This is my fault. I just assumed you broke up because you never mentioned him. Please believe me when I say I never would have, uh, kissed you or any of it if I'd known."

My cheeks flaming now, I can't meet his gaze. I stare at the coffee table, sweeping my hair out of my face compulsively. "I know. It was an accident. Just a miscommunication."

Reed nods slowly. He stands, his demeanor stiff. "Well, I should . . ."

My heart sinks. New nerves knot in my stomach. I don't want this to ruin my new friendship, not when I was just feeling like I'd found my place. The visions of the life I wanted to show Patrick suddenly look precarious, like photographs held over fire.

"Yeah," I say anyway.

Reed walks to the door, still rubbing his face in disbelief.

I sit on the couch, motionless. Everything I'd just found sort of nice in our present setting—the dark, the quiet—now feels painfully stifling.

I'm turning off the TV when Reed speaks from the door. "Hey, see you at improv tomorrow, though?"

I feel a small weight lift off my chest. He's not going to avoid me. I won't have to leave the new space I'm finding for myself, won't have to rebuild somewhere else. "Definitely," I say, not ashamed of the relief in my voice.

With a forced smile, he walks out.

I pick up my phone. I have to tell Patrick, even though I did nothing wrong. Our iMessage conversation glares up intimidatingly from the screen. Chewing my lip, I hover over the keyboard, growing more nervous with each passing second I find nothing to say. Telling him feels impossible.

Which is why, I decide, I won't do it over text. In person, I'll have the opportunity to read his facial expressions, reassure him more easily and more emotionally, escape the impersonality of thin type on our white screens. I'm not even putting the confession off irresponsibly long—Patrick will be here in one week. In one week, it'll be the ideal time to clear up this hopefully comedic misunderstanding.

I put my phone down. *One week*. Patrick will understand.

Thirty-Seven

I SIT IN THE same chairs I did when I picked Patrick up for Thanksgiving, listening to the same sounds of luggage tumbling down the carousel while I wait, watching the same flight information board. The baggage claim is emptier now, only travelers arriving for red-eyes populating the airport. It's late, the traffic outside slow, the whole floor seeming spacious under the uniform lighting.

This time, I'm here on my own. I got my license in February, and I've spent every day since convincing my parents to trust me with the car for this very occasion.

I drove with impeccable care despite having woken up this morning with excited jitters in every square inch of my body. I was *not* going to wreck the Subaru on the way to Phoenix Sky Harbor International Airport.

Every time someone walks out of the narrow tunnel from the gates, I lift my head. I know my hope is premature—Patrick only just texted me saying he landed. When my phone vibrates in my lap, I glance down immediately, eager for an update from Patrick on his progress through the terminal.

My shoulders slump when I read the message. It's not Patrick—it's Lacey.

Did you tell him yet?

I pause with my thumbs over the screen, dread pushing in next to my anticipation, twisting one more knot into my stomach. I type out my reply.

Not yet. I will.

Lacey's become one of my closest friends this semester, since I joined improv and she started dating Joe. She's funny, has incredible human intuition, doesn't mind how much I third-wheel her relationship, and is a straight shooter. It's why I shared with her the details of my unfortunate accidental date with Reed, which hardly crosses my mind except when I'm running rehearsals of how I'm going to tell Patrick. It helps that Reed hasn't mentioned it even once. All I have to do is explain everything to Patrick and I'll be free to erase it from my mind entirely.

You know the sooner the better.

I sigh. Lacey's right. The hard part is doing it. I reply speedily, knowing it's not Lacey's fault I want this conversation over.

I know. I will as soon as I can.

I'll have plenty of time, I reassure myself. Patrick and I will have the entire *week* together. The length of the visit feels incomprehensible, though I know it's just the psychological trickery of long distance, the product of deprivation.

Even so, it sets my heart racing. I hardly believe there was a time I took for granted that I could see Patrick every day. Those memories hurt now—the simplicity of having lunch with him on the grass, sharing class periods, walking home from school in the Phoenix heat.

Of course, back then it was the old Patrick. The old me. Not the new us we've become. I can't wait to fill seven whole days with him.

I look up, and finally my timing is perfect.

Patrick emerges from the hallway, no shadow of travel weariness in his features despite his rumpled windbreaker and airplane hair. I shove my phone and Lacey's reminder away as I stand, my eyes misty, my heart pounding with happiness. He hasn't seen me yet. It's the sweetest prelude.

I spring over to him, watching the moment he catches sight of me, joy filling his entire face. He speeds his steps, like even the seconds separating us feel unnecessarily long. When we crash together, I burrow into his chest so hard it hurts, wanting to wrap myself completely in his familiar smell. His face presses into my hair while his embrace holds me close. It couldn't possibly be close enough, yet it's everything I could ever want in this moment.

I pull back just enough, and like he hears my unspoken request, his lips meet mine fiercely. I don't want to let go, ever. But I want to take him home. I want to talk to him. I want to look at him. I just *want*.

After I've had a few moments fill of him, I step out of his arms. Patrick looks like he's caught in the same crush of everything he wants. He stares like he's memorizing me.

"Hi," he says, a little breathless.

"Hi there." I'm smiling so hard my face hurts.

"We're that couple now," he informs me.

"Which couple?" The lightness in my chest is incredible. I feel on the verge of laughing or crying. It's the weightless-ness of falling or flying—I don't know if there's a difference.

Patrick pushes a strand of my hair behind my ear with dizzying tenderness. "The couple who runs into each other's arms at the airport. You know the one."

I laugh. I do know. I remember the couple I saw last time I picked up Patrick. How I envied them. "Oh, *that* couple," I say. "I guess we are." I lean up to kiss him once more, just because I can.

His next question comes out murmured, meant for my ears only. "Do you feel it, too?" He puts my hand on his chest, where his heart is racing. It matches the pounding of my own pulse, interlocking rhythms playing the same song. "Just see-ing you is the most incredible sensation," he continues. "Like I just got off a roller coaster. Or gave a speech to a standing ovation."

I curl my hand over his. "I feel it," I say quietly.

We just stand for a moment, enjoying the silence.

"Let's get you home," I say eventually.

Patrick raises his eyebrows playfully. I shake my head with joking disapproval. I decide now isn't the moment to tell him what happened with Reed—there's no need to ruin the magic of his return. We walk to the parking lot, every step carrying us closer to three months' worth of daydreaming. I don't let go of his hand until I'm behind the wheel and absolutely have to.

Thirty-Eight

IT'S PAST MIDNIGHT WHEN I pull up in front of my building. The quiet outside is the settled quiet of suburban nights— the lights in every unit off, no echo of cars on pavement, only the low music of unseen crickets. Patrick took the last flight out of Austin after school and a Young Dems meeting, not wanting to wait for morning. Getting out of the car, I feel an expansive elation I don't remember from our previous visits. I'm not stressed about fitting in a million things. I just want to be with him.

We walk inside, where we find Robbie sleeping on the couch, our old quilt not fully covering his gangly frame. In the dark, illuminated only by her phone screen, my mom sits at the kitchen table listening to a podcast with her head-phones in, waiting up for us.

She waves, then gives Patrick a quick and quiet hug. "See you in the morning," she whispers. Patrick nods, smiling. With a yawn, she heads for bed.

Silently, we carry Patrick's suitcase down the hall into

Robbie's bedroom. His eyes roam over every darkened detail of my house, and I know I must've done the same when he led me into his home in Austin. Like he's finding everything a reminder—a reassurance—of the fact that he's really here.

I shut Robbie's bedroom door softly behind us. Facing Patrick, I wonder if he notices what I do—the charge starting to fill up the room. "You must be exhausted," I say, my voice hushed.

Patrick's eyes drop for a split second, then return to mine. He puts his hands in his pockets, his expression somewhere close to sheepish. "No," he says. "Not at all. You?"

Warmth pools in my stomach. It's exactly the response I'd hoped for, and fire licks the edges of the unspoken questions hanging in my pause. I don't want to say goodnight yet, not when I just got him back.

"No," I reply.

"Well." Patrick swallows, stepping closer. "What do you want to do, then?"

The warmth in my stomach turns hungry. Stepping up to him, I place my hand on his chest. He follows my movements intently, his gaze going half-lidded. "Want to come to my room?" I ask. The question comes out precarious, piled high with what I'm hoping for.

He nods, wordless. There's delight exploding under his tender expression, like he knew this was coming but still is overwhelmed by it.

With the house dark, I lead him by the hand to my bedroom. When he closes the door behind him with noiseless, deliberate movements, I don't turn on the lights. The stillness feels electric, the hush like a roar. I lie back on the pillows of my bed, pulling Patrick down with me. When our lips meet, I shiver from how good it feels. How much I like having Patrick in my bed. It's the realization of a long-held promise with more promises yet to come.

I let my hands roam under his shirt, then lower, to his waistband. He moves back to give me better opportunity. My heart pounding, I start undoing his belt.

"Hey, Siena?" The trepidation in his question pauses me. I look up, concerned. Which is when Patrick smiles. "How's your wrist feeling?" His eyes sparkle playfully.

I laugh, then clamp my lips shut, scared of waking up the house. "It feels great," I say flatly. When I returned from Austin, my wrist took two weeks to get back to normal. I've nearly forgotten the injury over the past months.

"Good." Patrick's reply is nearly inaudible, the kind of low murmur I feel everywhere. "Any other reason we should stop?"

The hunger in me sharpens, digging deeper. The weeks and weeks of waiting were not easy—especially when I had to hear Lacey describe her sex life with Joe in too much detail. But never did I consider deciding long distance wasn't worth the lonely delay. There is—I've learned over two visits, seven months, and one thousand miles—nobody else I could want. Looking back, those weeks feel like nothing now.

"No reason I can think of," I say. "Oh, and"—I reach for my nightstand drawer—"I have condoms."

"Me too." Patrick pulls one out of his pocket.

I laugh, quieter this time. "You brought that on the plane?"

"Yes, I did," he replies, unabashed, even proud of himself. "If the opportunity presented itself tonight, I was *not* going to be empty-handed."

I pull him to me, kissing him hard. His mouth is hot, his fingers trailing down my sides to where he can slip them under the hem of my shorts. He's touched me like this countless times. I've pressed my mouth to his neck, felt his chest heaving against mine, guided his hands to where I want them. Tonight, though, it's different. His breath is ragged, my face flushed. We've built up to this moment in every *I miss you, I love you, I'm thinking of you* across three months.

I slide my hand beneath his waistband, and he buries his head in my hair, sighing into the shell of my ear. There's no doubting how much he wants this now. It sends a thrill through me, knowing how he must have envisioned this moment a hundred times, like I did, from his bed, miles and months away from this one.

It's not New Year's Eve in an empty house after a romantic day spent in a new city. We have to be quiet, Patrick is fresh off the plane, and it's almost a hundred days after I first wanted to do this. None of it matters.

I shed my clothes, knowing I wasn't just waiting these past months for Patrick. I was waiting for this.

Thirty-Nine

WE'RE TEN MINUTES LATE to brunch with Joe the next morning. It's because we overslept, which honestly was probably inevitable, what with the late night we had.

While I'm opening the gate to the restaurant's patio, Patrick's hands inconspicuously find my waist. It's been this way the whole morning. I've been craving constant contact with him. Patrick seems to be no different—the quick kiss as we rushed out the door, the hand lightly on my leg in the car on the way over, his fingers entwined with mine while we hurried up to the restaurant. It's wrong to call it hunger, because I could feed hunger. This is insatiable.

Joe is seated under the blue palo verde tree growing in the center of the patio. It's flowering now, carpeting the ground with yellow petals. Joe, wearing the Ray-Bans I've hardly seen him without since he got them for Christmas, is perusing the menu. Patrick and I slide onto the bench across from him, sitting closer together than is strictly necessary for the length of the seat.

"Sorry we're late," I say in what sounds like one word.

"No problem." Joe looks up, folding the menu. "Good to see you, dude," he says to Patrick.

"Yeah, I'm really glad we could hang," Patrick replies with enthusiasm. I have to smile. Not that Patrick isn't excited to see Joe—I just know everything looks a little shinier this morning. His leg presses into mine under the table.

Joe's eyes dip to where my hand rests on Patrick's arm. Removing his sunglasses, he gives us a once-over. Something inquisitive flits into his expression. "So," he says casually. "What'd you guys do last night?"

Midswallow, I choke on my cucumber water. While I cough, Patrick rubs my back, not entirely selflessly. "Oh, I got in pretty late," Patrick replies, going for Joe's innocent delivery and failing.

"Did you," Joe says neutrally. His gaze is hyperfocused on us.

"Um. Yes?" Patrick sounds like he's starting to panic.

Joe looks to me. In control of my water situation now, I swallow. I know what's coming.

"You guys had sex," Joe says, monotone and succinct. I've been friends with Joe long enough to intuit how much delight he's hiding under his dryness. He's loving this.

"Joe!" I say sternly. "You can't just . . . say that."

"Why not?" Joe shifts easily in his chair, looking completely comfortable. "You could be a little less obvious. You're practically in his lap, and I'd bet my life Patrick's hand is on your leg."

Patrick guiltily puts his hand on the table, where it notably had not been before.

"Congrats, by the way, man," Joe adds.

I clear my throat pointedly.

His eyes moving to me, Joe looks playfully remorseful. "And congratulations are in order for the lady as well," he says, placing his hand over his heart.

"Thank you," I say, pleased. I fold my napkin in my lap, matching his show with primness of my own.

Joe straightens up. "Is that why you were late?" He makes a face. "Did you just—"

"*No,*" Patrick exclaims, looking mortified. I fight my smile. He's strangely cute when he's scandalized.

"I mean, it's cool if you did, though," Joe says, goading while sounding reasonable. He crosses his arms, like he's half expecting I'm going to confess to our sexcapades right here on the restaurant patio, in view of the moms with strollers ordering parfaits behind us.

"Joe . . ." I say, scolding.

Right then, with impeccable timing, the waitress swings by, pausing over us. "Need a couple more minutes to look over the menu?" she asks.

"Nope." Patrick jumps on the diversion. "I'll have the"— his gaze drops to his menu—"oatmeal," he says wildly, like it's the first thing he saw.

I hide my smile behind my menu. Patrick doesn't even like oatmeal. While Joe orders, I evaluate my choices. I've been to this restaurant before—it's old, with the sort of established, hometown-breakfast-spot charm blog reviews or chic interior design can't touch. I usually go for the huevos rancheros, but today, I know I'm going to need something Patrick will want to share or he'll be starving by lunch. I choose the French toast.

When the waitress leaves, Joe looks ready to resume his interrogation. Patrick preempts him. "So when are we going to get the whole group together while I'm here?" he asks.

I meet Joe's eyes across the table. He frowns a little, and I don't know quite how to respond. Joe seems similarly silent. The moment stretches long enough for Patrick to notice. Uncertain, he shifts his gaze from my friend to me.

"What?" he asks. "Is everyone, like, out of town for break?"

"Um." I pause. "I don't know, actually."

"We haven't really hung out with that crew in a while," Joe explains delicately. "I'm not sure what they're up to."

Patrick doesn't hide his surprise. "Oh," he says, one downward-sloping syllable. It's the first time I've seen him look somewhat lost in this place that, until recently, he considered home. Whether consciously or unconsciously, he moves his knee so it's no longer touching mine.

"It's just, since Joe started dating Lacey and I dropped MUN, we've been sitting with the drama kids at lunch," I say. While my voice is gentle, my mind is going over three months of text conversations. I haven't mentioned our old friends much, but I guess Patrick didn't realize just how much they'd faded from my life.

Patrick nods, failing to hide that he's still flustered. "No, yeah. That makes sense," he says with effort. "I know you've been hanging out with everyone in improv."

I say nothing, feeling guilty. It's not hard to make out in his eyes the shape of the hopes he's packing up. He probably had looked forward to some kind of homecoming party like last time.

"Which," Joe says, grasping on to the subject change with enthusiasm, "speaking of improv, you're coming to the match tonight, right? And the party after?"

Patrick perks up, though I know him well enough to recognize he's still a little deflated from the news of the friend-group changes. "Definitely. I can't wait to see Siena perform." His hand finds mine again, and the way his excitement pushes aside his disappointment is incredibly sweet. Our midsemester show tonight is why Patrick made sure to fly in last night. He was adorably nervous about flight delays and cancellations and wanted to make sure he had an airport buffer to get to Phoenix in time for the performance. His determination joined the long list of reasons why I love him—right between how he donated the proceeds of his first lemonade stand to the World Wildlife Fund when he was six and how he tears up whenever characters break up in a movie.

"Don't get too excited," I say, feeling the warmth of flattery in my cheeks. "I'm not that great, but I'm learning. Reed is really the star."

Joe's eyes cut to me. I determinedly ignore the question in them.

Oblivious to our silent exchange, Patrick sips his water, which he's nearly finished. He sets his glass down. "It's funny," he starts, "I had chem with Reed last year, but I never got to know him. Now I feel like I know him so well through all your stories."

"He's excited to hang out with you," I say earnestly, dodging Joe's gaze.

The comment wins me a smile from Patrick. He releases my hand. "I'm going to run to the bathroom before our food comes," he says quickly while he slides off the bench.

Once he's gone through the modern farmhouse doors leading inside the restaurant, Joe fixes me with a stare, eyebrows raised. "You haven't told him," he says without a moment's pause.

I don't rush to reply, instead drinking from my glass, focusing desperately on the pleasant cool of the ice against my lips. Inside, I'm curling in on myself. I have to do it, I know I do. I'd planned to this morning, but we overslept and had to rush to get here. "I will," I say, exasperated. "When he got in last night, we had sex, and then I didn't want to ruin the moment. There just hasn't been the right time."

Joe's expression flattens further. "You know you have to tell him before the party. It's *at Reed's house*," he points out.

"I know it's at Reed's house," I snap. His reminder irrationally pisses me off. Does he just think I haven't done this mental math? Whenever I've envisioned this night I've been really looking forward to, reintroducing Patrick to my new friends while flushed with the giddy glow of the improv match, I knew it would be in Reed's basement. It doesn't matter.

Joe sobers, his hard-ass demeanor softening. "Siena, he can't be the only one who doesn't know. It's not fair."

My frustration falters. In a second, it goes out, like a snuffed candle. I sigh. "I know. I know," I say, repeating the words to drive them home to myself. "You're right. I just . . . don't want anything to wreck how good things are between us." It's hard to voice out loud, because it's hard to imagine. What I've found with Patrick since he moved is some happy, surprisingly flourishing version of what we once had. The idea of it being poisoned by basically nothing is unbearable.

Looking sympathetic, Joe straightens his silverware, thinking. "You guys have a strong relationship," he says gently. "I mean, you have to in order to handle long distance. He'll understand."

I nod, feeling comforted to hear the reassurance I've repeated silently to myself over the past week. "Yeah. He will," I say, mustering force into my voice. "I'll do it right after this."

Patrick emerges from the farmhouse doors, smiling at me in the intimate way I've started to recognize since last night. It sparks something quietly wonderful in my chest. I spin the feeling into new confidence, holding on to everything I know I have with Patrick. He *will* understand. Our relationship has never been stronger. This will be nothing.

Forty

THE REST OF BRUNCH is remarkably easy. With my plan made, I feel like I'm relieved of a stomachache I didn't notice I had. Patrick asks with enthusiasm about Joe and Lacey's relationship, I summarize some of our plans for the week, and the hour passes quickly on the sunlit patio. My French toast is delicious, with syrup running rivers down the powdered sugar. Patrick, of course, has half.

Walking out to the parking lot once we've paid and hugged goodbye, I feel clearheaded. The day is open ahead of me, full of opportunity. I just have to get through this one thing first.

When we get into my car, I don't start the engine. I face Patrick. "I have to tell you something," I say, no waver in my voice.

"Okay," he replies readily. He's smiling, his eyes energized, but I can't match his expression. When I take a deep breath, his smile fades, like he's realizing something is coming. "Is this about last night?" he asks hesitantly.

I reach for his hand, hating that I even let his head go there. "No," I say emphatically. "Not at all. Last night was perfect."

Worry clouds Patrick's expression, like my words haven't entirely assuaged him. He releases my hand to press his palm to his jeans. "You're making me nervous," he says, looking at me sideways.

"It's nothing." I curl my fingers to avoid reaching for his hand again. I'm desperate to reassure him. "Really," I continue, "it's not even a big deal."

"Siena," he says with the first hint of sharpness. It spurs my next words out quickly.

"I accidentally went on a date with Reed."

Patrick blinks. He stiffens, his eyes going distant. I feel myself lean forward, anxious to know how he's taking it. "You—what?" he splutters. "When? *How?*" He doesn't look mad, just bewildered. My heart starts to unclench.

I'm reaching the easy part, I remind myself. The facts. I can give Patrick the facts. In direct light, they cast no shadows. "It was a week ago," I explain evenly. "Reed asked me to dinner. I didn't think anything of it. We're always going to eat as a group, and I just figured no one else was interested this time. But then, at the end of the night, Reed tried to kiss me."

"He *what*?" Patrick interjects immediately. Now he does look a little mad.

I rush to continue. "I stopped him, obviously. Nothing happened. He . . . thought I was single. I explained I wasn't, and he was honestly really embarrassed." I wince remembering it.

The moment remains a dizzy collision of recollections. The rush of hot surprise when he leaned in, then the painful awkwardness of pretty much everything afterward.

Patrick stares out the front window, his jaw rigid.

The sight frays my confidence. I'd come in on the momentum of enjoying the morning together, on Joe's comforting words, on the collective good of everything with Patrick this year. Finally, the momentum is slowing. The fear is catching up. The worries I've outrun for the past week, since the evening with Reed, are finding me here, in this suddenly claustrophobic seat of my mom's car. *What if Patrick doesn't understand? What if everything is somehow ruined?*

I search his face frantically for signs of what's going on in his head. Suddenly, I wish the engine were on so I could run the AC. The inside of the Subaru feels incredibly small right now, the stale air suffocating.

"Say something," I plead. Even though I did nothing wrong, I can't help being nervous. It was just a horrible misunderstanding. Really, Reed handled it like a gentleman—he wasn't indignant or self-pitying, and he didn't drop me as a friend, either. I wondered if he'd be awkward with me in improv, but when we had practice the next day, he just waved and kept on calling out audience suggestions for the game I was performing in.

It was nothing. It genuinely was.

"Do you like him?" My boyfriend's voice comes out low, like stone with sharp edges. He hasn't moved. He's still staring out the windshield, his shoulders squared.

I was prepared for this question. It's an easy one. "No. I promise, Patrick," I say, the feeling in my voice undeniable. "He's just a friend."

His chin slanting only slightly in my direction, Patrick glances at me out of the corner of his eye. "He clearly didn't think so."

I reassure Patrick. "He understands. He just—missed the memo I had a boyfriend." I flash a faint smile, hoping I can massage a little levity into the conversation.

"*How?*" he shoots back, evidently not embracing the humor.

"I don't know." My voice shrinks. I remember what Reed said. *Did I really never mention Patrick to him? Not once?* The thought shames me. But telling him that would only hurt him.

Patrick closes his eyes, taking a deep breath. When he lets it out, he finally looks at me, some of his anger faded. "I just don't know him," he says unevenly. "I don't really know any of your new friends. Even though I went to school with them for eleven years."

"That's what tonight's for," I offer immediately. "You can get to know them. The after-party will be at Reed's house. He . . . really wants to apologize to you in person."

"That's not necessary," Patrick replies, understanding working its way into his voice. "It sounds like it was just a . . . mix-up."

"Yes," I say, the word leaving me with a sigh of relief. Guilt of another color steals into me. My panic over Patrick's reaction feels wildly wrong suddenly, entirely out of step with every reason why I love the most considerate guy I know.

I'm reaching for my keys when he stops me.

"It's just—" He sounds hesitant, like he doesn't really want to reopen the conversation. Which means he's honestly still upset. The realization hits me with a fresh punch of remorse. "Well, you have this new friend group now," Patrick goes on. "Is Reed why you stopped hanging out with Garret and Alicia and everyone?"

I return my keys to my lap, my forehead creasing. "No," I say, my confusion now mirroring his. "I would have found new friends regardless of Reed." The heat in the car is becoming insufferable. Still, I don't want Patrick to feel like I'm rushing this conversation to its end.

"Why?" Patrick asks softly. "Was what we had last year so horrible?"

"It wasn't horrible." I pause over my next words, ones I hadn't planned. They're harder to figure out. "Just . . . MUN, our old friends—I fell into them because we were dating. When you left, I realized I didn't really fit there. I only thought I did because I fit so well with you."

While Patrick nods, he still looks sad. His eyes won't meet mine, indecipherable depth in their brown irises.

"Whatever it is you're thinking, you can tell me," I say.

He gives me a pained smile, hesitating. "Are you going to want to replace me, too?" he finally asks. There's real vulnerability in his voice.

It sends sympathy washing over me. He's feeling sort of the way I did in Austin, I realize, when I worried he was only with me because of our history. I put comforting conviction into my voice and look right into his eyes. "Patrick, no. Don't you see the fact that I'm still with you even when I've changed who I hang out with, what extracurriculars I'm in, means that I *want* to be with you? I love you."

Now his smile gains strength. It lights something up in me, my sympathy changing into relief, like paper and gunpowder into fireworks. He leans forward and kisses me on the forehead. "I love you, too," he says.

"Everyone changes in their senior year," I say into his shoulder, halfway to a whisper. "But I'm still me."

"I know," he replies, holding me close.

When he withdraws, I fiddle with my keys. "If you're uncomfortable going to the party tonight, or even the show, I'd understand," I say, my voice empty of reservation.

"No," he replies firmly. "It'll be okay."

The maturity of his response makes me swell in a way I really, really like. "Do you have any other questions? About Reed, or the extremely not-a-date?" I ask.

Patrick's expression darkens slightly at the reminder, but I watch him push past it. He shakes his head. "Long distance requires trust," he says solemnly, "and I trust you."

"I trust you, too." It's out of my mouth instantly.

I put the key in the ignition. I *do* trust Patrick. Not just in this one way he means, either. I trust him to work through the hard stuff with me, to handle the strains of distance well. I trust him to trust me.

Forty-One

I WALK THROUGH MY front door with a spring in my step. The hard part of the visit is over. Now it's time to enjoy the rest. We have the whole day waiting for us, and the only difficulty is choosing what's next when everything sounds wonderful. We could hang out at my place, or we could go to the park and read in the sun. Or I wonder if Patrick would want to hike in the desert hills. I latch on to this final idea— the perfect combination of the old and new us.

In the living room, Robbie's playing video games on the couch, soldiers exploding on screen while he frenetically rounds corners. Dad is seated at the dining table, slowly eating a sandwich and half watching the TV. It's not the first time I've noticed his curiosity about *Call of Duty*, although I'm pretty sure he's too scared to pick up the controller himself.

"So I'm going to sleep in my room tonight," Robbie declares.

He's not even looking up, his eyes fixed intently on the game. I notice he's not wearing his headset like he does when he's doing one of his three-hour bro dates where he and his friends kill strangers online.

With my keys in my hand, I pause near the doorway. Patrick lingers amiably next to me, not picking up on my sudden suspicion. But I know Robbie well enough to understand there's something unnervingly specific in his remark.

"Robbie," Dad says, pulled from watching my brother's virtual warfare. "We talked about this. You said Patrick could sleep in your room. It's rude to go back on your offer."

I watch my brother, my mind working. While I'm not sure where Robbie's going with this, I'm certain it's nowhere good.

"Yeah," he replies reasonably. "But that was before I knew Patrick would be sleeping in Siena's room. I don't see the point in me sleeping on the couch when my bed is empty."

There it is. Robbie's play here crashes over me like a cascade of cold water. I guess he still resents that my boyfriend is allowed to stay over, even boot him out of his room, while his girlfriend doesn't get to come to Thanksgiving. Nevertheless, this retaliation is brutal.

I'm conscious my dad's focus has shifted to me, and I carefully control my expression even though I'd like nothing better than to rip his controller out of his hands and flush it down the toilet. Patrick puts his hands in his pockets, suddenly looking very interested in the credenza near the door.

"Robbie, that's not true," I say diplomatically. "Patrick slept in your room. Remember how I woke him up in there at ten?" I ask, proud of myself. I'm mustering rhetorical precision I never managed in Model UN. I'm not technically lying, either. While Patrick and I took the opportunity to sleep in the same bed together—which felt almost as real and intimate as sex itself—we weren't careless. Patrick set a quiet alarm on his phone for six a.m., then stole into Robbie's room before my family woke up.

My brother pauses his game. Instantly, I realize my question was the wrong move. When he faces us, looking innocently curious, I glare. "Then how come," he starts, "when I woke up in the middle of the night and realized my phone was dead, I went into my room for my charger and found the bed empty?"

Next to me, Patrick physically wilts. To his credit, he fights through what I know is immense mortification to face my dad. "I'm so sorry," he says.

I'm grateful Patrick spoke up, because I'm incapable of doing so. The specific wrath reserved for siblings has locked my jaw.

My dad lets out a long-suffering sigh, and I fire Robbie a glare that promises payback for putting us all in a position no one is enjoying. With Mom at work, Dad's the one left to deal with this particular parenting issue, despite how much he'd obviously rather be watching *Call of Duty*. In fact, there's probably very little he wouldn't prefer doing. There's very little *I* wouldn't prefer doing, either.

"Siena," my dad finally forces out, "can I talk to you privately?"

I nod, then follow him like a prisoner to execution toward

my room, hearing what is unmistakably the sound of a pillow hitting someone and Patrick saying, "What the hell, man?"

I step into my room, where I sit down on my bed. Immediately, I hate the choice. It feels uncomfortably symbolic of the conversation I know is coming. Dad remains standing, leaning his elbow on the dresser with the posed stiffness of a department store mannequin. We've always had a pretty good relationship, founded on the mutual understanding we have nearly nothing in common. Right now, I feel those differences stretching the seams of what we have to get through.

"Did you have sex?" Dad asks clumsily.

I close my eyes from the fast Band-Aid sting of the question. While it's horrific to hear, I'm actually grateful he came out with it directly. Maybe it'll shorten the length of this unendurable discussion.

In the same spirit, I reply, "Yes."

Dad pauses. "Did you use protection?" The question comes out in a weird, struggling monotone.

"Yes."

He nods, looking faintly reassured. "Would you like to go on the pill? You know condoms have a small failure rate." He's saying these sentences like he's reading them from a PowerPoint presentation he really doesn't want to be giving.

"Oh, um." I blink, feeling the first flicker of something besides wanting the conversation to be over. "Yeah. I guess I would," I say. I hadn't really considered the idea. Up until last night, I'd been so focused on having sex for the first time, I hadn't given much thought to how to do it routinely.

"I'll call your doctor. Set something up," Dad says, seizing on having something concrete to do. He shifts, nearly knocking over the framed photo on my dresser. It's of Patrick and me from when we went to Castles N' Coasters, the mini golf course in the background, Patrick's arms around my waist. With unnecessary precision, Dad returns the photo to its place. "Do you have any questions?" he asks.

"Nope," I say with urgency. Dad seems to relax, which makes me straighten up, itching to start for the hallway. "Is that all?"

Dad frowns. "Did I miss something? I've never had The Talk before." He says *the talk* like it's a proper noun, which makes me smile involuntarily, imagining some manual parents have stuffed under their mattresses with the title in block letters.

"No. You did great," I reassure him. "Just"—I start cautiously, my heartstrings pulling me—"you're not mad that Patrick slept in here last night?"

The stiffness leaving his expression, Dad moves from the dresser to sit in my desk chair closer to me. "I'm not mad," he says earnestly, with unmissable kindness. "You could have told us and spared poor Robbie, but, well, your mom and I have known this was inevitable. We're glad it was with Patrick."

While half of me is dying from embarrassment, the other half doesn't hate hearing him say it.

"You know, I'm proud of you," he goes on. "Of the relationship you two have. It's really remarkable to witness your kid growing up and giving her heart to someone who deserves it." When he stops himself, staring past my blinds into the white sunlight outside my window, I have the impression it's because he might cry if he continues. I feel myself smile a wobbly smile, touched. Dad stands up, clearing his throat. "Be respectful of Robbie, though, okay?" he says seriously, like we've crossed over the conversation onto firmer ground. "It's a small house. We don't need him getting any ideas."

I don't fight my laugh. Dad permits himself a small smile. In fact, this *would* be my opportunity to throw Robbie under the bus the way he did me by revealing I'm not the only sibling who's had sex. I decide to be the bigger person and hold my tongue. Robbie will probably never know to thank me, but whatever.

When we reemerge from the hallway into the living room, we find Patrick sitting on the couch with Robbie. Now both of them have controllers. When Patrick sees my dad, his demeaner changes instantly. He pauses the game, cutting off the cacophony of video-game gunfire, and stands up in the silent living room.

"Robbie, you can have your room back," my dad pronounces.

Patrick nods, looking solemn. I wonder if everyone notices the small way he slumps, or if it's only me. "I understand," he says. "I can call Garret or Joe. I'm sure I can stay—"

Dad holds up his hand, interrupting Patrick. "You two are practically adults. You can share a bedroom for a week."

Patrick's eyes fly to me. Grinning, I watch the relief on his face—the feeling of having his sentence commuted—change into excitement mirroring mine. We'll have a whole week sleeping in the same bed. Of Patrick's smell when I wake up, of resting my head on his chest, hearing his heartbeat while I drift off.

"Wait, really?" Robbie's voice interrupts my imaginings. "Does that mean I can invite Erica for a sleepover, too?"

"Absolutely not," Dad says, unsurprisingly, considering Erica is Robbie's girlfriend of, like, two weeks.

Robbie drops his controller onto the couch. "That's totally unfair!"

"Robert," Dad's tone turns steely. "When you've been with the same girl for three years, you're welcome to have her spend the night."

I laugh, earning a dirty look from Robbie. Shrugging, I shoot him raised eyebrows and a silent *You deserve this.*

Slouching into the cushions, Robbie returns his gaze to Dad. "That would mean having the same girlfriend for all of high school," he says plaintively, like Dad's requesting the equivalent of winning the Nobel Prize.

"Yes," Dad replies, satisfied. "Yes, it would."

"That's impossible," Robbie says in defeat.

While he reaches for his controller, I catch Patrick's eye, and some private joy passes in our shared look. Though Robbie was being flippant, the ring of truth in his words fills my chest. What we have *does* feel impossible. Not climbing-Mount-Everest, winning-the-lottery impossible. The impossible of someone knowing you as well as you know yourself, of fitting more into one week than into three months. The impossible of seeing the same sunrise over and over.

My dad was right. It is worth being proud of.

Forty-Two

WHEN I WENT TO my first improv performance, I didn't
know what to expect from Reed's description. I didn't know
shows, or *matches*, consisted of a series of games chosen
from a long list, played competitively in teams of four or
five. I didn't know some were more sketch comedy while
others involved doing impressions or singing songs, or
that points were determined by the audience or the referee.
Since I joined, Reed has enthusiastically explained the tradition of ComedySportz and how we exist within a *venerated
legacy*—his words.

When Reed first mentioned me auditioning outright,
one of my images leapt into my head. Me free to invent ridiculous situations on the spot in the drama room. Doing Kate
McKinnon and Amy Poehler impressions and then working
out my own characters. Lounging with the earbud-sharing
drama kids on the planters every lunch. *Improv Siena.*

For the first time, the idea felt right. I don't know if the
evidence I'd seen of Patrick fitting into his new life opened

my mind or if I'd just found something I really felt resonated. Whatever it was, it stuck. I auditioned. Now I'm here.

Tonight, we're playing the only other Phoenix school with a ComedySportz club, unlike our usual matches in which we divide ourselves up and face off. It's a home game, meaning we'll perform in the West Vista drama room. In the periwinkle of dusk, Patrick and I head toward campus from the parking lot. I'm wearing my team "uniform"—a green WVHS Improv T-shirt, black shorts, and white knee socks. The campus is mostly empty, populated only by others like us walking up from their cars for the show.

It's surreal, holding Patrick's hand in these hallways like we've done thousands of times. With how quiet the campus is, it feels like every morning he walked me to class—I remember hair wet from morning showers, eagerness in sleepy eyes, catching each other up on our nights. I've gotten used to not walking to class with him in the early light this year. In ways, I've even enjoyed it. It's given me the chance to talk to people I hadn't before, some of whom have become new friends.

Still, it's really nice having Patrick here. Even if it's temporary.

I tighten my grip on his hand. "How does it feel to be back?"

He doesn't reply immediately, instead pausing for long enough I glance over to study his expression. He's looking off into the distance, out over the small garden of malnourished roses in front of the main office. "I don't know," he says.

Something in his tone surprises me. I didn't expect the question would stump him, or cast shadows over his face.

"Weird, I guess," he finally finishes.

I feel my smile fade. It's not the response I was expecting. Patrick's repeated often how much he misses West Vista. I thought he'd love the chance to return, to be back on literal familiar ground, in familiar hallways, by the familiar rose gardens. His reaction saddens me a little, I realize. "In a bad way?" I ask.

His gaze shifts from the roses to the bench where we would sometimes eat lunch when we weren't sitting with our friends. It was sort of our spot, one more of our unspoken routines. Even though it was in full view of everyone, it felt inexplicably secret, special. In January, the Ecology Club painted a wildlife mural behind it, making the spot a purple-and-orange Phoenix sunset.

"I just . . . don't know how much I belong here," he says.

I look around. Sure, not everything is the same, like the mural. But really, campus has barely changed since we were freshmen. I don't know why it's jarring him so much. Unless . . . it's not the campus that's different, but him.

"You do belong," I say. "Just maybe not the same way you used to."

He nods, still looking sad. I pull him to a stop in the middle of the hallway, then kiss him.

"You belong wherever I am. Okay?" I say.

I'm not sure if it's going to help. It's a platitude, wide and soft, and I hope it's enough to fend off what I'm starting to understand he's dealing with—the difficult, complicated realities of leaving your home in your last year of high school. It's the truth, though, and I do want him to know it.

From the way he smiles, I think he does. "You're right," he says.

We resume our route to the drama room, his hand still in mine. I hold on to my reassurance, hoping he feels it as much as I do.

Forty-Three

WHEN WE REACH THE drama room, it's packed. I keep hold of Patrick's hand while we walk in, literally pulling him into my world.

The cheerful prelude to the match is something I've gotten familiar with months into my improv career. It's one of my favorite parts of our performances. The room is structured like a small amphitheater, with wooden seats rising on platform levels up from the small open space in the front, where props are already set up for the show—goal posts and a scoreboard. Right now, however, there's no distinction between the stage and the seats. Everyone is everywhere. Groups of friends, classmates, and siblings sprawl out of the rows, mixing with people in improv uniforms. It's communal and a little electric.

Reed and Lacey stand in the center aisle in green shirts matching mine. They're talking to Joe, who's sitting in one of the middle rows. When he sees us, he waves us over, gesturing to the seat next to him, which I realize with a swell of gratitude he's saved for Patrick.

Looking at Patrick, I give him a small smile. There's this shift I've noticed when we go from just us to us with friends. We go from two people to *one* couple, our interpersonal inner workings going quiet. It's a nice feeling, though tonight there's something new in our quiet undercurrent— what Patrick said outside. We have different connections to this place, these people. It means that when we're with them, we're pulled apart, just slightly. *Patrick and Siena*, not *PatrickandSiena.*

We walk over to Joe, Lacey, and Reed.

"Hey, guys," I say. "You remember Patrick?" I feel awkward, like I have to introduce Patrick to Reed and Lacey even though they went to school together for years.

Patrick seems to be feeling some of the same awkwardness. He stands beside me, his shoulders hunched.

Lacey pulls him unhesitatingly into a friendly hug. "We remember," she says brightly. "It's great to see you again."

"Yeah, you too," Patrick replies. It's a hollow imitation of his usual warmth, and my heart sinks. Studying his expression, I see the weight of it on him, the feeling he no longer fits here.

Reed puts out his hand. "Hey, man," he says to Patrick, the picture of friendliness. Unlike Patrick, *I* know Reed well enough to recognize rare self-consciousness in him. He genuinely still feels guilty for our date mix-up.

Patrick grasps Reed's hand readily, like I knew he would. The handshake is a little stiff, but they're trying. Then Patrick's posture straightens, like he's shaking something off. "Hey, so," he starts with more color in his voice, "explain to me how this whole thing works. It's a comedy show but also a sports match?"

I slip my arm around his waist, pulling him closer. Of course he wouldn't let Reed in on whatever remaining resentment he might feel. Patrick's too kind for that. The gang starts in elaborately explaining the rules of ComedySportz, not that we really follow rules outside those we make up ourselves. While Lacey delves deep into the ever-changing concept of fouls, Ryan Escuela, our referee for the night, calls everyone to find their seats.

The group starts to disperse, and I'm left momentarily with Patrick, still holding myself close to him. "You good?" I whisper hopefully.

"Totally," he replies. It's his smile I find comforting more than his words—a small flash of his usual self. "Break a leg," he says, then gives me a quick kiss. He sits down next to Joe, and I make my way to the West Vista side of the stage.

Joining Reed, Lacey, and our team, I feel my heart pound with pre-performance adrenaline. I lean into it. I haven't been a performing member of improv for long, but as the match begins and my teammates take the stage, I'm swept up. Not in the funny voices or ridiculous scenarios we concoct—in the feeling of throwing myself into something unfamiliar, figuring it out as I go. Every day is something new.

I don't go on until the middle of the match. When the ref blows the whistle, I take the "court." Lacey and I and two players from the opposing team start a game where we portray famous party guests. Reed and the other team's captain have to guess who is who. It's a little awkward, even embarrassing. Still, I jump in feetfirst. Reed guesses in minutes flat, and Lacey and I walk off in hysterics, sweeping him up with us on the way.

Glancing into the audience, my face still flushed from laughter and the effort of the scene, I spot Patrick.

He's applauding like everyone else. Only, something is off. I can't miss the oddly sour look on his face or the deliberate, plodding way he joins in. For a moment, my entire focus narrows in on studying him, decoding where his mind is right now. It's strange how hard private currents like these pull, toward whatever the person you love is feeling.

I realize I'm surprised by that small, insistent awareness. It's something gone from the more independent life I've started living. Where usually I'd just be in the moment, watching the new skit, now I'm wondering what's wrong. I wouldn't say I'm resentful of this new concern, exactly. It's just there.

Then the ref's whistle blows sharply, returning me to the stage.

Forty-Four

REED'S AFTER-PARTIES AREN'T REALLY parties. Everyone hangs out in his game room, which is spacious, with the kind of carpet your feet sink into and decor reflecting his dad's interest in sci-fi movies. Reed hosts us pretty much every week. It's low-key—though there are drinks out, no one ever gets wasted. Sometimes people even bring homework.

I settle into my usual beanbag under the *Empire Strikes Back* poster, this time leaving space for Patrick next to me. We're not the first ones here. The room is filling up, people taking their customary positions in an easy, practiced choreography. With no music yet, indistinct conversation floats through the room. Joe and a few of the guys turn on the Nintendo Switch to play *Super Smash*, while Julian and Taylor film content for their channels in the back behind the couch. Reed sits in his regular seat on the ottoman next to me, scrolling his party playlists on his phone.

I know exactly how the night would normally go. I'd talk to Reed, or I'd cheer on Joe while he crushes everyone in whatever video game they've put on. Probably Lacey would enlist me in a game of mafia or charades.

Tonight, though, it's the first day of spring break. The energy is higher, everyone noisier, the room livelier with the fresh gleam of freedom. For me, spring break isn't the only difference. For the first time, I have Patrick with me.

I nudge his elbow. "So what'd you think?" I ask. We hardly had the chance to talk after the show since I had to help everyone clean and then volunteered to drive three people here. While Patrick was quietly polite in the car, I couldn't help wondering if he still seemed off. He's probably somewhat uncomfortable with Reed, which I can't say I don't understand. Reed really is impressively charismatic onstage and always a crowd favorite.

I know Patrick, though. If he just has the chance to hang out with Reed, he'll embrace him like he did Joe.

"I loved it," he says. "You were fantastic. Everyone was."

It's what I wanted him to say, and yet the way he says it sort of crushes me. He recites the short sentences like he's reading them to the mirror. I'm left gazing into the gulf separating his words and his expression, his posture, his everything. Hurt, I don't reply. Did he hate the show? Hate improv? I know my involvement must seem out of left field, but I figured he would be supportive no matter what.

When Lacey shouts excitedly from the couch, Patrick's eyes shift to the TV like he's searching for something else to focus on. Lacey has a controller and is holding on to victory for the moment while Joe, lips pursed, looks like he knows he'll never live his impending loss down.

"Hey," I say softly. "What's wrong?"

Patrick faces me, putting on a smile. It isn't a real one. "Nothing. Just watching the showdown." He turns back to the screen, closing the door on this conversation before I can follow up.

I watch him for a second, stung even though he's said nothing unkind out loud. On paper, he seems entirely pleasant. But in every flat reaction, every false reassurance, he's lying to me. I wonder briefly if this feeling is something I've forgotten over the past few months. Then I realize it's nothing I've ever experienced.

"Siena, please?" Reed's voice next to me pulls me from my thoughts. When I look over, I find sympathy in his eyes, like he overheard Patrick's brush-off. "My phone likes you better than me," he says, holding said cracked iPhone out to me.

I take it, laughing. It's a running joke between us, that only I can get his phone to connect to his speakers. "Which playlist do you want?" I ask, tapping the Bluetooth switch. "AstronAughts or Nine Ts?" The second one is written out *TTTTTTTT*. It's Reed's '90s hip-hop playlist.

"Ooh, tough one." Reed rubs his chin, facetiously pondering.

"Nine Ts," we say in unison. I smile. Reed laughs.

Sure enough, the next second, the speakers chirp with the "connected" noise, and music pours from the speakers, the warm bass rhythm of A Tribe Called Quest's "Excursions." I hand Reed his phone. "Uncanny," he says, shaking his head.

"Maybe if you didn't drop your phone twice a day it would like you better."

"Please," Reed replies loftily. "I dropped my phone *once* in front of you."

"Um, three times at least," I counter.

"When?"

I hold up fingers to count off my examples. "Once getting out of your car last week. Once when you dropped it on your chest lying on the couch and thought no one was looking, and—"

The beanbag shifts under me. I glance up to find Patrick's stood suddenly. Without looking at me, he huffs off to the counter in the back. My surprise souring into worry and something less charitable, I note the tension in his shoulders, the quickness of his steps. There's no denying it now. He's definitely pissed.

Conscious of Reed watching, I feel my cheeks flush. "Sorry, I—" I say, the end of the sentence sticking in my throat. *I what? I'm sorry my boyfriend is ruining his second night here over one innocent misunderstanding? I'm sorry he's not supporting my new extracurricular and new group of friends?*

I get up, then follow Patrick. Now *I'm* pissed.

When I reach the counter, my eyes widen, my anger forgotten for a moment. Patrick's pouring himself a drink. "We should go," he says, with force in the syllables. "I don't fit in here."

I inhale evenly, fighting to remind myself he's probably just hurting because of the Reed date thing. Still, the way he's handling it annoys me. "You're not *trying* to fit in. You've hardly said two words to anyone who wasn't Joe since the performance," I point out. Patrick says nothing. Instead, he sips from his red plastic cup. "And since when do you drink?" I ask sharply.

Patrick meets my gaze, his eyes flashing. "Are you suggesting I should have told you every time I took a sip of alcohol over the past few months?"

I clench my jaw. "No," I say, fighting to keep my cool. "But you could have mentioned it once. You're the one who said we should keep each other in the loop."

Patrick takes a long, deliberate sip.

"Yeah," he says, "well, you could have mentioned some stuff, too." His voice holds venom I knew—I *knew*—was roiling under his flat politeness.

The room feels hot, sweat suddenly noticeable under my clothes. With the combined noise of the low music, the video game, and my friends filming on their phones, I don't know whether I'm grateful for the privacy or overwhelmed by the clamor. I'm done holding on to my composure. Patrick had the right to be upset. He did *not* have to tell me he trusted me and it was okay when it wasn't.

I don't say this, though, because Reed comes up to us, hands deep in his pockets. "Hey, I don't know if this is about me or not, but I wanted to say I'm really sorry for what happened, man." He speaks contritely to Patrick. "I never would have taken her out if I'd known she wasn't single. Siena corrected me immediately. It was a complete accident, and it's not her fault at all."

I cringe a little. Reed's timing was not ideal. Patrick pauses, eyeing him, and I watch his instinct not to be rude wrestle down his irritation.

"Reed, your apology is really not necessary," Patrick says. "This is between me and my girlfriend."

Reed nods. "Right. I'll, um, go then." He gives me a concerned glance, then returns to the couch.

My gaze follows the retreating denim jacket he put on over his improv shirt. It's obvious Reed feels like crap. Which is unfair, because he said the exact right things. He was graceful and honest, and now he feels guilty.

It fuels the fire in me when I round on Patrick. "I don't get what this is about," I hiss. "In the car, you said you trusted me. You said you *wanted* to come here."

Patrick does something I've seen him do only once or twice ever. He rolls his eyes. "Siena, come on," he says harshly. "You clearly spend a lot of time with these people. You have all these new routines, these inside jokes. You're an expert on Reed's fucking phone."

"Yeah, because they're my *friends*," I reply.

"Exactly," Patrick says. "Your *friends* who you didn't bother to tell about me."

My mouth, ready for my next retort, snaps shut. Silence widens between us, except it's not silence. It's music, conversation, *Super Smash*. Instantly, I understand why coming here, seeing how enmeshed with this group I've become, has hurt him. Comments I heard in Austin replay in my head in incriminating loops—everyone saying how excited they were to meet me, how often Patrick had talked about me.

Here, my friends didn't even know I was dating him. The contrast crashes onto me with painful weight.

"Reed didn't know you even had a boyfriend. Not to mention me," Patrick goes on, pressing the wound. "You never mentioned 'my boyfriend, Patrick.' Not once."

"I'm sorry," I say, nearly in a whisper. Patrick's eyes find mine. He's mad, but he's listening. "Shit, I'm really sorry," I go on. "I—I understand how you feel like I don't care about you or I'm embarrassed of you or something. It's none of those things. Not at all."

Patrick exhales through his nose. "Please explain it to me, then."

I collect my thoughts. It's important I get this right because the idea of Patrick hurting over this in ways he shouldn't is unbearable to me. I speak quickly, like I'm stemming the bleeding from a wound I've inadvertently ripped open. "Okay, when you lived here, I kind of felt like everyone knew me as Patrick's girlfriend, half of *PatrickandSiena*. Which, of course, I'm proud to be your girlfriend. But we'd been together so long I started to feel like people didn't even think of me without thinking of you. Like I had no identity of my own."

I swallow. In the past months, I'd let those memories drift out of sight. I'd started feeling like half of a person instead of half of a partnership.

"When you left," I continue, "I sort of saw it as an opportunity. I wanted people to see *me*. I made all these new friends, and I needed them to know me before they knew us," I finish, desperate and pained and proud to have said it.

His anger deflating, Patrick looks only hurt. I can read it in his eyes. It's the longest pause until he speaks. "I can understand that . . ." His voice sounds hesitant, like he's picking his path over rocky ground.

I hear the unfinished part of his sentence. "But what?" I prompt him. "You can tell me. Please, I want to work through this."

"But . . ." he repeats slowly. "I guess it still stings. I talk about you endlessly to my friends, and . . . I like being part of *PatrickandSiena*."

I nod, listening to him seriously. With effort, I settle the fear I'm beginning to feel. This conversation could become a wedge pushing in between us—if we let it. "I think we're just different when it comes to this," I say gently. "It doesn't have to be a bad thing, though. We just have to make sure both our different needs are met."

Patrick sets his drink down, silent.

Tentatively, I take his hand. "I brought you here because I *do* want my friends to know you," I say earnestly. His grip is loose on mine, but he's holding on.

When I squeeze his hand, he squeezes back. The distance in his eyes is fading, and with inexpressible relief I feel the end of this fight coming nearer, like a rest stop on the long drives my family would make out to LA or Las Vegas.

Patrick looks out into the game room, where everyone's hanging out, oblivious to us. "You're right," he says with somber resolve. "I don't know if I fit in here. But I want to try."

"Thank you." The words rush out of me.

He smiles stiffly. Lacing my fingers in his—saying *I'm*

here with you—I lead him back to the party. This time, I'm determined to make more of an effort to let them know him. To let him know them. While I want to be independent, I don't want Patrick to feel unloved.

It's a balance. With long distance, I've gotten used to balance. How much time I should spend with my friends or spend on my phone. How much to live my life between visits or live my life waiting for them. How much to miss someone or to enjoy what I have every day. I've gotten comfortable finding my footing on each uncertain path.

This is just one more to walk. Patrick and I will navigate it like we have the rest.

Together.

Forty-Five

WHEN I WAKE UP, I don't move. Because for the first time, I'm waking up in Patrick's arms.

I nuzzle closer while he dozes, enjoying the way my sheets wrap me in his scent. Sunlight warms the room. It's perfect.

After our conversation last night, the party improved. I could see Patrick honestly working to get to know everyone, to join in, to have fun. Still, the strain never quite disappeared. It was unreasonable for me to expect it would. I shouldn't push for him to fit in with these people the first time he's ever hung out with them. Sure, he knew them vaguely last year, but I see them nearly every day. We weren't going to have the same experience. Which is okay. What's more, he doesn't *have* to connect with my friends the way I do. It's okay for us to have separate groups and distinct social lives. It just matters we're making the effort.

"Hey," Patrick says softly, his voice rough with sleep.

I shift to look up into his eyes. Even bleary from waking

up, they're bright, lit with the same contentment I'm feeling. "Hi," I say.

He stares, and I let myself enjoy the love in his expression. It's kind of incredible, everything it took to get us here. From managing months and months without each other to nights like last night, where we were stressed and sad, and yet still we've ended up right here, right now.

"Thinking about something?" Patrick asks.

I trace a line on his bare chest. "Just," I say, "Love Despite Reasons."

He smiles, then presses a kiss to my hair. "Love Despite Reasons," he repeats.

We let the rightness of those words sit for a few lazy seconds until I speak up. "What did you want to do today?"

"Hmm," Patrick says seriously. I make a game of guessing what he'll say—I remember his immediate interest when Taylor mentioned the newish independent bookstore near school. "How long do you think we could get away with staying in bed?" he asks instead.

I laugh. "Depends how much awkwardness you're prepared for when we emerge to my entire family eating breakfast ten feet from here."

"Fair," he replies. He falls silent, his eyes leaving me while he thinks.

I know what's making the question difficult. Neither of us wants to repeat last night. We need something stabilizing, something easy and authentic. Something us. While I'm pondering the options, I hear my phone buzz, rattling on the nightstand. I roll over, finding a message on my group chat with Reed and Lacey. Lacey's wondering if anyone wants to go with her to get coffee.

Normally, I would volunteer in a heartbeat. Instead I pause, fingers hovering over the screen. Today is for Patrick, no matter how glad I am I have new friends who know me for me. Decisively, I type out my reply.

Can't. Plans with Patrick.

I hit send. When I'm returning my phone to my night-stand, it vibrates once more in my hand. I glance down to find Patrick's name on the screen. For a second, I don't even recognize the oddity here—I'm used to waking up to texts from Patrick. Then the humor of it steals over me. I unlock my screen to read the message he's sent from right next to me.

Let's Do Rex's.

I smile, the idea fitting perfectly into the plan-shaped space I'd been searching to fill. It's exactly what we need. Reliable, familiar, pressure-free. I face Patrick, finding him lying in bed, holding his phone coyly on his chest.

I type out my reply while he watches.

It's a date.

Forty-Six

IT TAKES ONE MUFFIN, too much coffee too quickly, and ten minutes for me to realize this was a mistake.

Rex's feels wrong. Nothing is different—we're at our regular table, the papers in the newsstands are folded and old books on the bookshelves are leaning the way I remember, and they have the same radio station on they were playing in summer. Still, something, somehow isn't right.

I remember how in the weeks leading up to Patrick moving, Rex's had started to feel like a sign of our stagnant relationship, an espresso-scented existential cage. This isn't that. Ever since Thanksgiving, Rex's has gained a rosy glow from my memories here with Patrick. It was where I *didn't* break up with him, twice. It was where we said we would throw ourselves into the lives in front of us while staying together. I'd been excited to return here with him.

Now it's like the reality doesn't match up to my daydreaming. Or like this place no longer fits us.

Patrick sits across from me, idly stirring his drink, staring out into the room. He has a nervous, expectant look in his eyes, and I'm pretty sure he's searching the room for some ineffable flaw, some hidden explanation for why we're having such an empty time. With every passing second, I'm hunting for scraps of something to say, a conversation to start, anything. I find nothing—nothing except one persistent fear. I've never not had something to say to Patrick. I've never spent this long with him in person since he moved, either.

What if it's no coincidence? What if this stilted silence isn't just the random misalignment of this particular plan? We worked when we were having brunch with Joe or distracted by my improv match and Reed's get-together, but not now. What if being together for seventy-two hours has changed us back into people who no longer connect?

No. I refuse to believe it. Just because we've outgrown Rex's doesn't mean we've outgrown each other. If we've changed so much we no longer fit here, we've still changed for the better.

Patrick faces me again with a smile like room-temperature milk. The widening conversation-less quiet is physically uncomfortable, prickling in the joints of my fingers and my knees wedged under the table. Desperately, I say literally the only thing I can think of.

"I almost broke up with you right here."

Patrick blinks, understandably caught off guard by my sudden confession.

Instantly, I feel worse. I want to shrivel up in my seat. *Why couldn't I have just commented on the weather?*

"At Thanksgiving?" Patrick asks. His lips twitch with real amusement, not the feigned version I just saw. He . . . doesn't seem surprised.

Incredulity steals over me. "Wait. Did you *know*?"

Patrick pops a piece of scone into his mouth. I realize he's drawing out the moment, *enjoying this* for some reason. "I was really glad you didn't," he says once he's swallowed.

I wait to feel guilty for how poorly I hid my intentions. Instead, seeing the knowing, even satisfied expression on Patrick's face, I'm unable to keep myself from laughing. "Why didn't you ever say anything?"

"Why didn't you go through with it?" he counters.

I slouch forward, elbows on the table, reliving the memory. The details hold the same magic they did then. Silent streetlights, wet clothes on skin. "I pretty much knew I wouldn't when you kissed me after we went in the pool," I admit. In Patrick's expression, some of the knowing softens out, like he's recalling what I am. "But the first time I planned on breaking up with you was the day you told me you were moving," I go on.

Patrick's eyes flit wide. *This*, I know instantly, is new information. He pauses—then, decisively, even fiercely, reaches for my hand resting on the table.

I grasp his fingers, just a little nervous. I didn't say it to upset him. To me, those almost-breakups feel inconceivably distant in the past, far from whom we've become. It's just a conversation, no longer a possibility.

"I had no idea." Patrick stares at the foam collapsing on

his cappuccino. His eyes snap up like he's realized something. "Siena," he says, his voice sharpening slightly. "I literally asked you if you wanted to break up. I practically handed it right to you."

I smile, remembering he's right. "You did," I say. "But you said you were leaving, and it gave me second thoughts. I just . . . kind of figured we'd fizzle out over long distance."

His hand in mine, Patrick raises an eyebrow. "And?"

I know my answer immediately. It makes my heart swell and my smile widen. Imagining me right here, having the doubts I had, is nearly funny to me now. It feels like a different world. A different life.

"We didn't fizzle out," I reply.

Patrick's eyes warm with fondness. "No," he agrees. Something wry flickers over the corners of his mouth. "So you're saying I have long distance to thank for still having you?"

"Yes and no," I reply, matching his playfulness. "You have yourself to thank."

This time, when quiet settles over us, it's comfortable. We're left with shared smiles. Then Patrick's gaze shifts from me into the crowded café. He frowns. "Maybe that's why it feels wrong here," he muses. "I didn't know how often I almost got dumped here." When his expression goes grave, I'm not completely certain whether he's joking. "We should go before you start having doubts again."

I laugh, not letting go of his hand. "We should," I say. "Not because I might have doubts. But because this . . . isn't us," I say. Putting words to the idea feels like lifting it from my shoulders, placing it between us where we can contend with it together. "Not anymore. I think . . ." I trail off, ideas forming in my head. "I think maybe instead of bringing each other into our respective worlds, or trying to return to our old one, we need to go and create a new one. Just us."

Patrick's eyes focus on mine. Excited inquisitiveness lights his expression. "What did you have in mind?"

In reply, I step out from the table. Patrick follows me wordlessly. While this place, these very seats, have been checkered and crisscrossed with miscommunications, right now, there's no need for either of us to speak. I know exactly what we're going to do, and I know he's with me.

Forty-Seven

CONVINCING MY PARENTS WASN'T hard. In the kitchen, I presented the points I had rehearsed with Patrick on our way home from the café. We're both eighteen. We're both licensed drivers. It's only three hours away. We'll only be gone one night.

They listened patiently, then relented easily. I couldn't help suspecting the really persuasive thing was none of my points, but the fact I would be going with Patrick—the most trustworthy guy imaginable. After the way he handled the sprain incident, I know my parents feel safe in the knowledge he'll be looking out for me. It's ironic. I was annoyed when he immediately told my parents I'd gotten hurt. Now it's what's earned us this privilege.

I don't blame them for the way Patrick's presence reassures them. I feel safe with him, too.

We get underway fast, the idea changing suddenly into something we're really doing. My dad gives me a speech on camping rules that lasts three times longer than his sex talk, and we dig out the old camping gear that hasn't been used in at least five years from the storage box in the garage. The cloth is dusty, the battery in the lantern only working due to some miracle. We pack everything into the trunk of my mom's car, with even Robbie helping to heft sleeping bags. Then we're off.

The drive is gorgeous, the road cutting down the naked landscape like only the highway knows where it's going. Sitting in the passenger seat while Patrick thumbs the wheel to the music, I love the thrill running through me. We're embarking on something new for us both. Our first trip without parents, without classmates or chaperones. Just us. There's no pressure, no imbalance of who's the outsider and who isn't. We're navigating our own new corner of the universe, content just to be with each other.

Patrick darts me glances as he drives, grinning whenever our eyes meet. We sing to our favorite songs, loud and horribly off-key. When we're not singing, we talk, or we take in the shifting scenery we're moving through. First, we pass through desert. It's not flat stretches of nothingness—not in spring. The desert in spring is vibrant, with flowers unfurling in the trees, and patches of earth more green than beige. Everywhere is the recognizable saguaro cactus, found only in this small slice of the world. Their geometric arms point calmly skyward, each one up to hundreds of years old.

When we start the climb into Flagstaff, we leave the

desert below, winding our way into pine forests and mountains. The colors change to browns and greens. In places, we even see snow. In our final hour, we return to the desert, the greenery ceding once more into sand.

What never changes is how *huge* everything is. The expanses of open land, the towering trees, the sloping forms of the mountains—the *sky*, soaring over us. It's the sort of sky everything expands into—hopes, possibilities, dreams. The drive feels out of the reach of the rest of the world, Patrick and me in our own perfect in-between.

Once we've reached our destination, it takes us time to get through the line of cars and ensure we have a camping spot for the night. With the logistics figured out, we park and get out. Dust coats the sides of the car, with beige in every crevice of the tires. It's noticeably dry outside, the heat brittle on my skin. When I close the passenger-side door, I'm invigorated, the feeling of standing after so much sitting a luxurious relief.

Patrick says what I'm thinking immediately. "Bathroom first?"

I nod. We take the necessary couple minutes—very necessary, given the three hours we spent in the car—then follow the signs. It doesn't take long before the sight opens up in front of us.

The Grand Canyon. Its vastness is incomprehensible in one glance. I stare past the small gnarled trees, tracing with my eyes the canyon sloping down to the basin in endless rolling contours. I'd thought our drive was magnificent, but those shifting landscapes were nothing next to this enormity.

Patrick and I walk the Trail of Time, which isn't much of a hiking trail. Instead, it's paved, the pathway running along one side of the canyon with sweeping views. Plaques line the walk, taking us through the Grand Canyon's geological history. Each step represents a million years in its development, meant to help visitors comprehend time on the earth's impossible scale.

I've taken this walk before. We both have, on field trips in grade school and family vacations. I've seen the Grand Canyon half a dozen times. But when we walk to the edge to look out over the view, the afternoon light shining on the purple and orange and red in the rocks, I'm hit with how different right now is.

Patrick's arm encircles my waist. I'm conscious of how I've stood in this exact spot, felt the desert wind laze lightly up from the rock faces to sweep my hair from my forehead. Still, it's new somehow. I'm older, with Patrick standing by my side, sharing our growing love and trust. It's marvelous how something so familiar can remain so exciting, so unexpected. So unlike anything else I've ever seen.

I think of the path we took to this remarkable point, literally and figuratively. We walked through time together, watching lifetimes build on lifetimes, forming new foundations, layers, colors while the years continued on. With each step forward, I know everything will keep changing.

I notice the Colorado River, the thin band of blue in the

heart of the basin. Once, it flowed on flat ground. The river didn't shape this breathtaking place over night. It worked day by day until something miraculous was created in the middle of the desert.

I lean into Patrick, and we gaze out to the horizon together.

Forty-Eight

WE FUMBLE TO PITCH our tent, poles poking every which way in our hapless efforts. Patrick has some success stomping the spikes into the dirt the way my dad explained. But then we have no idea which extendable rod goes where. The best we do is some sort of three-sided structure before finally, thankfully, one of our neighbors kindly takes pity on us.

The camper, an outdoorsy-looking twentysomething, promptly undoes every single part of our handiwork. Patrick and I can't contain ourselves. Exchanging one embarrassed glance, we're suddenly laughing until our sides hurt. Our good-natured rescuer has the poles and the canvas up in minutes.

Inside, Patrick and I eat the food we packed, enjoying the half seclusion of our gray polyester walls amid the soft sounds of nature and other campers outside. When the sun sets, we sit outside, heads tilted up despite our necks hurting. We can see every star in the sky. They're not just individual pinpricks on flat black. This far from the city, they sparkle over the night in swaths of glitter.

The temperature drops, and we return to our tent, zipping ourselves in. With the distant sounds of other campers out for spring break drifting over to us in the clear night, we begin getting ready for bed.

There's just enough room to stand in the small tent. I pull off my tank top to remove my bra. My back is to Patrick, but when I hear him stop moving, I know he's looking.

Smiling softly, I unhook the clasp and let my bra drop to the floor of the tent. I don't feel cold, even though I should, with only the thin tent protecting us from the desert night. Here, now, temperature isn't the only kind of heat to be found.

I wait until I feel Patrick's hands brush my skin, then wrap around me, his fingers splaying on my stomach. Expectation collides with the thrill of reality in me—the fact that I knew this was probably going to happen makes each second of it happening no less exciting.

Twisting to kiss him, I lean until my back presses against his chest. The night softens, cool enough to raise goose bumps on my arms as I strip off my leggings. The sound of our breath fills the tent, our heartbeats echoing through the canyon not far from here.

We don't speak, because we don't have to. There's something special in having sex for the second time. The first time is an event—the second time is a promise. It says, *We do this now*. I find it hard to remember I once wanted fewer promises with Patrick. Now there's nothing I want more.

When we move together, I feel our years of history and the changes that come with them pulling us ever closer, reminding me of everything we've shared and everything we still will.

Forty-Nine

SUNRISE PAINTS THE CANYON pink. We got up early enough to pack our gear in the predawn light, moving quietly to not wake the people whose tents we passed while we carried our stuff to the car. It had its own magic, Patrick's and my morning conversation consisting only of the occasional whispered exchange as we worked next to each other. With everything packed up, we found our way down a trail for a better view of daybreak.

Sitting side by side on the ground, I rest my head on his shoulder, grateful for this getaway and wishing it didn't have to end. It was exactly what we needed. Hoping to memorize every detail, I study the way the rosy light finds new crevices and draws new shadows on the rolling rocks.

We stay silent until Patrick elbows me gently. "See why I love Arizona yet?" he asks.

Smiling, I glance up into his satisfied expression. "I *guess* so," I say, with more sarcasm than I feel.

Honestly, there's deeper truth in his remark than I think

he knows. Coming here with him has reminded me there's always more to discover about things I already found familiar. If I've learned one thing this year, it's that you can't totally know a person or a place. And there's something wonderful about that.

Patrick stares out over the canyon, looking content.

"I'm surprised you didn't apply to any colleges here," I go on. I say it earnestly, with no pressure or hinting inquisitiveness. While my college decision was made the day I got into UCSB, Patrick's remains open. So far he's gotten into Stanford, UCLA, and University of Michigan, but not every school has released decisions yet.

The other couples I know are also dealing with this conversation right now. Some are splitting up, some are committing to trying out long distance, some are lucky enough to have gotten into dream schools near each other. The one rule everyone agrees on is not to choose a college for a significant other.

Which is why I've patiently kept myself from prying into Patrick's decision-making process. It's the least I owe him, what with my own choice confirmed. I'm guiltily conscious of the position in which I've put Patrick—it's not my fault, but because he knows where I'm going, the decision has landed on him to either join me or not. If he goes to UCLA, we'll be two hours apart. If he goes to Stanford, or farther, we won't. Knowing him, it's pressure I'm certain he feels, pressure I don't want to worsen.

Even if we do end up far from each other next year,

I've contented myself that it'll just mean four more years like this one. The possibility doesn't frighten me, honestly. While love might grow from certain circumstances—points in your life, places, or shared experiences—it's not just the composite of them. When it's real, it's out of the reach of those things, something you hold on to even while they shift.

With Patrick, it's real.

"I don't need to apply to schools in Arizona to come back," he says, his voice light with confidence. "It'll always be my home."

"Mine too."

He hugs me tighter. The shadows are shrinking on the colored canyon walls, sunlight setting the stone on fire with vibrant hues.

"I did make my decision, though," he says, hesitancy hiding in his voice. "About college."

I straighten up, shifting on the ground to face him more fully. "When?" I go over Patrick's and my college-related conversations in my head, wondering if I missed something. "I thought you needed to visit some campuses first. What changed?" I ask. I'm not mad, just intensely curious.

"Um." Patrick idly picks up a small rock next to his shoe. His gaze moves from the yawning canyon in front of us to me. "The day before I flew out here, I heard from PLME. I got in," he says. "I don't need to visit campuses to know med school is what I want."

My eyes widen. "Why didn't you tell me you got in?" I'm

starting to feel like I misread the undercurrent in his voice. Maybe it wasn't hesitancy. Maybe it was excitement.

While this settles onto me, I realize I . . . don't share his excitement. It's not Brown, not the distance. It's medical school this early. I'd wondered if maybe getting into other colleges would help him consider other options, keep his mind open. Instead, he's fixated on PLME. I want to cross into the rest of our lives with him—but I don't want a combination of parental pressure and a stubborn, outdated sense of self pushing him.

"I know how you feel about med school," he says delicately, his gaze dropping to the small stone. "I wanted to make sure I knew what I was going to do before I brought it up again."

"So . . ." I search for sense in what he's telling me. "It's only been a couple days and you know for sure?"

"I do," he replies, sounding steady. "It'll mean more long distance. Of course, I understand if—"

I wave off the question before he can finish it. "I don't care about long distance. Don't you think it's possible you're making this commitment too early? Why not just go to Brown, then apply to med school when you're done? Give yourself a chance to try more things?"

Patrick pulls farther from me. When he curls his fingers, pressing the rock into his palm, his eyes flash. I'm surprised by the anger in them. "Like what, Siena?" he snaps. "*Improv?*"

The sharpness he puts on the word stuns me. I feel my

cheeks color. My momentary hurt catching fire, I'm suddenly pissed. "Yeah. Like improv," I reply hotly. "What's so wrong with it? What's wrong with putting yourself out there to try something new? Like we've been doing since you moved. We're so young—I don't see why you need to decide now what the rest of your life will look like."

Patrick laughs, the sound harsh and too dark for the sunlight now shining on his face. It's a warning without a message, something ugly on the horizon I can't yet make out.

"You know, maybe you *should* have kissed Reed. Otherwise, how do you know you don't want to?" Mocking rings in Patrick's question. "It's what you're saying, right? You can't commit to anything unless you've tried all the alternatives."

Despite the desert sun having reached me, I feel my blood freeze with cold fury. It's there in his voice, the rare sneering quality I've nearly never heard from him. I hate how he's treating me like a debate opponent, with cutting deliberateness in his rhetorical devices. I'm not having it.

"I didn't *want* to kiss Reed. I *want* to be with you," I spit out each syllable. "But sometimes I feel like you only want to be with me because it's part of your plan. Just like med school. You just stick to things instead of ever wondering if you really want them."

Pain joins with the exasperation in Patrick's features. He's losing his grip on his cool debating posture, I note, expecting to feel grimly satisfied. Instead, it only makes me sadder.

"Haven't I shown you that's not true?" he protests. "I've tried new things. I've made new friends. I've embraced Young Dems instead of Model UN. I live in an entirely new city. I hike now, for fuck's sake."

"Those things don't hurt anyone!" I raise my voice recklessly.

Patrick's anger fades for a moment, overshadowed by confusion. "What's that supposed to mean?"

I flex my fingers compulsively, feeling wound up. I'm charging headlong into insecurities I hardly ever voice even in the quietest parts of my mind. Still, I don't stop. Something pulls me forward. "You didn't *quit* Model UN. You had to replace it. You didn't move on your own. I'm just saying if you *did* want to break up with me, you would never do it. Just like you'd never disappoint your mom and walk away from med school. You're too nice."

The moment the words leave my mouth, some warped sense of remorse falls over me. This was *not* the way to have this conversation. My final sentence is suddenly everywhere, in every grain of dust under us, in the prickly heat of the new morning. I shouldn't have been accusatory, but he does need to hear it.

Patrick's jaw clenches, his expression hard. He's enraged.

Good, I think. He shouldn't shy away from unpleasant feelings.

"You're one to talk," he says. His voice is steel. "You wanted to break up with me but couldn't go through with it out of pity."

Sweat springs to my palms. "It wasn't pity."

His glare says he doesn't believe me. "Now that we're talking about it, I'm curious why you did want to break up with me before I told you I was moving. There had to be some problem. Some reason you were unhappy."

I recognize the impulse driving him. He's digging into the hurt, doubling down on the fight. If he thinks I'll retreat, though, I won't. While I'm not enjoying this argument, I think it's one we need to have. I won't end it just because it's ruined the view.

"I needed the chance to grow and change, and I felt like you were holding me back," I say honestly. Reaching these confessions is like looking over the edge of the canyon. It's scary, but not in a bad way. "I wanted to do new things, and whenever I suggested them to you, you refused. You just wanted to go to Rex's every Saturday, wanted our lives to stay the same. But long distance changed everything."

Patrick's expression flickers like a candle buffeted by the breeze. "You never told me that," he says, softer. "You were going to break up with me without even telling me why you were unhappy?"

"I didn't break up with you, though, did I? But Patrick..." Everything has ebbed out of my voice. Carrying this forward feels like dragging something up a cliffside. I just have to keep going. "When you came for Thanksgiving, I asked you about going to Reed's party, and you said no without even thinking. You didn't want what I wanted. You didn't *want* to want what I wanted."

Patrick drops the rock he's holding. It rolls haphazardly off the path, down the incline, and out of sight.

"You didn't tell me it was important to you," he finally says. "If you had, of course I would have gone. Haven't I proven I'll do anything you ask of me?"

I reach for his hand. "You have. And we didn't break up," I remind him. "Long distance made us stronger. It ended up being the chance we needed to solve our problems. The freedom *I* needed to figure out my life with our relationship in it."

"You didn't need to wait for long distance to *solve our problems*," Patrick replies. "Everything you're saying now, you could've said to me over the summer."

I open my mouth, then close it. I'm not exactly skeptical of what Patrick's saying, but not convinced, either. This summer, I remember *not* feeling free to voice any of this. While it's easy for him to assure me in hindsight how he would have handled something, he *has* changed over the past year. He's not the same person I would have had this conversation with last summer. I'm not the same person, either.

Patrick looks out over the canyon. The sun is up now, its light shining on what was minutes ago shadows, and yet I feel utterly in the dark. "Sunrise is over," Patrick says hollowly. "We should go."

"Yeah. We should." My voice matches his. We're exhausted. The fight has ripped out every spark of the energy we woke up with. I stand, swiping dust from my shorts. The fight isn't over, but I have nothing left to say. I stand by my feelings, by everything that got us from there to here. Even so, I understand it would be hard to hear. I owe him time to think.

We walk back to the car together, hurting and a little heartbroken, knowing the magic of this place is gone.

Fifty

WHILE I DRIVE, PATRICK just stares out the passenger-side window. His body is turned from me. The incredible views outside—the flat reaches of the desert, the sand scattered with flowering plants and the striking cacti—hold none of the wonder they did when we drove in. Instead, they're prying reminders of what we can't enjoy with our words hanging over us.

I focus on the road, not wanting to reopen the fight while I'm driving. Still, I steal glances at Patrick whenever I'm stopped, wondering desperately what he's thinking. It'll be fine, I reassure myself. We're stronger for having shared our insecurities and worked out our conflicts in Austin. It'll be no different now.

When I pull up to the curb in front of my place, Patrick doesn't get out.

He faces me, pale. I have my hand on the handle of my door, eager to escape the confines of the car, my legs stiff and my eyes exhausted from the drive. It was the longest I've ever done behind the wheel.

None of those things matter when I see the misery in Patrick's expression. I lower my hand, feeling dread pool darkly in my stomach. He's never looked this unhappy. Not even when he told me he was moving.

"I think . . ." he starts. His gaze drops to the seat, a strange vacancy in his expression, like staying in the moment is a struggle. He inhales, then exhales. I watch him with mounting worry. "I think we should break up," he says.

I don't react.

I can't. Something happens to my sense of each passing second, the world outside of us warping into indecipherable, meaningless shapes. I'm suddenly very focused on my breathing, on the hollow hum of the silence now stretching in the car. It's not possible I heard him right. I feel like I'm in a dream—the ones I used to have early in our relationship, when I wasn't sure how long we would last. How could this happen *now*? Three years in and in love.

"I know it's not the *nice* thing to do," he continues, his eyes flashing on the word. The next second, remorse swallows his flicker of resentment. "But I can't be with you." His throat wells, and he clears it, the noise harsh and pained. "I can't be with someone who hides unhappiness until the right circumstances luckily come up to fix it. We don't fit together, Siena. Maybe we haven't for a while."

The reality of what's happening finally hits me. Emotions pour over me. Panic, fear, heartache. I feel them in different places, one numbing the tips of my fingers, one clutching my chest with invisible claws, one writhing nauseatingly in my stomach. "That's not true," I protest. I've never heard my voice like this. Thin, high-pitched with pleading. I force myself to continue, hasty and desperate. "We fit together. We had a fight. It was a bad one, but we still love each other." I feel like I'm speaking fundamental truths, which makes it disturbing how unconvinced he seems by them.

"I thought so," he says. "But now . . . I think the only thing holding us together was the fact that our relationship existed over hundreds of miles of distance. We could pretend we were together when really, we kind of weren't."

His words hurt immediately. I feel like I'm still in the canyon, on some trail, with the rocks and dirt eroding without warning under me. I'm sliding, stinging and afraid, with no idea where I'll land. Tears leap into my vision, burning my eyes. I blink, pushing them away, and find anger replacing them. "I can't believe you would throw this away. I guess you *don't* love me," I say. "Not the way I thought."

Patrick flinches, just like I intended. I can tell he wants to protest, to say he loves me.

It's an old habit, I realize with horrible clarity. Nothing more. Patrick bites back the reassurance, resignation closing up his expression.

"It's better this way," he says instead. "For both of us. You can finally do everything I was holding you back from."

We've reached the moment I knew, consciously or unconsciously, was coming. The moment I've been fighting since this conversation started. There's impassable finality in Patrick's voice. Something within me gives in, collapsing under the weight of what's happening right now. Where I felt sadness, fury, spite, fear—now there's only helplessness. A tear trickles down my cheek, and I wipe it furiously.

Patrick's gaze follows my motion, his own eyes watering.

"I'll get my things and go stay with Joe until my flight home," he chokes out. He's still struggling to sound composed, like he's insisting on not crumbling even though he already is.

I don't miss his offhand word choice, the way he refers to Austin. He's never called his new city home.

"Whatever you want," I say. The syllables sound unreal. Distant. I'm still in shock, emptied out by the likes of some emotional ice-cream scooper. I fling reassurances into the open space. *We'll talk about this in the coming days. Couples break up and get back together all the time.*

Patrick nods. He grabs his backpack from under the dash, then pauses with his hand on the door. "By the way," he begins, his voice softer, some of his tearfulness gone. "I want to go to med school because I like helping people. Like how I took care of you when you sprained your wrist." He hasn't met my eyes. Now he does. "You just didn't notice."

I think back to our hike. Every detail of the morning returns to me, reforming into new patterns. The way Patrick patiently bandaged my wrist, kept his calm while he tended to me, knew exactly what to do. Hot guilt knifes into me. I should have seen his passion, just like he should have seen how much I wanted things to change over the summer.

Maybe he's right. Maybe we *don't* belong together.

"I guess we both made the mistake of deciding who each

other was," Patrick continues. Something seems to disappear out of him, drifting off into the day. "It doesn't matter now," he says.

He opens his door without waiting for me to reply. I stare after him for a moment, then straighten my fingers, stiff from the steering wheel. With cold comfort, I remember there are logistics to get through. I have to let him into my apartment, help him get his things, make sure he gets to Joe's. I grasp onto these small concrete realities. I can focus on pushing myself from each to the next.

I swing open my door and speed my steps to catch up with Patrick one last time.

Fifty-One

I STAY IN THE kitchen, holding in my sobs. The apartment is crushingly silent, the rustles and other small sounds of Patrick's every movement from Robbie's bedroom painfully clear in the stillness. Thankfully, my family isn't here. Contemplating the explanations I'll have to give them is just not something I'm ready for right now.

Instead, I focus on the grain of the wooden kitchen table where I'm sitting. Minute by minute.

I know Patrick won't take long to pack since he'd only just gotten here. The realization is its own harsh reminder—it hurts to remember how yesterday, only yesterday, we woke up looking forward to a whole week together for the first time in months. With the midday sun heating the room, I sit, giving him space and needing space myself. It's not enough to stop me from overhearing his voice from down the hall. "Hey, Joe? . . . Yeah, we just got back. Um. I have a favor to ask, man." He sounds strained, unlike himself.

I walk out to the living room. I don't want to hear more.

Patrick returns a couple minutes later, suitcase in hand,

his eyes tinged the slightest shade of pink. My gaze falls from him quickly, straying elsewhere. Seeing the most familiar face in the world to me outside my family is doing no favors for my emotional state.

"You have a place to stay?" I don't know how I force out the question.

He nods. "I'll see y—" He cuts himself off, the painfully vacant look I saw in the car coming over him once more. It's ironic how even now we're thinking the same thing. No, we won't be seeing each other. He'll return to Austin and be out of my life. For good.

"Right," I muster. "Well, bye, Patrick."

"Bye," he replies. He rushes to the door, leaving so fast I know it's because he's holding back his own sobs.

When the door shuts, I feel it echo in my heart. The tears I've been fighting don't come, though. It's like I'm emotionally overloaded, facing feelings huge enough I'm simply unable to recognize them. I walk mechanically down the hall, into my room, where I calmly collect the pictures of Patrick I have on display. The one on my dresser, the postcards he's sent me. I place them in a drawer, not ready to throw them out even though I know I'll have to.

I sit down on my bed, waiting for the pain to crash over me. Immobilize me. Rip me apart. Still, the waves don't come. I just feel numb.

When I hear the front door open, everything in me focuses on the sound. For the cruelest second, I think it's Patrick, coming back to tell me he was wrong. He doesn't want to break up.

Of course, it's not him. Robbie's and my mom's voices

echo down the hall. They're in the kitchen—I hear cabinets opening, the thud of the fridge door. *Putting away groceries,* my mind dully informs me.

I know I can't avoid the other painful conversations I have in store. I'll have to explain. Admit. Relive. There's no point in putting it off.

Slowly, I get up, and suddenly I feel sick. Feverish, nauseated, like the emotions I can't let in have burrowed into my body, demanding to be felt in some way. I put one foot in front of the other, moving in a daze out of my room, into the hall.

When I reach the living room, my mom looks up from the brown Trader Joe's bags on the counter. "Hey," she says brightly. "How was your trip?"

I can't reply. This ill feeling and the horrible weight of what I have to say paralyze me.

Mom notices. Frowning, she glances past me. "Where's Patrick?" she asks. From her voice, still light and normal, I know she doesn't really get it yet. She thinks the question is idle, easy, with some simple reply like *He's in the bathroom.* Her eyes return to me with closer scrutiny when I hesitate.

Robbie puts down the paper towels he's holding. His unbothered expression is fading into one a little more wary. Even he knows something is wrong.

"We broke up," I say.

It is, somehow, what releases everything. Like heartbreak was hiding just past a door with a three-word key. My shoulders shake. My chest catches. Finally, sobs tear through me.

Fifty-Two

FOR TWO DAYS, I barely leave my room. I don't text Patrick—I feel betrayed, broken. He doesn't text me, either. Nevertheless, I repeatedly flick my thumb to light up my phone screen to check. Every time I do reminds me of how he's no longer my background. Every time I look at our messages reminds me I no longer have the heart emoji next to his name.

He's still in Phoenix, I know. I could text him. I mean, I *could* walk over to Joe's. Still, I've never felt farther from him in my life.

I spend the days watching YouTube videos on bedroom makeovers, then rearranging my furniture, occupying myself with the simple, meaningless changes. I eat my meals at my desk, not ready to make casual conversation with my family. I know they're upset, too. They miss Patrick.

What's more, they don't believe this is truly over. It's the real reason I can't endure family dinners or even morning coffee. I know if I venture out, I'll have to face the papercut edges of gentle questions, of *why* and *who* and *how*. I just don't have the heart to walk them through what went wrong in Patrick's and my relationship. Nor can I bear to look at our breakup myself yet, either. My mom will just tell me to fix it. She'll want to nudge, bend, push things into the shape they once had. But I know it can't be fixed. And maybe it shouldn't. We probably are better off for breaking up.

It still hurts enough I can't contemplate leaving the house, though.

My room just feels safer somehow. Sheltered. The rest of the world is where I was with Patrick. Walking with him, going to school with him, or in recent months, living with the quiet knowledge of the invisible tethers tying us. Which means now the outside world is where I'm conspicuously *not* with him. It offers endless reminders of what's different. Whereas my room is just my room.

On Thursday, I have big plans to stay in bed until noon. Another side effect of the breakup—I've never slept this much my life. But my lying in bed is interrupted by Robbie barging through my door when I'm just drifting back to sleep in the morning light.

I clumsily check the time on my phone. It's 9:03 a.m. I groan. "What the hell?" I ask. Rolling over, I pull my comforter up, covering my face. "Get out."

Robbie ignores me. He yanks the covers down, then promptly sits on my legs.

"Robbie!" His weight is enough to make me kick and sit up, pulling my feet under me.

"You need to go outside today," Robbie declares.

I rub my eyes, not certain I've heard him right. Underneath my irritation, I feel stealing in the familiar dull pain I've learned to live with this week, like it does whenever I wake up. I push it down, focusing on my brother. He smells bad. He's wearing nylon shorts and one of his beloved Under Armour shirts, which is tighter-fitted than his sister wants to see. It's obvious he just worked out, and now his sweaty butt is sitting on my bed.

I glare, hopefully marshaling my sleepy eyes into some semblance of defiance. "Did Mom send you in here?" I fire back. This is classic Mom. She's been hovering for days, passing back and forth in front of my door when she's home from work. Sending in Robbie is just her newest ploy, and not her best one.

"Of course Mom sent me," Robbie replies, bouncing lightly where he's seated on my mattress. "But she's not wrong. For once."

I roll my eyes, not amused. "Well, tell her you tried. I'm not ready yet."

Robbie doesn't budge. "Nah. You're going out today," he says. "It's the only way to *get* ready. I know it sucks about Patrick." I frown, waiting for his flippancy to piss me off further. Strangely, it doesn't. While *sucks* is quite the understatement, it's not exactly wrong, and frankly, millions of more poetic words couldn't really capture how shitty I feel. Robbie goes on. "Nothing in here is going to make you feel better. Trust me. I'm experienced with breakups, since I've had *five* different girlfriends." He doesn't hide the pride in his voice, which makes him sound like he's thirteen. "You, on the other hand, have only had the one boyfriend," he concludes.

"Let me get this straight," I say flatly, eyebrows raised. "You're saying you have more experience than me at getting dumped."

Robbie nods. "Yes, exactly," he confirms. He doesn't look offended in the least.

It makes me laugh, just a little. The feeling is weird in a nice way, muscles I haven't used waking up in my chest. It is, I realize, the first time I've laughed in days. While this recognition is nearly enough to tip me over into crying, I don't let myself. "Okay," I challenge him. "What's your expert advice?"

"Easy," Robbie says, leaning back on his hands. "Text every guy you know and ask if they want to hang out. Then hook up with the first one to reply."

This time, when I laugh harder, it has the force to pull me out of the reach of tears entirely. It's wonderful. Like being human in ways I was starting to smother under my sleep-filled mornings. However, it's *horrible* advice, which I kind of love. "Robbie, I'm not doing that," I say.

He shrugs, unfazed. "It's how Erica and I got together."

I honestly don't doubt Robbie means what he said. Still, I'm not sure our situations line up. "I was in a relationship for three years," I say gently. "I'm not trying to jump into a new one."

"Fair. But you're really bumming me out just sitting in here. Like, the vibe is not good." He sounds earnestly concerned. "It's not like you don't have experience being without

Patrick," he points out. "Just do whatever shit you normally do when he's in Austin."

I close my mouth on my unformed reply. Staring at my younger brother, I realize he's made a great point. His expression has lapsed into his usual high-school-boy neutrality, like he has no idea he was just sort of wise.

While I sit speechless, he stands. "Besides," he says, "if you don't get out of the house, you're going to have to see me and Erica making out every time you leave your room to pee. She's coming over in twenty minutes." He walks to the door.

"Hey, Robbie?" I say to his back, stopping him. "You're a cool kid, you know that?"

Robbie's noncommittal expression falls away instantly. He grins his most bro-ish, goofiest grin. "Yeah," he says. "I had a suspicion." He lifts his long arms to smack the door jamb on his way out.

I don't lie back down when he's gone. For the first morning since Monday, I don't want to. The fact Robbie cared enough to threaten me with the sight of him making out with his girlfriend was unexpectedly fortifying. What's more, his recommendation was something I hadn't considered myself. Most of my life since September *hasn't* involved Patrick. It dawns on me suddenly that post-breakup, long distance might just be a blessing.

In one swift motion, I slough the comforter off my bare legs. I get out of bed, then face the window, where our second-story unit overlooks a street of small houses and similar complexes, satellite dishes and power lines. With new strength, I start to remember everything I've forgotten for the past few days. I've built routines, friendships, hobbies that are completely separate from my relationship. Patrick and I don't need to divide up our friends or worry about seeing each other in the school hallway. I can return to my life without Patrick without missing a step.

So I will.

Fifty-Three

I DON'T FOLLOW ROBBIE'S charmingly crass advice down to the letter. But I do text Reed and Lacey. I told them earlier in the week that Patrick and I had broken up, and promptly the next morning I received three pints of ice cream from DoorDash. I would text Joe except I know Patrick's staying with him.

Lacey replies to my invitation first.

Wish I could! Tutoring today, though.

I should've figured. Lacey tutors chem, and her schedule is packed right now with the AP test coming up.

When minutes pass while my phone stays silent, I put it on my desk, flicking on the phone's ringer. Determined for today not to be a sweatpants day, I shower quickly, then stand in front of my dresser. Opening my drawers, I have the strange sense I'm reinventing myself, dressing to be someone new. I haven't been *Single Siena* since I was fifteen. I want to feel confident and look composed, not like some slouchy version of me. But I don't want to seem unlike myself. Shorts? High-waisted jeans? Something button-down or more casual? Preoccupied with my choices, I jump a little when my phone chimes.

I check the screen, finally finding a reply from Reed.

I'm free. What did you have in mind?

For a second, I feel guilty about hanging out with Reed one-on-one. Then I remember I have absolutely no reason to.

Over the next half hour we work out our plan. I had, in fact, nothing in mind. I hadn't thought past being with other people. When Reed decides what I need is a mindless movie, he sends over a showtime, and while I haven't heard of the movie, I don't care.

Twenty minutes later, I'm walking from the parking lot to the theater. It feels good to be outside. I decided on white denim shorts and a black T-shirt, and the sunlight warms my arms in the best way. Enough to feel it, without the uncomfortable prickling of impending sunburn.

I'm grateful to Reed for jumping into this, making the decisions when I didn't have the heart to myself. He's been great—not just because he sent me ice cream. Since the breakup, he's texted me comforting, concise messages, ones I knew came from a friend rather than the guy who tried to date me once.

When I step up to the curb, I find him standing outside

the theater, in front of the row of movie posters, some of them misaligned in their cases. He has his hands in the pockets of his UCSB hoodie.

Reed committed to the school the first day he could, just like me. Seeing the UCSB logo reminds me of the future in front of me—one without Patrick. It's striking enough I nearly slow my steps on the pavement.

It's not entirely sad, though it's not entirely easy, either. While I won't have Patrick, I will have wonderful things in my life. I can go to college with my friend. Move on. For the past few days, I've felt like my vision of the future had faded into gray scale. Now I'm realizing it's just shaded in slightly different colors. I'll be okay.

When Reed catches sight of me walking up, he opens his arms, his face sympathetic. The gesture is very Reed. Grand, even performative, yet I have no doubt the emotion underneath is 100 percent genuine. I walk into his hug, not minding the tears stinging my eyes. Burying my head in his shoulder, I take the much-needed comfort, his smell reminding me of nights hanging out in his game room or sitting next to him in the drama room watching Lacey perform. He says nothing, just holds me until I step back.

Wiping my eyes, I laugh a little. "I'm okay," I say. "I don't look like it, but I am."

He smiles, the expression lighting up his features. Then he squints in what looks like concern, his swoop of black hair shifting with the movement. "You know, you can't be okay until you've had popcorn. Experts have even prescribed gummy bears."

I return his smile, knowing it doesn't capture the happy-sad cyclone in me. "Well, if experts say so," I reply. I follow him into the theater, grateful beyond words I got to know him this year.

We stand in line for concessions. Reed is perfect. He makes me laugh and provides exactly the kind of easy conversation I need, engaging enough to distract me without demanding too much. We get popcorn. We get gummy bears. In the cool dark of the theater, I tear up remembering every time Patrick and I sat in these same cloth seats. How many movies fill three years of dating? Forty? Fifty? Reed notices, politely checking his phone until I wipe my eyes with one of the napkins I grabbed.

This is how sadness works, I'm starting to understand. It doesn't always just press down on you hard enough you stay in bed until noon. It fights dirty. It kicks your heels when you've fixed your eyes forward, elbows you somewhere soft when you've relaxed. Determined not to let it win, I exhale, then breathe in. I'm met with the glorious, *glorious* smell of popcorn. Reed was joking, but he wasn't wrong. It does make me feel kind of better.

The movie turns out to be pretty terrible, but in the best way. Reed and I crack whispered jokes to each other, share eyerolls, and find ourselves rooting hard for the characters despite the dysfunctional plot. When the credits roll, I feel impossibly light. I had . . . *fun*.

We walk out, dropping our popcorn and candy in the garbage. "Hey," I say, my unlikely mood giving my voice strength. "Thanks for doing this. It really helped."

"You don't need to thank me. I had a good time." He holds the door to the hallway open for me. "So I'm thinking of hosting a charades night this weekend. You in?"

"Considering I have absolutely no plans, *hmm*." I pull a conflicted face, feeling up to humor. "Tough to say."

"I understand," Reed replies, faux sympathetic. "Maybe you can pencil me in between listening to sad music and lying down in a dark room."

I laugh, shoving him lightly. We emerge from the hallway into the lobby, into the sunlight, headache-inducing in its sudden vibrance—and right in front of us, Patrick and Joe are waiting in line for concessions.

My laughter dies on my lips. I freeze, pulling my hand from Reed. Cold guilt slams into my stomach. Patrick's eyes are on us, ringed, I notice, with dark circles. It's unquestionable he just saw me laughing and playful with Reed.

Too many thoughts topple over in me. I don't want Patrick to think I've moved on and am going on a date, especially not with the one guy he was vaguely threatened by. Even though Patrick was the one who dumped me. Even though I have every right to move on. I just feel like I would be disrespecting our three years together to go on a date three days post-breakup. Most of all, I definitely don't want Patrick to think I meant to hurt him by going out with Reed. I did this for myself.

I expect Patrick to face forward or to glare. For betrayal or judgment to flash over his features or sharpen the straight lines of his posture.

Instead, his eyes shift not to Reed but to the UCSB logo emblazoned on his sweatshirt. Hurt crashes over him. While the change in his expression is subtle, I'm now struck by one more painful result of how long our relationship lasted. I don't need dramatics to know exactly what Patrick is thinking. He's seeing into a future painted in new colors, too. A future he'll have no part of, but he's just learned Reed will.

The worst part is, even though we're broken up, his pain reaches me, too. I feel it in my heart like it's my own. When we were long distance, the invisible tethers connecting us had felt like lifelines. Now they're still there, and I realize each one has a hook on the end, ready to pull out some new piece of me.

Because I still love him. The simple admission reopens every wound I'd gotten to stop bleeding. Just because we're over doesn't mean my feelings for him disappeared overnight. They haven't faded, even if a movie with a friend can help me hide from them for a few hours.

Patrick finally rips his gaze away. He steps forward in line. I watch him for a moment, muted, a silent war raging in me of wanting to explain myself and not. Joe gives me an apologetic glance and follows Patrick. I'm not upset Joe's sticking with my ex for now—I'm glad Patrick has someone to lean on the way I have Reed.

My vision going watery, I nearly stumble out of the theater, bursting through the glass doors without really knowing where I'm going. Small sobs have started to escape me. People give me worried glances, which I pay no mind to. I'm fleeing from feelings I know I can't outrun, desperate to find somewhere I can break down in private.

Reed's hand on my elbow steadies me gently, and I let him lead me to his car, where I climb into the passenger seat. I shut the door in time to really cry.

Hunched over, I shudder, sucking in ugly breaths. They're unmistakable proof of how pathetically fragile my lifted spirits were. I'm not *Single Siena*. I'm shattered, wearing the stupid costume of some imagined self.

Reed leans across the gearshift, giving me a shoulder to cry on. "Take however long you need," he says comfortingly. He rubs my back while I'm crying too hard to reply.

I thought I could return to my life because I'd built so much of it without Patrick. The reasoning feels ridiculous now, like the front of a house I hadn't realized had no walls. None of this will be easy, not even from a distance. Patrick was part of my every day, in hundreds, thousands of ways. He wasn't *one* piece of my world—he was part of the materials in *every* piece.

I'll be thinking of him even when he's not in the movie theater to run into. Because despite the distance, Patrick was everywhere for me.

Summer

Fifty-Four

"YOU KNOW HOW MUCH I care about you," Joe says.

I watch him carefully. He looks heartfelt, a little sad, but sure of himself. We're in his family's kitchen, dumping ice from the freezer into the expansive kitchen sink. Most of the party is outside, but it's too hot to leave the drinks in the sun. While up-tempo music drifts in through the screen door, Joe and I break up clumps of ice to surround cold Cokes and Spindrifts.

Outside, past the CONGRATS, GRAD! balloons, parents and grandparents sit at folding tables and recently graduated seniors congregate by the pool. It's one of those Phoenix days where you just defy the heat, everyone seeking shade or resigning themselves to sweating through their semiformal party dress. I won't pretend I'm not grateful Joe and I took the opportunity to head inside to work on the drinks within the cool, white walls of his kitchen, though.

"It's just that," Joe goes on, "I don't want this to get ugly. I want us to walk away friends, because you mean a lot to me."

I shove the can I'm holding into the ice. "What are you saying?" I ask, guarded.

"We should break up," Joe declares. "Before college."

I stare, taking in the contrition in his eyes, the way he rubs one elbow with what looks like nerves. In the years I've known Joe, I'm not sure I've ever seen him this way. Like he's uncertain, or he *is* certain and he doesn't like it. He looks fragile.

I nod. "Pretty good, actually."

Joe's sympathy shifts into delight. The change comes over him quickly and completely. He straightens, smiling, and grabs one of the remaining cans of sparkling water from the counter. "Yeah?" he asks. "You think so?"

"You were firm but kind. Clear but not demanding," I confirm.

He breathes out, his eyes moving off of me. He sticks the can into the ice, then claps his hands like he's psyching himself up.

I note his gesture with alarm. "Wait," I say. "You're not doing it *now*, right?" I glance outside to where Lacey and Reed sit with their feet dangling into the pool, hanging out with some other people from improv.

Joe frowns. "No," he says, following my eyeline to Lacey. "This weekend. That way we have the rest of the summer to go back to being friends."

In the softness of his voice and the way he gazes out the screen door, I catch the shadow of the sorrow he put on moments ago. The genuine version this time. "You're totally sure you want to end it? You guys are so great together," I say gently.

Contemplativeness flits out of Joe's features. He gives me a flat look I probably could have expected. We've been having variations on this conversation for weeks, since he first shared his plans with me. "We're great together now," he replies with emphatic patience. "When we're *together*. But I do not want to do long distance."

Joe's going to Berkeley, Lacey to Vassar in New York. I'll concede they've picked one of the longer long distances they could have.

"Long distance isn't so bad," I say quietly, unable to help the wistfulness in my voice, even vulnerability. Months after Patrick's and my breakup, it no longer hurts to remember what we had. Instead, it brings something like a shy smile to my lips. My memories of Patrick are happy. I'm grateful I have them. I'd imagined our relationship was something *we* were building. Now the relationship feels more like the scaffolding around me, removed once it was no longer needed and leaving me standing.

Joe looks doubtful. "Come on, Siena," he says. "If you and Patrick couldn't make it work, no way Lacey and I can."

I roll my eyes. It's pretty much reflexive, not resentful. There's no point trying to win Joe over on this one. I've made the effort. We're just playing out old lines in this familiar script.

With my last Spindrift stocked into the ice, I follow Joe outside. The heat hits us like heavy curtains, leaving me wondering if I could just return to the kitchen, possibly to stand in front of the fridge with the door open. Instead, I hear someone call my name. I turn to find my parents with Reed's, lingering near the doors in the shade of the house.

Joe gives the group a once-over, then heads to join Lacey, sending me a *you're on your own* glance.

I walk over to the parental group, trying not to look hesitant. I've met the Kims a few times, even had a couple family dinners with them during the three weeks that Reed and I dated. It didn't work out. I knew it wouldn't, kind of. It was the definition of a rebound. With some distance from my relationship with Patrick, I genuinely had wondered whether I would find something real with Reed. Instead, during movie nights, walks in his neighborhood, and collaborations on perfect playlists, spending time with him had let my wounds heal while I wasn't looking. The pressure-free fun had gotten me over Patrick and led me back to my life. It was nice, but ultimately Reed and I both decided it wasn't going anywhere.

We've remained friends since our split, but I never know how to act around his family when I see them at his house or at improv matches. I reach the group, and Mrs. Kim's over-eager smile gives me the sense the slight discomfort is mutual. "Reed mentioned you'll also be trying out for the improv group at UCSB?" she says, phrasing it like a question.

"I'm going to try," I say, returning the smile. I don't know if I'll get in since I'm such a newcomer to performing, but Reed's been helping me prepare. It's what helped us stay friends instead of lapsing into post-breakup uncertainty—we spent lunches playing modified versions of improv games. "If not, though," I go on, "I'm sure I'll find something else to join when I get to campus."

"Are you excited for next year?" Mrs. Kim asks.

My smile bursts wide. "So excited." I no longer cringe when people ask me about my plans for next year. I have an answer, and it's the kind I want. Not for forever. Just for now.

This year, my senior year, the one I'm ending on this patio in the sweltering summer heat, on my own and surrounded by new friends and old, has only made me more confident in where I'm going and how I'm getting there. I'll keep trying new things, never closing myself off to what could change me. Senior year has been hard, even bruising, but it hasn't been without so much I've loved. Improv, adventures with friends, even writing for the lit journal. I've used my freedom to find out who I want to be.

I've seen myself as different selves this year. *SienaandPatrick. Improv Siena. Writer Siena. Single Siena.* What I'm starting to realize is that I was none of them, and they weren't me. Because I'm *Siena.* Everything else—they're pieces of the me I'm still becoming.

"I'm glad she and Reed will have each other there. A little piece of home," my mom says with satisfaction. She's in unusually high spirits today, puffed up with maternal pride, wearing a floral dress she bought for this occasion.

"You're just glad you have Reed's number," I say, lightly teasing, "and you can text him to spy on me."

Mom's indignation is theatrical. "I wouldn't do that!"

While my dad laughs, I raise my eyebrows innocently. "What was I thinking?" Smiling slightly, I leave them to what will no doubt be energetic speculation on our college lives. Relishing the faintest suggestion of the summer breeze, I head in the direction of Joe, Lacey, and Reed.

Reed's removed his feet from the water and sits with his knees drawn to his chest while Lacey lets her long legs dangle, bronzing in the sun. When I reach them, they're discussing the trip we're taking next month to stay in Lacey's aunt's cabin in Flagstaff. "If we pack light, we can all fit in one car," Reed is saying.

I know exactly which car he means. Using savings from his part-time job staffing the public library's checkout desk, Reed recently purchased a used four-door Jeep Wrangler, which he treats like it's a human child. Kicking off my sandals, I sit next to Lacey, sliding my feet into the tepid pool.

"Okay," Lacey says measuredly. "But how does packing light fit with cornhole and camping gear and shots?"

Reed looks like he was waiting for the question. "Have you seen my trunk space?"

"Not this again," Joe says, shaking his head.

I lean back on my hands and close my eyes. I'm looking forward to the trip. Joe and Lacey will be broken up by then, which I know is a factor in Joe's timing. He wants the week in Flagstaff to mend their friendship. It'll be a little awkward at first, but it'll also be days of exploring the town, hiking, and hanging out with friends I hope I'll keep long past high school.

The sounds of their convivial bickering slip into place with the small talk of the other guests, the water surrounding my toes, the sunlight in the crystal-clear sky, everything fitting together into one of those unexpectedly perfect moments. It feels like summer.

While I watch the ripples my feet create in the water, I'm reminded suddenly of the last time I sat here. With Patrick by my side. The memory makes me smile. It had been the first night I'd started to realize how much I'd overlooked in my own boyfriend. The night it all began to change between us.

I loosen my grip on my thoughts, letting my imagination wander to what Patrick might be doing right now. Maybe he's with friends—Vic or Carly, Ross or Yi-Ping—or maybe he's hiking on his own, outdoors under the same sun. I envision graduation parties like this one, celebratory dinners with Mel and Greg. He would have graduated with his new high school class. He probably missed Phoenix, at least a little.

With space from our breakup, I haven't only learned how not to be heartbroken. I've come to realize there were things Patrick was right about and I was wrong about. Our relationship was never the problem. Long distance was never the solution. *I* was keeping myself from voicing how stuck I felt—out of pessimism, stress, uncertainty, inertia, or some stifling combination. I could have spoken up, and he would have listened. I could have worked to find myself, regardless of him. I was indecisive in my own life and in my relationship for too long.

Ironically, I needed our breakup to see it. To see how nothing changed without him, not really. How I still had to fill in the blanks myself.

I should have worked on myself the way I wanted to

instead of projecting my insecurities onto our relationship. What's more, I shouldn't have pushed him to find similar questions in himself. Some people *do* know what they want for themselves and their future, even when they're young.

He was right in so many ways. I know it now.

For the first time in months, I open our text conversation on my phone. It stings a little, dim pricks under scar tissue, seeing our final messages. They're painfully innocuous, texts coordinating our drive to the Grand Canyon. But now, the sting is faintly sweet. I'd be lying if I said I didn't think about him. I think about him almost every day—whenever I see something that reminds me of him, or hear a joke I know he'd laugh at. For a while it was hard. I'd tear up and have to hide my eyes behind sunglasses, or something would ignite in me and I'd find myself suddenly furious.

This month, something shifted in me. The missing became warmer, comfortable. I know if I text him, I'll be okay if he doesn't reply. I'll be okay if he does.

I type without thinking, then hit send.

Last Days Relaxing?

Not really expecting an answer, I put my phone down. My hair slips off my shoulders, my heartbeat steady and sure. I refocus on my friends, on everything I've found and built and relearned on my own.

Fifty-Five

WITH EVENING DESCENDING OVER the rooftops outside the window of my room, I'm researching hiking trails on my computer. In the hour since we got home from the party, my toes still haven't entirely unpruned, and I nestle them into the rug under my desk while I click through photos and online maps. I'm trying to balance Joe's insistence on not too much climbing with Lacey's desire for panoramic views, and predictably, it's not easy.

I scroll a list of trail photos, deciding this one won't work. The path to the vista is too steep. For Joe, not for me—I bought hiking boots just for this trip. *With decent treads*, I hear in my head. I smile. Closing out of the tab, I'm ready for the moment to fade, the way they always do. But this time, it doesn't.

With impossible timing, Patrick's name lights up my phone screen.

I don't hesitate. I unlock my phone, finding his message sitting in our conversation, innocently familiar, yet jarringly new.

Lately Downright Repetitive.

I laugh, holding my phone with my thumbs hovering over the screen. I have to hand it to Patrick—his sense of humor is never showy, but he's surprisingly clever with the LDR game.

Chewing my lip, I consider my reply. I want to keep the conversation going, no matter the destination. It's just nice to talk to him. When I type out my response, I'm surprised how naturally it comes. The instinct is still there, even if the context is different.

> Any tips on finding a simultaneously easy
> but also beautiful hike in Flagstaff?

Once it's sent, I stare out the window instead of returning to my computer. Dusk is right on the edge of night, the sky navy over one remaining strip of yellow.

I don't ignore how my heart skips when he replies quickly.

> I haven't hiked there, but give me a
> minute to check my go-to blogs.

I read his text over, then over once more, like I'm Nancy Drew searching for a secret code. Doubt starts to steal into me. Maybe this is weird. Maybe Patrick is only doing this to be nice, and he doesn't actually want to talk to me.

No, I remind myself, closing off the line of thinking.

Patrick proved to me he doesn't do things just to be polite when he doesn't want to do them.

Impulsiveness grabs hold of me. I reply before I can convince myself otherwise.

> Thanks. I'm glad you texted back, by the
> way.

There's nothing from him for the longest stretch since his LDR message. It feels like a full minute. *He's checking his blogs,* one voice in me says. *He's tired of talking to you,* says another. His response quiets them both.

> I'm glad you texted.

It flips a hidden switch in me. I want to ask him *everything*. Millions of questions. How he's doing, what his final semester was like, whether our relationship is a fond memory to him. I know there's something I have to say to him first, though, before we can restart any form of friendship.

> Hey, I know this is a thousand years late,
> but congrats on getting into med school. I
> should have said it sooner, but I want you
> to know I think it's really incredible. You'll
> be a wonderful doctor.

I put my phone down. I'm self-conscious having written

so much. Even now, Patrick is probably the only person I would send such a vulnerable message to. It's okay if he doesn't reply, I reassure myself. I'm okay. I've been okay for months. I don't need closure or whatever from this. I—

My phone vibrates.

I reach for it with a speed that exposes my lies to myself.

> **Thank you for saying that, Siena. It means a lot.**

I watch his typing bubble pop up, then disappear over and over. Biting my nail, I find myself hoping he doesn't hold back whatever he's debating saying.

Finally, his text comes in. My eyes race over the small type.

> **My mom is still subscribed to the WV lit journal. I read the story you had in the final issue. I loved it.**

His praise warms me from the inside out. I stayed in the lit journal just to give it a chance, wondering where it might take me. While it's not as important to me as improv, I was proud of the last story I wrote when I saw my name in print.

It didn't feel like this. It's funny how kind words from Patrick gratify and please me in ways nothing else does, like the only key to one very specific door in my heart. The piece I wrote was fiction about packing for college, and it was about leaving Phoenix, but also probably a little about Patrick leaving me.

I'm going to thank him when three more texts from Patrick hit my phone. They're links to blog posts describing trails in Flagstaff. Pulling one knee to my chest in my desk chair, I scroll through, touched by his immediacy and the effort he took finding them. He dropped everything to help me out. It's the way he is—or the way he is with me. I'm no longer sure where one starts and the other ends.

I read on, to his message following the links.

> Okay, the first one is a little harder than the others, but it's short and the views are the best. The second one would be a crowd-pleaser, but it'll be packed if you don't go early. The third one is kind of a drive, but it might have everything else you're looking for.

> Wow. Thank you. Seriously, I've been staring at maps for the past hour.

In reply, Patrick sends one more link. It's for hiking boots—in my exact size, I note. I laugh out loud in my empty room.

> You're hilarious.

Am I? Because I'm being totally serious.

My laughter subsides into a smile. Real and uncomplicated, not sad. It feels nice to joke with Patrick. The distance is there, but it's not vast the way I expected. It's the distance of neighbors, not strangers. On the whole, this conversation is nothing like I would have imagined, though I've never imagined it.

Surprisingly, recognizing that puts the first hint of nerves into me. Because there's enough here now, enough said over the past fifteen minutes to warrant me telling Patrick something I've come to understand over the past few months.

Can I say one more thing?

You don't have to limit yourself to one.

I pause. It's hard turning difficult thoughts into sentences, but I try, typing carefully.

I'm sorry I expected you to change just because I was changing. It wasn't because I didn't like who you were. I really loved you for exactly who you were. I guess I just wanted permission to change myself, but I know now I should have just talked to you. I didn't need long distance to let me

quit MUN or join improv. I could have done
those things when you were here. If I had, I
wonder if maybe we'd still be together.

When I press send, the giant block of text floats into our conversation, immediately embarrassing me with its length. I promptly panic and type out and send another message.

Not that I'm, like, trying to get back
together or anything. I just still care about
you and wanted you to know I'm sorry.

Even though I have no idea what he's going to say, I exhale in relief when Patrick's typing bubble pops up. He hasn't been totally scared off.

The what-if game keeps me up at night.
I don't know what the answer is, but I
appreciate your saying that. I care about
you too.

I read and reread his first sentence. It lights a little spark in me, the flame small yet steady. How many nights? Does he think about me as often as I do him? He has to. What we had was real. Even though he was the one to end it, walking away from us couldn't have been easy.

My phone vibrates in my hand.

> I'm sorry too. I could have made more
> room for you to grow in our relationship.
> Looking back, I see how often I shut you
> down. I never wanted to stifle you, but I
> know, in ways, I did.

It's entirely the response I hoped for, and the Patrick I remember. I'm the one who led us onto this subject, so it's sort of on my terms. The fact he's following me here graciously fills me with gratitude.

I reply, emboldened by his kindness.

> We both made mistakes, but I don't regret
> what we had.

> Me neither.

Moving from my chair, I lie down on my bed, smiling at the screen. I send off my next message.

> Long-Due Reconnection.

> Literally Doubtlessly Right.

We continue the LDR game, sometimes with interruptions for more conversation, late into the night.

Fifty-Six

I FINISH MY DINNER when everyone else is only halfway done—except Robbie, who's probably two-thirds there.

In other circumstances, I would've savored Mom's mac and cheese, the warm smell of which fills our kitchen. Right now, however, I'm close to jumping out of my seat. My knee bounces under the table, and I'm expecting the glare I receive from Mom when I check my phone.

My dad, who's giving the mac and cheese the respectful pace it deserves, eyes my plate in confusion. "Did you guys not eat before you drove down?"

"Nope," I reply quickly. In fact, Joe, Lacey, Reed, and I had lingered in Flagstaff until the last moment we could without risking heavy traffic on the way home. Reed dropped me off outside about an hour ago. The trip was perfect with the exception of the mild discomfort between Joe and Lacey when we got there, which gradually disappeared over the first day spent walking in the wilderness while sunlight glittered through the trees. Joe and Lacey settled into respectful friendship, helped by the collective understanding this might be the last time the four of us hang out like this. I want to believe we'll remain close through and after college. But I also know people change.

Mom frowns. "Would you like more potatoes?"

On other nights, I really, really would. They're the kind she's roasted into crispy, salty wedges. "Nope," I say. "I'm good. I really want to go unpack, so I might just head to my room." I push confidence into my voice, hoping I sound convincing despite inventing this on the spot. In reality, I couldn't be less interested in unpacking right now.

It was the wrong thing to say, I realize quickly.

While Mom's expression hardly changes, I detect the new suspicion settling over her end of the table. "Plans tonight?"

"No," I reply.

Yes. I *do* have plans. Plans currently returning life to the butterflies in my stomach, including some I've never felt before.

"You just spent a whole week with your friends," my dad says. "Can't we have more than twenty minutes with you before you go do whatever it is Reed has planned tonight?" He sounds less stern than disappointed, which is sweet and makes me feel guilty.

"I'm not going to Reed's," I say honestly.

Mom, however, is never one to miss an evasive response. "Who do you have plans with, then?" she asks, her voice still light and insinuation still sharp.

Finally, frustration starts to cut into my excitement. My knee stops jumping under the table, and I meet my mom's stare. "I'm not going anywhere," I reply firmly and again not falsely. Robbie quietly reaches for more salad.

~ 357 ~

"Then tell us more about your trip," Mom counters.

I check the clock on my phone. There's no way I'll get out of this discussion in time if I keep debating my mom. Instead, I stand sharply. Part of me wishes I could explain why I *can't* explain what I'm leaving to do. It's not that I don't want to tell my parents what my plans are. I just . . . don't know what my plans mean yet. "I'll tell you tomorrow," I say measuredly. "I have a call right now."

Mom blinks. Genuine interest flits over her features. "With who?"

I can't stifle my groan. "Does it matter?" I shoot back. I'm certain I have, like, fifteen seconds to get to my room and open my computer.

"I'm just curious," Mom replies.

I feel a flush rising into my cheeks. This was not the discreet exit I'd envisioned.

"Oh, come on," Robbie says. "It's obviously with Patrick."

The room goes still, except for Robbie, who finishes loading lettuce onto his plate. With gusto, my brother spears his salad with his fork.

"She's been texting him under the table for weeks," he elaborates past his bite.

Suddenly, the passing seconds feel like my second-most-important problem. I give Robbie the most vicious glare I can muster. Once a traitorous little brother, always a traitorous little brother.

"Patrick?" Mom and Dad repeat in cartoonish unison. They sound pleased—too pleased. This is exactly why I didn't want to tell them. The hopes I've held on to for this call feel fragile enough that the prodding of one person—let alone four people—could crush them.

Honestly, I ought to have known someone in my family would notice. Patrick and I have continued our casual texting over the past weeks. Even in Flagstaff, I found myself sending him pictures from our hike while Patrick kept up a steady stream of questions and conversation. In moments, I was hit with such intense déjà vu—when I was sneaking glances at my phone while surrounded by friends, or waking up to find a message from him waiting for me. Sometimes it hurt. Sometimes it felt like flying.

While I would often have to remind myself we weren't together, the new ebb and flow of our conversation made it easier to remember, if not effortless. There were times when we'd text for hours on end, others when we'd go days without hearing from each other. Always, though, we'd find our way to the conversation again.

It feels healthier, in a way. While there's no pressure to communicate every little thing, our connection is still undeniably strong. Our steady back-and-forth is its own sort of loving. I don't know what it means. This call is supposed to help me figure it out.

"You're talking to Patrick?" Mom's curiosity has converted fully into enthusiasm. "Are you two . . . ?"

"No," I reply immediately. Then I remember exchanged photos, new jokes, and déjà vu, and the picture complicates. "I don't know," I amend.

"They won't be anything if you don't let Siena leave," Robbie interjects, in what I need a second to recognize is actual helpfulness.

Mom is silent until she abruptly smooths her napkin. "Well, what are you waiting for? Go! Say hi for us."

While she practically shoos me out, I catch Robbie's eye, knowing we're sharing the same internal eyeroll. I walk quickly to my room before I'm waylaid by any further questions. Grabbing my laptop, I sit down on my bed with my earbuds. My heart pounds. I can't name the emotions coursing through me. I just know they're *there*. With the rush of feeling intense and everywhere, I move my finger to click Patrick's name on the screen.

He picks up immediately.

"Hey," I say, failing to sound nonchalant. My voice is tight, breathless. "Sorry I'm late."

Patrick is in his room. It's searingly familiar despite my having only seen it on my one visit to Texas, and I have the sensation of peering into a dream. He's sitting at his desk, the light from his lamp illuminating his face. "No problem," he says. "It's good to see you."

They're trivial words, but somehow, their lightness lends them weight.

His eyes roam over the screen, taking me in. He looks slightly different, his hair a little shorter and a little lighter from the summer sun, his nose perhaps a tad sunburned. But his eyes—his eyes are as warm as I remembered. The feeling hits me square in the chest. It's some strange relief to have him in front of me again. Like coming home.

I grin, and it does me in a little. Tears prick my eyes. I've shed plenty of them over Patrick in the past few months, but never this kind. I want to cry from how good this feeling is.

Patrick is feeling the same. I see him, pixelated over the mediocre Wi-Fi, and I know he is. He's grinning one of his unrestrained, ebullient grins I used to love so much. His eyes are watery, glinting in the lamplight. When he laughs, I know it's not because this is funny. It's out of pure joy.

I laugh with him, wiping a tear from my eyes. "It's really good to see you, too," I say.

The joy in me changes into a warm ache, one I identify instantly, effortlessly. I love him. I never stopped. Not over weeks and months, over silence and sporadic conversation, over new starts and old rhythms. In all that time, it hasn't dimmed. I settle into my cushions, content just to know this, to have him on my computer screen in my lap.

"How's your family?" Patrick asks. It's a nothing question, yet from him, right now, it's everything.

I fill him in with enthusiasm, catching him up on Robbie's antics and my mom's lovingly overbearing inquisitiveness. I ask him the same, and about his friends, and about his summer. And the minutes pass, and the hours. Suddenly, my computer is nearly out of battery and I'm reaching for my charger, not wanting this to end.

Patrick doesn't want it to end, either. It's obvious from how he hasn't stopped smiling pretty much the entire time.

I'm coming to appreciate that one of the luckiest things in the world is never running out of things to say to someone. Patrick and I don't, the entire night. When my throat begins to hurt from talking, I check the clock on my computer screen—then recheck it. It's nearly one in the morning. Which means it's even later for Patrick.

"Crap, it's late," I say. "You should get some sleep." I hope he hears I'm only being considerate. I certainly don't *want* to hang up.

Patrick's eyes dart to the clock in the corner of his screen, widening a little when he sees the time. "I probably should," he says reluctantly. "But . . . this has been a lot of fun." He doesn't say it like he's closing something off. It's half of an invitation.

"It has," I agree, ready to supply the other half. "We should do it more often."

I feel something unfamiliar when the words leave me—the constraint of distance. If there weren't thousands of miles between us, I would ask him out on a date. I hope he knows, though, that another call wouldn't be as friends.

I'm on the verge of clarifying when he speaks up. "Actually, Siena, I have a question for you," he says, just slightly louder and faster, a spring-loaded sentence.

I straighten up, nerves and excitement rushing into me. I should be exhausted, but I'm pretty sure I've never been more awake.

He meets my eyes in the camera. "You asked me once why I liked you. I didn't give you a good answer."

"I remember." It was Thanksgiving, when I doubted we were going to make it. I was searching for a reason to stay instead of finding that reason in myself.

"I didn't give you a good enough answer because I didn't *have* a good enough answer." Patrick rubs his palms together. In the gesture, I know he's nervous just like me, one of infinite details of him encoded in my mind probably forever. He goes on. "I just liked you for obvious reasons—you're kind, you're smart, you're pretty. I think I took liking you for granted."

I say nothing, not hiding from how this hurts. While Patrick's and my relationship is over now, it's difficult to hear it was founded, in part, on *just because.*

"Siena, what I know now is how incredibly insufficient, lazy, and just plain wrong I was," he says.

His words are once more an electric current.

"I should have liked you for your constant curiosity, for the way you find opportunity everywhere. I should have liked you for how you helped me realize what was exciting in my life here. I like you for your courage, Siena—the courage it takes to not know yourself yet and find the question inspiring instead of intimidating. It's incredible. It hasn't been easy since we split up, but it's let me see you—us—more clearly."

My reply jumps out of me. "You said *like.* Present tense." It's not as if *everything* he's just said didn't nestle itself into the most precious part of my soul. Just, the one word stood out.

Now Patrick smiles, eyes brimming. "I said *like.*"

Heart thudding, I feel my expression match his. "Well. You don't need my forgiveness. I should have been better to you. I regret things, too. But I'm glad we're doing this."

"I'm really glad," he agrees. "So glad that . . . Well, Siena, do you—would you want to get back together?"

It's indescribable, hearing my hopes out loud. While he continues, the happy haze of what he's said wraps over me with the warmth of desert sun, the cracked-soda fizz of sweet delight, and the hugeness of canyon nights.

"I know we're going to different states for college, and it would mean more long distance," he says. "But I don't care. I want to be with you. However I can."

Now I'm crying for real. Tears spill down my smiling cheeks. I'm nodding, unable to speak just yet. When I find my voice again, it comes out choked with joy. "I've tried a lot of new things this year," I muster, telling the story of a year in nine words. "But, Patrick, by far the worst was being without you."

Patrick's smile touches me through the screen.

"So yes," I say. "Yes, I'd like that."

End of Summer

Epilogue

SHOULDERING MY BAG, I pass people quickly on my way through the terminal. The Austin airport is packed with end-of-summer travelers, and I dodge past children and duck around luggage. I'm hurrying like I'm about to miss my flight.

Except I'm going in the opposite direction.

I ignore the plethora of guitars and homey restaurants I noticed on my first time here, ignore the squeaky sound my shoes make on the well-trod tile. I hardly hear the airport announcements and calming music looping over the loud-speaker. My focus is fixed entirely on reaching one thing. Baggage claim.

In fact, I've more or less focused on nothing else for the past few weeks.

Each day has carried me closer to huge changes, ones finally starting now. Tomorrow, Patrick starts the long road trip to Brown. It'll be days of driving, with nights in road-side hotels. When he'd invited me, I'd said yes immediately.

We'll make the trip together, then I'll help him move in and see his campus before I fly home. I'll be back in Phoenix in time to pack up my own car and drive to California for my UCSB move-in.

Right now, however, college in the imminent future is not what's speeding my steps. This trip will be the first time I've seen Patrick since we got back together. It has my body humming with anticipation.

While things have been incredible between us the past few weeks, I've lost count of the times I've pictured being with him in person. Our first video call opened gates in my heart, letting me hope for and envision everything I'd learned not to.

I push through the crowd, emerging into baggage claim, my head swiveling wildly while I search the open room. In front of me, a family moves—and there he is.

I stop, the airport seeming to disappear. He's beaming at me, one hand in his pocket. It's impossible how real he looks, how reachable. I feel the breath leave my lungs, and then I'm rushing up to him, running, closing the last distance between us.

We don't crash together. For a moment, we just stand inches apart, drinking each other in. It's not only for the sensation of looking forward just a little longer, although the deliciousness is undeniable. Staring into his eyes, inscribing every detail of his face in this moment into my memory while only inches separate us, it feels like saying, *We've done this. We've* been *apart.* Apart in where we lived, apart in our romantic lives. *And we kept loving each other anyway.* No matter how hard the universe pushes or pulls, forces or withholds, some stories just aren't meant to end.

"Hi," Patrick says, the word wobbling on the edge of everything.

"Hi," I whisper.

Then I throw myself forward, into his arms, kissing him with months of pent-up emotion. It's a perfect kiss, fit for every cliché. With our lips meeting, and Patrick's frame fitting mine exactly the way I remember, and gentle devotion struggling with desperate need in his arm encircling me, I let every thought in my head vanish into this moment. It's fireworks in my heart, exploding over the skyline of the rest of our lives.

"I didn't think I'd ever get to do this again," he says softly into my hair. Happiness isn't the only thing in his voice. There's recognition, too, of the fact that happiness sometimes lives where sadness used to dwell.

I pull back, giving him a playfully accusatory grin. "I did figure that was your goal when you dumped me."

Patrick rolls his eyes, his smile matching mine. "You're never going to let me forget that, are you?"

I pause like I'm considering. Even so, I'm unable to help myself. My hand finds his, entwining our fingers, enjoying every innocuous spark of skin on skin. "I definitely expect you to make it up to me on this unsupervised road trip," I say.

Patrick's eyebrows rise, which was the reaction I'd hoped

for. I don't keep my satisfaction out of my smirk.

His expression settles into pleased confidence, which is, well, hot. "I plan to," he says. He throws an arm around my waist, pulling us hip to hip as we start to walk out of the airport. "I've been thinking," he continues. "Long distance relationship. LDR. I don't know if it's quite right."

I look at him out of the corner of my eye while we step into the Austin sunlight. "No?" I ask. "We *are* about to be even longer-distance than before."

Patrick looks unmoved, his face lit up and carefree. "It doesn't matter. The distance doesn't matter. It doesn't define our relationship, because we'll always have this—being together—eventually. It's more like a Temporarily Distant Relationship."

I nod, intrigued. "TDR," I say, then pause, thinking. "True Devotion Remains. Time Delivers . . ." Here, I falter. "Robots," I finish. While Patrick laughs, I go on. "It might be a harder game to play than LDR."

Something sparkles in Patrick's eyes. "Possibly," he says. "But what's wrong with trying something new?"

My smile overtakes me. I decide how wonderful it is that you can fall in love with someone over and over. I imagine changing on our own while our connection stays the same. And I wonder if it's possible to look into a sky exploding with color and think it's a sunset when really it's a sunrise.

We walk toward the car, toward the next couple days we'll spend together, and I know that even when we part, my love for him isn't going anywhere.

Acknowledgments

When we were dating long distance, every time we would part felt vastly daunting, while every time we would visit felt dazzlingly full of opportunity. Years later, every book we write feels some of both. We're immeasurably grateful to the people who've made the opportunities possible, and who've helped us navigate the daunting parts.

Without our agent, Katie Shea Boutillier, none of what we've had the joy of publishing would be possible. It feels unreal that this is our sixth book together. We knew from your very first email that your enthusiasm and passion would make you the right champion for our work, and we've been proven right year after year. Thank you for every strategy call and late-night email, for knowing when to trust us and when to push us.

The same goes for our editor, Dana Leydig—we recognize the exceptional good fortune of getting to work together for five novels. We remain honored by how you continue to help us find the profoundest resonance in each new story. You put such care and thought into every edit letter, striking the perfect balance of editorial insight and GIFs, and it never goes unnoticed or unappreciated (sorry for the double "un"s here—you know we can't resist). On *With and Without You*, we were delighted to also have the chance to work with Meriam Metoui, who helped us polish Siena and Patrick with precise care.

Writing each new book is in most respects the hard part—working with the incredible Penguin Random House team is the easy, joyous part. We thank our excellent copyeditors and proofreaders Marinda Valenti, Abigail Powers, and Sola Akinlana, whose keen eyes and grammatical wisdom never fail to improve our work. Kristie Radwilowicz and Theresa Evangelista's flat-out gorgeous cover is the perfect vision of Siena's sun-filled world, with desert vibes leaving us staring in delight. For straight-from-our-daydreams design (those sunset pages!), thank you to Kate Renner. For impeccable management of the process from manuscript to this lovely book, thank you to Gaby Corzo.

Tessa Meischeid, we feel unbelievably lucky to have you working on our books. You are the publicist authors dream of having. Thank you for sharing our work with the world and for becoming a real friend in publishing. Felicity Vallence, not only will we credit you forever for #Wibbroka, we look forward every release to your endless enthusiastic insight. It is not an exaggeration to say that when peers ask as about Penguin Teen, we always take the opportunity to gush about everything you do. James Akinaka, Kara Brammer, Alex Garber, and Shannon Spann, we're honored to be part of your incredible work engaging readers and inspiring a love of reading worldwide.

One other commonality of publishing and long distance: the importance of friends and family, who cheer on the joys while providing invaluable support during the difficulties. We're very grateful to have friends from every part of our lives—high school, college, and onward—who have gamely learned publishing vocabulary for us, not to mention following every step of our career (with a special nod to Charlie Hughes, the originator of Reed's "TTTTTTTT" '90s hip-hop playlist).

Not much is consistent in publishing except for the joy of the friends we've made in the writing community. This book was written entirely in the pandemic, and instead of writing retreats and coffee-shop dates, we are beyond grateful to our friends for their virtual support. To Aminah Mae Safi, for her levelheaded advice, fortifying kitty pictures, and weekly FaceTimes. Bridget Morrissey, for always being game to unravel timeline anomalies, not to mention uncommon loyalty, for being excited whenever we're excited and frustrated whenever we're frustrated. To Maura Milan—this book was outlined entirely during our daily virtual sprints. Thank you for asking the questions that kept this story moving and for roasting Siena's love for improv.

To Farrah Penn, Gretchen Schreiber, Rebekah Faubion, Diya Mishra, and Kayla Olson, thank you for the publishing talks and for exchanging manuscripts, wisdom, and enthusiasm. Bree Barton, Amy Spalding, Kristin Dwyer, Britta Lundin, Isabel Ibañez, Derek Milman and Brian Murray Williams, Sierra Elmore, and Sarah Grunder Ruiz, you've made our struggles manageable and our celebrations sweet. Lastly, everything starts with our families, who have made our dreams possible in every regard. We love you.

We reserve our final recognition for you who deserve it most: our readers. Some of you have followed us from our start. Some of you have just given us a first chance. Some of you have recommended us to friends. Some have shared stunning photos, delightful messages, or kind reviews. We write for you. With every new story, we're honored by your readership.

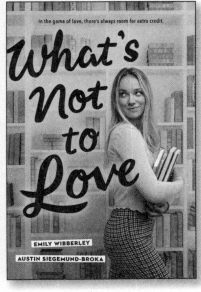